A Cowboy in Carpathia:

A BOB HOWARD ADVENTURE

Author's Expanded Edition

Teel James Glenn

Two-Gun Phoenix Publishing

A COWBOY IN CARPATHIA: A BOB HOWARD ADVENTURE-AUTHOR'S EXPANDED EDITION
A Two-Gun Phoenix Publishing Publication

A Cowboy in Carpathia: A Bob Howard Adventure-Author's Expanded Edition by Teel James Glenn

Edited by Sorella Smith
Cover Art by Dana Black
Book Design and Cover Formatting by Cookie Morris
Two-Gun Phoenix Publishing logo by Percival Constantine

Two-Gun Phoenix Publishing
8892 Yorktown
Southaven, MS 38671

twogunphoenix@gmail.com

ISBN: 978-1-971151-02-1

Dedication:

To the Master, Robert Ervin Howard; I only wish he could have known what he gave us all and that this could have been his path instead of the one he walked.

To David Burton, my brother who has gone beyond to sit and sup with Bob Howard—hold a place for me at the table…

Acknowledgments:

As no writer is an island, I am fortunate to be supported by my colleague Carol Gyzander who served as the first reader and initial editor on this manuscript. Thanks, E.T.

CONTENTS

The Who in Our When:

"I have sometimes wondered if it were possible that unrecognized forces of the past or present or even the future work through the thoughts and actions of living men."
Robert Ervin Howard in a letter to Tevis Clyde Smith

Robert Ervin Howard was born in 1906 in Texas, the U.S.A., and in our reality, he left the world in June of 1936. In the short time between he achieved the heights of creativity as few ever have. Howard began his professional writing career in his late teens, selling short stories, poems, and novels to a variety of markets including the famous *Weird Tales*, *Argosy All-Story*, and *Golden Fleece*, and creating iconic characters like Conan and Solomon Kane.

His prolific output was all the more remarkable because in his short life he never traveled more than several hundred miles from his Texas home, never met another professional writer or editor in the flesh and his writing skill was all self-taught.

In the end, as his mother lay dying from tuberculosis, his inner darkness won, and he took his own life.

In our world.

But in the world of this book and those that follow, I postulate a different path for him and for some other real people with no disparagement or judgment made.

So, come with me to a different time and place to a world of adventure and hope...

Prologue: Sacrifice

Cecilia Towne woke up alone in the dark stone-walled room, confused and frightened. She had long honey-blonde hair, now askew, and wore a modest, simple spring dress that was torn at the shoulder. She tried to remember how it had gotten that way.

Cecilia climbed unsteadily to bare feet shivering with misery. The floor was cold, damp stone.

She remembered leaving her parents' house and going to meet up with some friends at the village pub, but her mind was awhirl with strange images and memories. She had trouble remembering if she had ever made it there.

Cecilia saw her own shadow against the wall of the cell-like room, cast by the flickering light of a hurricane lamp. It made her shadow, distorted by the dancing flames, into a grotesque living thing.

She tried again to recall how she had gotten there. There was a handsome, angular face in her mind; she remembered him meeting her just outside the pub. Then he was sitting with her and she was laughing, and a faint memory of a drink that was more bitter than it should have been. Then it was all jumbled. She felt hands on her and darkness.

Cecilia gasped, "That toff—he gave me some sort of drug at the inn!" She staggered against the wall of the tiny stone cell. The smells of decay and death that filled the space assailed her like a punch to her gut, making her nauseous.

This can't be happening to me, this can't be real. Yet the ache of her muscles told her it was very real.

There was a sudden sharp pain on her back and she whirled with a cry of agony to look into the handsome but anger-twisted face of her tormentor.

"You need to learn some manners, bumpkin," his cultured voice proclaimed. Then the whip he held in his hand snapped and there was a searing pain across the captive girl's chest.

"Why are you doing this to me?" she pleaded in agony. "Please, in the name of God, stop!"

"You do not give me orders, peasant!" the haughty voice snarled. The whip snapped again and again till the flesh of the sobbing girl welted and oozed blood.

The tortured prisoner tried to protect herself from his attack, but the confines of the cell prohibited her backing away from the stinging whip.

"It's a shame there isn't more time before the moon reaches its zenith or I promise you that you'd have a lot more to scream about," the tormentor said with sharp tones. He grabbed her by her hair and pulled her from the cell into a narrow corridor then slashed her on the back again to drive her down a narrow stone hall.

Her jailer herded Cecilia like a wounded animal through a wooden door banded with iron. The door swung outward to reveal a large circular amphitheater with a sandy floor and a ceiling that faded into the darkness above. Torches sat on poles set around the area in a broad circle just inside the ten-foot wall that circled the entire space. There was a single, heavy metal gate on the far wall—beyond which was a dark mystery.

The girl dropped to her knees in the direct center of the space in the small circle of torchlight. She looked up to see the white face of the moon directly above through a distant pane of glass.

"God, please help me!" she sobbed hysterically. "Will you not save me?" she prayed.

It seemed that it was not God but the devil that answered her prayer, for the metal gate rattled open and a dark shape moved out of the shadows toward her.

The shape growled, Cecilia screamed and then the young girl could pray no more. Forever.

Chapter One: The Day the World Changed

I have liv'd long enough: my way of life
Is fall'n into the sere, the yellow leaf;
And that which should accompany old age,
As honour, love, obedience, troops of friends,
I must not look to have; but, in their stead,
Curses, not loud but deep, mouth-honour, breath,
Which the poor heart would fain deny, and dare not.

William Shakespeare, Macbeth Act V, Scene III

Hester Howard was not long for the world—her son Bob had known it before the nurse's pronouncement. Mrs. Green said Mama was gonna die real soon. There was no doubt about it; she would not wake from her coma. Mama looked like she was in a deep sleep, so frail, her breaths so shallow that her chest did not appear to move unless one looked intensely at it.

Bob had bought a plot of land in a cemetery for the family the day before so there would be certainty of a place. It seemed important, somehow with all the rest going on that Bob knew where she would rest. And he would rest beside her.

She had always been there for Bob with stories of their family in old Ireland, crossing the United States as pioneers.

She had been the only flower in the dusty dirt of Cross Plains, Texas. It was she who introduced him to poetry and literature.

She had instilled such a love for reading in Bob that he used to sneak into the closed library one town over, take a book or two to read, then return them when done. He was sure the librarians knew but they never said anything.

It was she that showed him, through those books, that there was something beyond the dusty horizon. It was in books he found a way out of the grime and ignorance of Cross Plains. And it was in writing stories that he realized he could escape the death and decay, and even triumph over it.

Yet the shadow of death had always been there; Mama Howard had been dying for as long as Bob could remember. His father, a country doctor with no bedside manner and little love for the profession that worked him hard and kept him poor, could do nothing to prevent it.

Bob had seen the procession of oil field workers, bullies, roustabouts and drunkards that populated the day-to-day reality of the town pass through his father's office. He had even accompanied his father to the sites of shootouts and stabbings and watched, slack-jawed as Doctor Howard ministered—oft times futilely—to the wounded. He had seen many men pass to the great beyond. Now his mama was going and he would be alone in the dying, dirty, boomtown.

That was why Bob had borrowed the old thirty-eight caliber revolver from his friend Lindsey Tyson. Now he sat in the battered old Ford in the driveway to the hospital working up the courage to use the gun on himself.

It was not that he feared death. He knew death. All his life death had been his constant companion.

No, it was that he feared life. A life of endless drab days, each blending into the next.

He looked out of the car window at the dusty street. He had seen that street for most of his life. That same street.

It was not the market in Samarkand, the Steppes of Russia, the field of Agincourt nor the plains of Aquilonia, yet on that street he had seen them all.

The men who walked Main Street in Cross Plains were the same as those of ages gone, yet to Bob Howard they were aliens. They had 'been,' he had not.

He had not left a hundred miles from his birthplace his entire life. Except in books. Then at fifteen he bought an issue of *Adventure* Magazine and knew he wanted to be a writer for it.

Words had been his passport and his hope. If only the magazines paid more, if only the magazines paid on time. If only.

He could not live on 'if only.'

Without Hester Howard's kind words, her quotes from poetry and tales of the family history, the words in the books were empty. And the empty space inside of Bob was suddenly more vast.

He hefted the gun. It felt very heavy in his meaty hand, and so very cold.

An odd thought fleeted across his poetic mind. *Wish it was Grandpa's gun.* It would seem somehow fitting if he used that old gun, but restoring it was one of those things he had just not gotten around to.

Time, he thought. *It is always about time.* There was never enough.

He thought about all the time he had sat alone in a room writing for the pulp magazines. All the time he had not walked across the London Bridge. All the time he had not crossed the Bosphorus. All the time he had not lived himself but given life to paper heroes.

Tears blurred his vision.

Now Hester was gone or close to it, there was no hope. No one to joy in his triumphs. The one other woman that had been in his life, Novalyne, who had listened to him and delighted in his visions of ages past, was gone as well—not to the great dark, but still beyond his reach. A destiny that was not his.

Alone. Time.

Time alone.

The thought of both was almost overwhelming.

"Time is a phantom, built by the mind of man..." He remembered one of his own poems. He remembered all his poems and more. His stories and his letters to friends like H.P. Lovecraft—Howie—the only chance he had to connect mind to mind with others. All of them, so far away.

The gun in his hand began to shake.

"I'm sorry, Mama," he said aloud, then quoted again, "I saw the temples topple, till I saw the idols reel, Till my brain had turned to iron, and my heart had turned to steel."

He cocked the hammer and put the barrel of the gun to his temple.

"For my road runs out in thistles and my dreams have turned to dust." His finger touched on the trigger lightly like a mother's kiss on a baby's eyes.

"I'm sorry, Howie," he said.

He thought again of all the crimson tales he had written, all his letters to his friend Howie Lovecraft where he extolled the virtues of the natural man, the barbarian. Men who lived each minute, fire in their veins and never a doubt in their minds but that life was the choice. How it was inevitable that such men would triumph over the constructs and artificiality of modern man.

Howie always argued for civilization.

"Heathens had no time to doubt," Bob abruptly said aloud.

The barrel of the gun was cold against his head.

"I can't doubt," he said in too loud a voice. "I ain't no civilized man, despite what Mama tried to make me."

The tears all but blurred the windshield of the car so he could not see the hospital anymore. "I ain't nothing like a civilized man, despite what Howie says."

His finger refused to tighten on the trigger.

He remembered a poem he'd read to Novalyne.

"My memories dim of a time of men
When truth and valor reigned
When just and friend were lived not penned

And love was a thing never feigned
Gods on high when I die
Let them pyre me not on my wishes or hope
That fails
Let me ride out instead with a helm on my head
On a Dragon Ship under full sails..."

He had to find that dragon ship.

He saw all the panoply of kings and armies, the roar of battle, the cries of grim, gray warriors who faced death with life, who squeezed each moment of life from the bloody grip of their enemies, and he uncocked the hammer.

"Only a civilized man would moan and gripe about a human passing," he said aloud. "Barbarians always chose to live completely till they die and savor every minute!"

He wiped his tears and put the gun in the glove compartment before slipping from the car to go sit by his unconscious mother, promising her he would find a way to honor her faith in him and see the world. Then he read poetry aloud to her quiet form until she passed to the great beyond.

So, on that day of June 11, 1936, the world changed...

Chapter Two: On the Pavement

"Civilized men are more discourteous than savages because they know they can be impolite without having their skulls split, as a general thing."
-Robert Ervin Howard

Bob Howard walked down Canal Street on the lower east side of Manhattan on a cold, September day soaking in the energy of the city. He was only in New York a few hours and already astounded by the sheer excess of it all.

It was his first time in any large city besides New Orleans, having never often left his small town in Texas. He was determined to make his fortune and see the world. Exactly how he was going to do it, beyond the fact that he had booked passage on a ship sailing for England in several months, he had no idea. He had no specific plans except to look up some publishers in New York before embarking, and with luck get some new writing assignments.

Howard was a writer. It was in his blood, his bones, his heart. He had been raised on tales of his family's past and had been making a scant living as a wordsmith for a decade. Now, with his mother three months dead, all her affairs finally settled, he was keeping his last promise to her in a bid to see the world.

No one in the dusty boomtown save her had understood Howard's need to write, to look to horizons distant and past, and touch the fantastic both inside and out.

She had always smiled when he told her of his latest story or the next one he planned to write. He renewed his promise to her spirit that he would live life to the fullest from this point out, not waiting in a small room for books to bring the world to him. He would go into the world and see it all for real.

To that end he had taken the small inheritance she had secretly hidden away for him and bought a train ticket for New York.

Robert Ervin 'Bob' Howard was a burly man just over six feet tall with wide shoulders, a friendly open face and clear blue eyes that some might call poet's eyes.

Those eyes were wide and startled and his smile almost constant as he walked most of Manhattan from the rail yards to the Empire State Building then down Fifth Avenue to spend part of his day in Washington Square Park and Greenwich Village. It was all so amazing to the stranger from the plains of Texas that he was constantly exclaiming, "I'll be darned!" with each new marvel he beheld.

He was as much a subject of awe to the locals as the buildings around him; he wore old cowboy boots, worn blue jeans, a dress shirt and tie, a tweed suit jacket and a battered cowboy hat jammed on his head against the gusts of winter wind.

If that had not been enough to establish him as a visitor to the city, he also carried a suitcase in one hand and a battered typewriter case in the other—surely badges of the tourist.

Now the Texan had wandered down Canal Street in search of a low-rent hotel he had read about in a magazine. He hoped he could get a room for the month he planned to wander the Big Apple before the steamship he'd booked passage on would set sail for England. Howard had finished a novella for *Adventure* Magazine while on the train, feeling a tremendous sense of accomplishment.

Added to that was a new excitement, knowing that later that week he would fulfill his own lifelong dream—to meet other writers in person!

From correspondence with his friend Howie Lovecraft, who was up in Massachusetts, the Texan had learned that on every third Friday of the month The American Fiction Guild met at an unassuming hotel on the east side of Manhattan.

The meetings were open to anyone who was 'in the word game' like Howard was. 'Pulpsters' they often called themselves. There were agents and editors there as well as writers at all levels of the pulp profession and Howard was excited to meet any and all of them.

Howard hoped to meet them, 'chew the fat' and even get some leads on assignments.

I guess I'll see Howie in the spring when I get back from Old England—hopefully when it's warmer up there in New England.

He'd walked down Fifth Avenue thrilled at the vista of the island above and below that the wide boulevard presented at a glance. In the writer's mind, it was old Alexandria, ancient Babylon or even fabled Atlantis and so much more.

I'll bet there are more people in one of these skyscraping buildings than in all of Cross Plains, he thought. *But just like all those empires that fell, even this one will pass away someday.* He looked at the determined and preoccupied faces of all those racing around him to seemingly no purpose and concluded, *Civilization is just not a natural state.*

When he'd reached Thirty-Fifth Street he stopped and like countless tourists since its completion, he leaned back in awe to admire the steel and stone needle pointing into the sky that was the Empire State Building. It was hard for him at that moment to even imagine such a spectacular sight succumbing to a horde of barbarian raiders, yet he knew it must someday happen.

Surely a Tower of Babel, he thought with a grin as he listened to the buzz of a hundred voices in many languages around him. *And in a blink of the eye of the Almighty it will join Rome and all the other fallen empires. Someday barbarians will eat meals on the cracked stones of it all.* He thought of the looming dangers in Europe of the Nazis in Germany, and the Japanese aggression in China, and realized that perhaps the day of the barbarian was not so far off.

Now as he walked along Canal Street, in search of the rooming house and marveling at the clothing shops and interesting curio stores, he became aware of the sound of a raucous crowd around the corner of an alley that was even louder than the general hubbub of the great city.

"Get him, Joey," a voice called out above the din. "He ain't got no defense."

"He can't take a punch," another voice said shrilly with a number of quick responses of "He's done alright so far!"

Howard rounded a corner to see a narrow alley between two buildings that was jammed with bodies—all working-class men but of every stripe from men in business suits to men in well-worn work clothes.

From the way the men yelled, their cries were focused inward to the center of the group. The Texan made a pretty good guess what was happening. He sidled up to one of the last of the crowd and asked just to be sure.

"What's going on, hombre?" Howard asked.

The questioned man, an overweight fellow in ill-fitting work clothes, who was sweating despite the cold, barely glanced at Howard as he spoke. "Big Carney is takin' on Joey O'Flynn! They been talkin' about this fight since Joey and he fought to a draw last year."

Howard could only push his way partially through the distracted crowd, but his height was sufficient to allow him to view the proceedings clearly. It was, as he had guessed, a bare-knuckles boxing match between two gladiators

The two men at the center of the furor could not have been more different; one was a tall shaven-headed negro who was muscular and lean. He had stripped to his narrow waist and showed a physique that might have been sculpted from ebony. His opponent was a few inches shorter but with a build like a beer keg. He was a red-haired fellow with almost no neck and fists that seemed outsized for his form. He wore a red plaid work shirt with the sleeves rolled up.

"Get 'em Joey!" called many in the crowd but "Shut the loudmouth up, Big Carney," many replied.

Howard noted that the calls for and against each man were, in many cases, across the racial lines—something he would not have heard back in his Texas town.

The two gladiators were both powerful boxers. Big Carney had a good guard, moving cautiously while Joey, relying on his massive forearms and shoulders to absorb punishment, had a more aggressive style. He advanced on the African with a steady steamroller-like attack.

Big Carney used footwork to move backward, launching lightning-swift strikes at Joey as he stepped backward and rolling with any of the powerful but slower blows from the redhead.

Howard watched the action with personal interest, having participated in a number of bare-knuckle matches in his hometown icehouse on Friday nights. The Texan realized that the redhead was fighting with anger in his movements while the black had a much more cool, technical approach.

"Grudge match?" Howard inquired of one of the watchers.

"Joey took a lickin' from Big Carney last year when the circus was in town," a fellow in a green fedora pulled down almost to his ears said. "Been takin' a ribbing about it since then."

A gray-suited slick came up to Green Fedora holding two singles in his hand and, as Howard watched, handed them to Green Fedora who nodded then slipped the money in his pocket.

"On Big Carney?" Green Fedora said. The gray-suited gent nodded.

Now the Texan noticed that other money was changing hands all around the circle of cheering men.

Across the crowd, he saw a thin fellow with a long nose, sharp features and narrow, dark eyes that gave him a vaguely rodential aspect who was taking bets for members of the crowd on that side of the 'pit.'

Just like the icehouse fights back home, Howard thought. *People really are alike all over.*

The fight in the center of the maelstrom became more intense as the rage in the red-haired fighter grew. He pressed harder at the African, the sheer force of his aggression continuing to drive Big Carney around the circle.

The black man, however had better footwork than his opponent and was able to avoid most of the force of the piledriver blows from the Irishman.

Howard could see that Big Carney was a boxer and Joey a 'fighter' but with enough brute force to cover the flaws in his technique. The true definition of 'slugger.'

"Gonna put down a bet, buddy?" Green Fedora asked the Texan.

"No thanks, *hombre,*" Howard said. "I don't know enough about the whole situation to risk my little poke on."

He did not know, but as he watched the situation became clearer by the moment as Joey pressed Big Carney a little too far. The African had waited for the Irishman to expend most of his power and now replied with a swift series of powerful jabs that stopped Joey's advance and began to stagger him. It looked like the big negro was going to win the match, his strategy had worked.

The redhead covered up and absorbed four strong shots. Howard watched him with intense concentration, seeing something that made him gasp.

Then suddenly, surprisingly, and with devastating effect, the redhead fired a fast combination of body blows that brought Big Carney to his knees.

The crowd went wild with screams before and against as the red-headed gladiator launched a rock-hard right cross that sent the negro to the ground.

The supporters of Joey quickly swarmed in around the victorious boxer and he accepted their praise with the humility of a presidential candidate that had been elected by a landslide.

Big Carney was nearly unconscious on all fours. The crowd that surged around him all but ignored the fallen fighter, with the few who had lost money on his defeat cursing him as they moved past.

Bob Howard watched it all transpire and felt his blood boil. He walked to the reeling Carney's side and knelt. "You alright, Hoss?"

The African looked up with slightly unfocused eyes, his lip bleeding and his cheek starting to swell. "I ain't never felt no human person hit that hard," he mumbled.

"I'm not surprised," the Texan said with distaste in his voice. "You weren't hit by no human; at least not by his lonesome."

He stood and in a loud voice aimed at the redhead and his supporters he said, "Joey done cheated y'all out of your honest bets sure as I'm standing here."

Chapter Three: Pie in the Sky

The crowd in the alley froze in eerie silence and all eyes turned to glare at the Texan. The sudden quiet allowed the sound of the busy metropolis to close in on the ad hoc arena.

"What did you say?" Green Fedora asked.

"I said that varmint is a cheatin' coward who would get himself shot if he tried that underhanded stunt back in Texas."

Now the redhead had pushed free of his admirers and walked toward the Texan.

"Who the hell do you think you are?" the Irishman asked.

"My name's Bob Howard, Mister, and I seen how you slipped a metal bar from your pocket then passed it to slimy over there when the crowd moved in." The Texan pointed at one of the redhead's supporters, a skinny fellow with a pock-marked face. The man looked at his accuser and his narrow eyes widened. He appeared ready to run from the alley.

"You're talking bushwa!" Joey snarled. "I don't like no country hick callin' me no cheat. I beat that shade fair and square; I'm the better man!"

Bob made a laughing sound and, faster than one would expect for a man of his build, raced across the alley. The Texan grabbed the skinny man by the scruff of his neck before he could bolt.

"Hey, let me go!" the man yelled but Howard took no notice and thrust a hand into the man's coat pocket. He pulled a short steel bar the size of a penny roll from the man's jacket and tossed it down at the redhead's feet. It landed with a loud 'chunk' sound.

Howard spoke to the crowd. "Joey slipped that from his own pocket when Big Carney was drivin' him back which is why he suddenly had 'iron in his fists' and then this here yahoo took it from him when the crowd rushed in." He turned to direct his steely gaze directly at the Irish fighter. "You better not try that kind of thing at a card game where I come from, fella, lest you want to get .44 caliber lead poisoning."

The spectators' eyes now turned toward the Irish fighter whose pale skin flushed red with anger and embarrassment.

There was dead silence for a long moment followed by a cacophony of curses as the bettors turned to collect their money back.

Joey was forced to hide among his supporters and had to withdraw from the alley post-haste as angry losers tried to recoup their losses.

Howard moved to Big Carney and helped the black man to his feet. There were welts showing on the African and his lip was badly split but he was grinning. "You put up a good fight, Big Hoss," the Texan said. "But that sidewinder was shootin' from ambush."

Big Carney, taller than the Texan by several inches, winced with the effort of his smile. "I'm glad you saw his switch, Boss. I was sure I was losin' my edge." The battered fighter showed no anger at his defeat; on the contrary, he seemed to be singularly happy at being 'vindicated'.

"You may have made yourself an enemy with that Joey fella, Boss," The negro continued. "His memory is pretty long—he done waited a whole year to sneak his revenge on me for beatin' him fair last time we played this town."

"You ain't gonna chase that polecat yourself?"

"No sir," the black said. He gingerly donned a shirt and suit jacket and picked up a fedora to slip on his shaved head. "Ain't no percentage in a negro chasin' no white fella, even in so open-minded a city as New York."

Howard nodded. "Can't say you're wrong there about it being open-minded, Big Hoss; even if I'm just in town today I could see it sure ain't Texas."

"You're pretty open-minded yourself for a Texan, sir," the African said, "no offense meant."

"None taken," Howard replied with an easy drawl. "It's one of the reasons I left—to broaden and open my mind, if you will."

"That why you come to New York?" The two were walking from the alley now, up Canal Street, and the Texan marveled at how such a pair attracted little or no notice but would have been a scandal back home.

"That and to make my fortune. And by fortune, I mean enough money to keep me fed; I have enough for rent on a cheap room but want to look for some work while I also look for writin' work. I'm planning to sail for Europe in three weeks but figured I could find some piecemeal somethin' to keep me in victuals till then."

Big Carney smiled and winced again. "Well, Boss, I think you just found yourself a job. You ever been to a circus?"

"I appreciate you treating me to a meal, Big Hoss," Howard said. "After I pay for my room, I really won't have all that much left for victuals."

The two men had walked to one of MacFadden's Penny Restaurants on the way uptown after Howard decided not to check his baggage into a ten-dollar a week hotel. Big Carney said the job at the circus came with room and board and that was inducement enough for the Texan.

The two men began to chat about life in general and a little about the Texan's chosen profession.

"I figure I've always been sort of inclined to tall tales, hearing and telling. I had an old mammy once tell me about Skili, the owl witches that haunted the night and hunted souls; I imagine they woulda sounded like that owl's cry Fact among the Cherokee the word for shape-shifting witches and a regular old horned owl is the same; Skili."

"I had an aunt what used to tell me such things," Big Carney said. "Seems she always had another tale out of the swamps or hills, kept us all amused for hours with her stories."

"Ain't all imagination," Howard said wistfully. "She'd sit with me some nights outside the café where she was a cook and tell me tales of things in the swamps of Louisiana where she come from and secrets of her Juju. Got to so as I could recite some of them old spells from heart. And my Mama used to tell me tales of fox women back there that did their own hunting; I suppose it's just the thing that makes a fella like me a tad bit suspicious of women, eh?"

MacFadden's Penny Restaurant was a godsend to the lower working classes, according to Big Carney. "I has eaten at these places all over the country, Boss Bob; it ain't exactly food but it can fill a man between real meals."

"I wish you'd quit that 'boss' and call me Bob."

"Maybe when we've sweated together a bit and in private but I likes to be careful." The African left unsaid what the Texan knew—being too familiar with the 'wrong' person was punishable in many parts of the country and even if New York was broad minded it was not a good habit to get into. As it was, places like the Cotton Club still did not allow the black talent to mix with the all-white patrons; and that was in Harlem itself.

Howard marveled at the meal; nine cents bought a hamburger made from what tasted like meat-flavored sawdust (four cents), a good hard roll (one penny), a cup of coffee that owed more to chicory than anything else (two cents) and a dessert piece of pie (two cents).

The unusual pair blended with the other down-and-out diners who all stood at high counters since there were no chairs which, it was said, encouraged good digestion, but in fact moved people through more quickly.

"So, what is your real name, or do you want I should just call you Big Carney?"

"My mama named me Biggles Charles Johnson, but you can imagine the ribbin' I got as a tadpole so I was Biggie from real young. Then when I joined up the circus, I just sort of became Big Carney."

"What made you join the circus?"

"Oh, I guess the chance to travel, Boss Bob—"

"Bob, please—"

"Well, Boss Bob," the big man said with a smile that told the Texan he was not prepared to take 'that' liberty—yet. "It was a way to see the country, go places a fella like me might not always be welcome—with a family around me, sort of." He looked around at the others in the restaurant. "But I like New York—a man can just be here and not be judged. And you get to meet new and interesting people."

"Well, a pleasure to know you," Howard laughed. "And to be deemed 'interesting.' Back home I was just 'odd.' And I appreciate this fine feast you have laid before me."

"We eat better at the circus, but I was a bit puckish after my little dance with Joey. Mister Maxim—he's the fella that owns the circus—sees we all put a good feed on. Says he can work us harder if we have full stomachs." He patted his flat stomach as if it were Buddha-like. "I agree."

"What's it like working there?"

The tall African shrugged. "It is a good job; a hard one, don't get me wrong, but a good one. A man is taken for who he is there, and what he does. Not what some rube's idea of how people should be treated cause of what they look like, you know?" A shadow seemed to pass across his battered features. "'Cept, of course, like in any group there is some-what holdin' to certain views on race."

"Oh?"

"I'm hiring boss now for the roustabouts," the African said, "but there's a few folk what don't think no colored should be in charge of nothin'."

Howard nodded with a sad expression. "People are the same all over."

"Yeah, so I've found as well," the big man continued. "But there are just as many and more that don't hold to those views and a husky fella like you will fit in just fine; nobody can put up a fuss."

"I don't want to cause no trouble for you. I'm sure I can find me something to tide me over—and I plan to hit some of the magazine publishers here in the city and try to get some assignments. I just need me some spending cash while I wait for my boat."

"I'm the boss for hiring. Work here until you leave for…where you say you going again? England? We always take on some locals when we open, and you can take time here and there to see your publishers; besides—I figure I owe you a few arguments since you saved both my reputation and my paycheck."

"How so?"

"Well, I done bet all I had on myself," Big Carney said. "This here is a victory meal that you helped pay for; have another piece of pie!"

Chapter Four: Writer to Roustabout

The two new acquaintances made their way across the busy street with the Texan pleasantly confused by the hubbub around him.

Once they were across the street Howard paused to take in the famed Madison Square Garden. It was a massive building, more impressive to the Texan than even many of the skyscrapers. It was two hundred feet by almost four hundred feet, with seating on three levels, and a maximum capacity of almost nineteen thousand spectators for boxing but had now been inside configured for the Maxim Brothers' Circus.

"We have a lot in back as well," the black man said, "and two canvas tents to work the animals in so we are only in the garden when we need to be. We open in four days. One of the reasons I was down near the bowery was looking for brawny types like you, Boss."

The large open parking area behind the Garden was a beehive of activity that seemed to the Texan to put the mad activity of the city itself to shame.

A horse training ring was set up outside one of the tents and a thin, pale man in jodhpurs worked a grey gelding on a long lead. He cursed the animal as it went through its paces.

A pretty blonde woman was watching from the side of the ring and when the trainer snapped his whip at the horse to hit it in the muzzle, she yelled at him.

"Klaus you can't keep hitting him," the girl said. "It just makes him stubborn." Her voice was distinctly New York which seemed at odds with her delicate features.

"I'll teach this devil some respect," Klaus said. His thinness was an ascetic thin. It was only after he studied him that

Bob vaguely recognized the rodential man's from Big Carny's boxing match on the Bowery.

"Not if you terrify him," the girl said to the trainer. "You gotta make him respect you."

"I'd rather have him fear me. These damn things ain't smart enough to respect nothin." He caught sight of Big Carney and Howard and sneered. "Like some other dumb animals I know of."

The Texan saw the muscular negro bite his lip at the clear insult and would have said something if he had not feared costing Big Carney his job.

"That is Boss Klaus," Big Carney said when the friends had passed the ring. "He's billed as the "Colossal Klaus," he has a horse act. The little lady with him is Miss Julie. She is his lead rider and his wife, though what she sees in him none of us can figure."

"Sometimes it's hard to figure females," The Texan said. "I ain't never got any of them figured at all."

"What fella does?" Big Carney laughed and Howard joined him.

"I saw that fella at your fight. He was taking money."

"He gambles everywhere we go," the negro said. "Some of us suspect he's got mob connections, but we never say so, ya know? It ain't healthy."

Inside the open-sided tent Howard and Big Carney found half a dozen burly men seated around a boiling pot of stew, chatting.

"Boys," the head roustabout said, "this here is Bob Howard. He's in from Texas and he's gonna be helpin' you fellas with the rigging. Bernie, show him where to stow his gear then you can all meet me in the center ring, and we'll set out what is what for tomorrow."

Bernie was a fireplug of a fellow that barely came to Howard's shoulder but who radiated both power and amiability. "Come wit' me, Bob, I'll get you settled."

The smaller man led the Texan to a sort of barracks with cots set up for the roustabouts.

"I ain't never been as far south as Texas," Bernie said. "I'm from Jersey myself. Heck, I ain't even been south of Trenton! I'm hopin' that the circus will take me with it this time when they go on tour."

"You don't work with them all the time?"

"Naw, just the last two times they come to New York. I met Big Carney at a bare knuckles match, and he invited me to work here. It's good food and the pay is good, and I like the people."

Howard smiled. "I gotta say I'm with you on that, Bernie."

After the Texan picked a bunk and stowed his gear beneath it the two men walked back across the open area and into Madison Square Garden itself where an army of workers was already rearranging the floor for the circus.

"The hockey teams are here when we aren't," Bernie said. "We have to move the seats and set down planking and sawdust by ourselves. Plus, they just did some repairs on the place so there is a lot of just plain junk around we have to deal with this time. That's why the circus came in two weeks early this time; more dough for us!"

And that is what the Texan and a dozen other burly men worked on for the rest of the day, setting the flooring of the building in place at the direction of the Garden staff.

Howard found himself enjoying the physical labor and the camaraderie. All the men were blue-collar types, some quite rough and ready, but all grateful to have the work and all a little enamored with the circus life.

While they worked the circus folk proper were beginning to rehearse in the space. Bob got to see the equestrian girl, Julie, as she rode around the outside of the arena while the workmen were laying the center ring's floor.

"Something, ain't she?" One of the men said when he saw the Texan looking.

The girl in close up was fulfillment of her distant image, with warm blue eyes and a ready smile as she worked the horse with centaur-like skill.

If she was aware of the men ogling her, she gave no sign, lost in the joy of the ride.

"Like a valkyrie come to earth," Howard said.

"Huh?"

"Yeah, she's somethin'," the Texan said. "Like she was born on the horse; I ain't never seen a better rider back home."

"You know something about horses?" Bernie asked.

"I used to ride. And my dad was a doctor, but in my area that meant animal doctoring as well, so I'd go on calls with him."

Just as he spoke one of the workers up in the seats dropped a wrench that clattered down the metal stairs with a sharp din that cut through the noise of the general work.

It was a sharp enough sound to startle the horse the girl was riding.

It spooked. The girl was able to rein him in, but the sudden sound was enough so that when a worker in front of the animal dropped a pile of boards, the resultant commotion caused the already unnerved animal to bolt.

Even a rider with the blonde girl's skill could not control the doubly frightened animal and the white stallion whinnied in terror and spun, fighting the girl's attempt to hold him. The panicked horse snorted in fear, and it was all the rider could do to keep from being thrown from the now maddened runaway.

Howard saw the girl's predicament immediately and dropped the planks he was holding. He raced across the arena before anyone else had even realized something was wrong.

Chapter Five: The Price of Heroism

The Texan had the presence of mind to grab for a coil of rope on a crate as he ran past some construction debris. He began waving his arms above his head with the rope in his hand. He knew that with the poor eyesight of the equine any object in front of it would appear larger and by holding his hands up he would be even more frightening to the beast than the sound that scared it.

The horse saw Howard and shied.

The beast veered off while Bob made a quick loop in the rope. The Texan ran at an angle to the startled horse while he twirled and tossed the lasso he'd made. His first cast was a good one and slipped over the animal's neck with an almost supernatural skill. He leaned back and the loop tightened.

The horse bucked and snorted but the rope held, dragging the Texan a few feet before he could lock his legs and plant his feet.

The other roustabouts moved to create a human blockade while Howard leaned into the rope, careful to only apply enough pressure around the runaway's neck to slow it down rather than bulldog it and cause it to fall over with the girl on its back.

The blonde rider, with the rope lead as a distraction, was able to regain control of the stallion. Howard choked up on the rope and walked slowly forward, pulling in the rope hand over hand until he was close enough to place a gentling palm on the muzzle of the horse.

"Easy, boy," The Texan said in a relaxed drawl. "Ain't nobody gonna hurt you none at all."

He continued talking calmly to the horse in a calm voice while the other roustabouts closed in to hold the animal.

The girl vaulted from the saddle and stood breathing hard, leaning against the flank of the stallion.

The horse gradually calmed down with Howard's gentle voice and one of the other men took the horse's reins.

"You alright, ma'am?" The Texan asked the girl.

She looked up at Howard and flashed a radiant smile. "I am thanks to you, cowboy, that was quick thinking."

The Texan colored and forced himself to tear his gaze away from her blue eyes. "I-uh- saw he was gonna spook just a hair before he did, and I've seen that look in a cayuse's eyes before."

"You know horses?"

"A bit."

"More than a bit, I would think," she corrected him. She put a long-fingered hand on his arm. It was surprisingly strong for so delicate a hand. "Thank you." She came up on her tiptoes and leaned in to peck the Texan on the cheek. "Everyone should have a cowboy standing by to help!"

The Texan colored again and the roustabouts nearby all snickered good-naturedly when suddenly a sharp voice intruded.

"What the hell is going on here?" It was the horse trainer Klaus. He strode across floor of the Garden directly at the blonde girl.

The much larger roustabouts parted to let the trainer through. He went directly to the girl and snapped at her, "What the hell are you doing with Champion, you idiot?"

"Klaus, I was just--" she began.

"I don't want to hear your stupid excuses!" The horse hearing his raised voice began to snort in discomfort.

"Ease off there, hombre," Howard said. "That ain't no way to talk to a lady." The burly Texan moved to interpose himself between the trainer and the girl.

"How dare you even address me you dung sweeper," Klaus hissed. He looked past Howard to stare daggers at the blonde. "As for you, I will deal with you later." He turned abruptly on his heels and strode off as if his pronouncement was final.

Howard clenched his fists so hard that his hand vibrated to keep himself from swinging at the trainer. The blonde girl saw this and put a hand on his arm again.

"It's okay," she said in a subdued tone as she watched Klaus leave then added, "I really do appreciate you saving me, Cowboy." She leaned in and planted another quick peck on the Texan's cheek before taking the lead line from one of the other men and walking the horse across the Garden floor.

Howard stood staring after her, his suppressed rage at the trainer's insults sending blood roaring in his ears.

"Let it go, Bob," Big Carney said, sliding up beside the Texan.

"I ain't so good at swallowin' that kind of guff," Howard said. "It comes hard to Texans."

"It comes hard to all of us, Boss Bob," the negro said with a deep sadness in his tone. "But youse gotta do it to get by."

Howard looked up at the African giant and gave a wan smile. "And sometimes even triumph, eh?"

"We hope so, Boss."

The roustabouts returned to their duties, but all afternoon Howard's mind kept returning to the placid beauty of the girl and the viciousness in Klaus's expression.

Bernie and the Texan were thrown together often enough that they were able to chat a bit as they worked.

"You write stories and people pay you?" The smaller man asked as they unloaded pallets of wood.

"Well, they're supposed to," the Texan said with a laugh, "But places like *Weird Tales* take a dog's age to pay."

"I just think it's pretty amazing," Bernie said. "I ain't never met a writer."

"Well, I ain't either," Howard said. When the Jersey man looked confused Howard added, "Where I grew up they kinda thought I was a circus freak for even reading as much as I did let alone the idea of makin' stories up and getting' folks to buy them."

He hefted a four by four off the truck bed and stopped to wipe his brow. "I've only corresponded with a couple of writers, Howie Lovecraft up in Boston most, but I hope to meet some while I'm in New York and get some assignments before I take off for Europe."

"Europe!" Bernie said with awe, shaking his head. "I'm just hoping to make it as far as the Mississippi. For a country boy you sure think big."

"Maybe," Howard said with a chuckle. "But I'm a country boy from Texas and that makes all the difference!"

That night in the dinner tent the hard-working men were a jocular group and Howard almost forgot the incident until he saw the blonde rider and the trainer enter the tent. The girl had a black eye.

There was a murmur of discontent as all those in the tent noticed the shiner. When the Texan saw that he started to rise but Bernie put a hand on his arm and a discouraging glance from Big Carney kept him seated.

"Let it be, Bob. It's happened before."

"And you've done nothing?"

"She always says it was just an accident, she was 'clumsy' or such," the negro said. "Nothing we can do till she wants us to."

"Or until he hurts her too bad?" Howard said. "Where I come from we know how to handle his sort--"

"It's not that easy," Bernie spoke up. "They are married and you can't risk your job. You can't save someone from drowning if they want to drown."

The Texan considered his words for a long moment then nodded. "I gotta tell ya, gents, this 'civilized' world of ours leaves me wanting something else most of the time."

Much of the rest of the meal was almost silent as the men were all afraid to voice their feelings about what they had seen. Eventually they began to converse again with a forced jocularity that spoke to how much they did not want to deal with Julie and her issues with Klaus.

"Attention, everyone," a balding figure in a loud sports coat stepped up to the head of the tent and got everyone's attention by banging on a table with a tin cup. "Are you all getting a good meal?"

The group all yelled, "yes!"

"That's Lou Maxim," Bernie whispered to Howard. "He's the managing owner."

"I know you've all had a hard day and you have a lot of work ahead of you still, but I wanted to thank you all and let you know that I appreciate all you do to make our little family successful. We open in a few days so you'll be working long shifts. We all will, but once we open, I'll stand you all to a turkey dinner with all the fixings!"

A cheer went up around the tent.

"See, I told you these were good folks to work for," Bernie said with a grin. "Now you know why I want to travel with the show."

"Same reason I joined up, way back when," Big Carney said. "That and we can be having this talk at the same table."

Bernie nodded, a little embarrassed by the obvious fact that there were no distinctions in the circus world as in the rest of society. At least not the same distinctions.

Howard acknowledged Big Carney's words but kept his eyes toward the exit. Big Carney could see where he was focused.

"Gotta let it go, Boss Bob," the African said.

"Some things just stay with me, Hoss," the Texan said. "But I'll walk it off and not scotch things for anyone."

"We'll head back in to lay more floor in about fifteen minutes," the African said. "Boys'll take themselves a smoke before we go in. Why don't you cool off outside?"

"Thanks," Howard said. He pushed away from the table and headed out of the tent to try and cool his anger.

The lights of Manhattan all but glared out the twinkling stars and the Texan was aware of the constant roar of traffic just out of eyeshot. Across the river New Jersey shore lights blinked mysteriously and ships out on the river seemed to blink in sympathy.

"Ain't no good," he whispered to himself after a time. "I guess I wasn't cut out to hold on to this job. I just gotta talk to that Klaus fella. And it's gonna be a serious talk!"

Chapter Six: Facing Up To It

Bob not quite sure where to go to find Klaus and Julie with a deep simmering need to take some sort of action. He was uncertain what, since simply beating the horse trainer with his fists as a solution to the 'problem' would be lowering himself to the abuser's level.

Still, he had to do something, even if it were only to talk to the girl and convince her to leave the brute. *Some knight in shining armor I am,* he thought as he wandered between the tents in the converted parking lot. *I'm just a ball of anger with no point to it--kind of like that varmint I'm after.* It was Howard's curse for being a poetic, empathic soul despite his country upbringing.

The problem complicated when he rounded the corner of one tent and almost ran smack into Lou Maxim.

"Easy there, big guy," the circus owner said. "You'll hurt yourself running around out here, lots of ropes and cables, you know?"

"Sorry, sir."

"I saw you in the food tent," Maxim said. "But I don't remember you from Philly."

"Uh, no sir," Howard said. "I just joined up today, Mister Maxim. Bob Howard." He extended his hand and received a surprising solid grip from the owner.

"Is that a Texas accent I detect?"

"Guilty, sir."

"We've played Dallas and Houston last season and gonna add San Antonio this coming season." The balding boss smiled. "I hope you will like it with us enough to stay for that tour."

Howard felt warmth from the man that explained so much about how the whole of the circus folk felt about each other; it was a family, and this big, jolly man was the father figure.

But there was more than jocularity in the man's eyes, a wisdom and sharpness. And Maxim showed that when he said, "You seem troubled, son."

"I gotta say, sir," Howard said, "that I do but I'm not sure just how to handle it. See, I know what's gotta be done,-- a lesson's gotta be taught someone, but I'm afraid if I do it my actions will--well, make me no better than the fella I plan on teachin' a lesson."

The circus owner pursed his lips then produced a cigar which he made a great show of lighting. He took two puffs before he answered. "If you feel that strongly, son, I'd expect the best thing to do would be to tell that person face to face what he is missing. I suppose you will have to hope that does what you want."

The Texan digested that advice for a moment while Maxim puffed away than asked, "Do you know where Mister Klaus and Julie's tent is, sir?"

"Ah, now the light dawns, it's that way, Mister Howard. You keep in mind we are a big family here. I started this show from literally a one-horse operation, putting on riding exhibitions in towns so small you if you blinked, you'd be out the other side. I've worked hard to keep this family alive and vital, but like all families we have our black sheep. But they are still family so, if an argument within the family happens it should be for the good of the family." Maxim's implication was clear to the Texan, and it helped to further temper his western fury as he moved away from the circus owner.

Once Howard reached the outside of the tent, he paused to catch his breath and try to cool his Gaelic temper.

I don't have to resort to his tactics, the Texan thought, *If I can bluff him into thinking I will*. With that decision he started to open the tent flap but a shrill voice from within stopped him.

"I don't care what kind of guff you want to give me, Schmidt," a strangely familiar voice said. "You got a marker and you gotta pay off."

"I just need another week, Jack," Klaus's voice answered. "I had no idea that cowboy would spot your idiot man's switch."

"It don't make no difference," the other voice said. "You owe me and that means you owe O'Bannon and he's one of the big boys."

"But I--"

"But nothing," the sharp voice snapped at Klaus. "Pay up by tomorrow night or it won't be me that comes to collect; it will be The German himself or one of his boys and they won't be asking nice."

Howard jumped back as the flap to the tent opened, hiding in the shadows while a familiar figure exited; it was another face from the boxing match; the one who wore a green fedora who he had seen cheat Big Carney.

Klaus stepped out of the tent to watch the man leave and cursed. "Damn bookie!"

"Klaus," Julie came out of the tent to stand by the trainer. "The tea is ready." She held out a cup to Klaus, but he struck the cup out of her hand so that the hot tea spilled on her. She yelped in pain.

That was too much for the Texan. Howard rocketed forward and grabbed the trainer by the collar and flung the smaller man bodily against the side of the tent.

"You need to learn some manners, boy. Where I come from we don't lay hands on women folk."

The trainer leaned against the canvas, stunned by being manhandled and stared at the writer. "You keep away from me, pathetic minion! I will have you up on charges."

"And I will have you in a hospital if you ever touch that woman again, and there ain't no jail that can stop me from keeping my promise to you."

The blonde girl flew to Howard and grabbed his arm. "Don't hurt him." She was still dripping from the spilled tea.

"I don't plan to, ma'am, but then, I don't plan to see you hurt none, neither. I ain't as patient as some of the folk-- I'm not about to just let things stay the way they are."

"But--"

"Sorry, ma'am," The burly Texan said as he took her by the elbow and escorted her. "But we have to talk away from this varmint." He turned back to stare daggers at Klaus.

"You don't move your lily-white butt out of here if you know what's good for you," the Texan warned. "Not till we say so."

The woman went willingly, if somewhat confusedly with Howard, who took her some distance away, looking back to be sure that Klaus did not exit the tent to follow them.

"Ma'am," Howard said when they stood out of earshot of the trainer, "I know it ain't no one's business but your own who you love or how, but that being said, it ain't easy for folks to turn a blind eye."

The woman's face was a canvas of conflicting emotions. Her eyes seemed on the verge of tears, but Howard could also see strength within them. When she finally spoke, it was slowly and deliberately, each word painful.

"I met Klaus when I was just a girl. He was so strong willed and sure of himself. And I was in a home that--well that was not a good one. My father drank and used to hit my mother around."

"You don't have to tell me this, ma'am, I'm not accusing you of doing anything wrong. I know from my mama that the heart don't make the smartest decisions sometimes--but--you have to save yourself, ma'am. It can't get no better, no matter how much he says it will be different or he will change--his sort don't. Not without a lot of outside help, which he ain't seekin'."

The Texan spoke tenderly with no condescension in his tone. "I said my piece to him, and now I'll just say one last thing. ma'am, then I'll leave you two alone. Only you can change your life; but you ain't in this alone-- no one that has friends is; and you got lots of friends. I'd like you to consider me one of them."

The two stood for a long moment, the girl looking up into his eyes but with her vision focused inward and she seemed to be looking at the panorama of her life rather than her hopeful Texan savior.

Chapter Seven: Another Match

Howard left her and went into the Garden, most of his fury spent by his conversation, but still full of nervous energy. He put himself harder into the labor that evening setting up bleachers, doing the work of two.

"You're full of vinegar tonight, Bob," Bernie said.

"Just turning lemons into lemonade," the Texan said as he hefted a large beam.

He continued to work with the other men that night, but his mind was still on his last sight of the blonde girl focused on an inner landscape, reflecting on the path that had gotten her to where a rough neck from Texas was lecturing her.

The Texas writer laughed to himself. The absurdity of the whole affair kept returning to him. *I'm just a country bumpkin, what do I know about the whole wide world? I should keep my opinions to myself. Miss Julie is an adult. I should stay out of it.*

He only half convinced himself, but the distraction of the physical labor helped. It was exhilarating to throw himself into the work and to enjoy the company of the simple but honest roustabouts.

When the men knocked off at midnight, they were all exhausted but with a sense of having accomplished something. The reshaped interior of the Garden was coming into focus for the opening little more than a week away.

Howard took an hour after the other men had hit the hay to pull out his battered typewriter and turn out his quota of wordage for the day--something he never failed to do despite any circumstance--even his exhaustion. He had been 'thinking' a story for *Dime Detective* Magazine all day and so it flowed quickly from his fingers.

When he finally hit his cot, he was asleep in moments.

The next morning began with a hearty breakfast that was jocular as dinner had been, with all the circus folk a boisterous and pleasant group.

"Is it always like this?" Howard asked.

"We open on next Thursday," Big Carney said when he saw Howard as the two men got into line for chow. "Everyone has lots of nerves and we have long hours. A little more than usual since we have to clean up the mess the renovations made. But it will even out after that."

"Oh yes, about next Friday, is it possible for me to get out early enough to go to an Author's Guild meeting they have here in the city once a month?"

"Oh, sure," the big African said. "By then it will just be maintenance on things; so we'll all have a lot more down time until we have to strike the show at the end of our run."

The news that he would be able to finally meet some other writers did much to buoy the Texan's spirits as the day's work began.

Things brightened even more when Julie came into the corral to work her horses. She was her usual perky self, solicitous to everyone but she cast a particularly broad smile toward the Texan.

Klaus was nowhere to be seen for much of the morning and when he did put in an appearance it was to make a quick check of the horse stalls. He studiously avoided eye contact with both Howard and his wife.

At lunch the Texan was amazed to see the blonde girl take a seat near him at the table.

"Enjoying your time here with the circus, Mister Howard?"

"Bob, please. And yes. The-um--people here are nice." When he realized what he'd said he blushed.

She giggled but her smile was gentle. "Yes, and sometimes the people who join the circus are nice as well." She made it clear she was thanking him for his intervention without trying to embarrass him further.

The other roustabouts thought her friendly smile was in response to Howard's public heroism of the day before. Both of them let the others continue to believe that.

"I think your 'conversation' with Klaus had a real effect," she said quietly to the Texan. "He was very docile today and even gentle. Caring. Like he used to be."

"I hope it makes a difference, ma'am."

"Please call me Julie. Friends should use first names."

"Julie it is then."

"Okay, Cowboy," Big Carney called from the head of the table, "Time to make the circus happen!"

"See you out there, Bob," the blonde said and waved him off.

The afternoon went swiftly for the Texan, now able to immerse himself in the work with no guilt or concern for the girl. Instead, he felt a little excitement for the prospect of meeting other writers the next Friday evening.

It wasn't until sometime after dinner, while everyone else was smoking and Howard was taking a walk outside the parking lot to stretch, that the Texan saw Klaus again.

The horse trainer was standing at the edge of the parking lot talking with Big Carney and the man in the green fedora that Howard recognized from the boxing match in the alley.

They were engaged in a heated conversation with Big Carney shaking his head at first but after some conversation he finally nodded assent.

The Texan hid in the shadows until Klaus and Fedora headed off and when the head roustabout came by let himself be seen.

"What was that all about?" Howard asked. "They tryin' to pressure you about the fight the other day?"

The tall negro laughed. "No. They wanted to get another fight going, said a lot of people want to see me in a fair fight against O'Bannon's new fighter. A fella they call The German."

"You gonna do it?"

"I figure, why not?" Big Carney said. "They're talking next weeknight the show closes. Just invited guests. Could be a big purse."

"Do you figure they'll be on the up and up?"

"After the last time word got out it wasn't so, yeah," the tall man smiled. "I figure they have to be honest, or nobody will ever bet on any match Tony or O'Bannon ever throws."

"Tony?"

"The guy with the green hat. He's the leg man for Red O'Bannon who runs the Irish mob here in the city."

"What did Klaus have to do with it?" The Texan asked.

"He brokered it," Big Carney said. "I guess he lost a lot on the match betting against me as well. And I gotta say he seemed a bit cowed." He raised an eyebrow and stared at the writer. "You didn't do nothin' to him last night, did you, Boss?"

"Now, Big Hoss, would I do something like that?"

Both men laughed together.

"You sure you can trust these guys?"

"Only as far as it's in their own interest to put on an honest fight."

Howard nodded. He was familiar with the gambling culture from back home in Cross Plains. There the 'rough' element had been a little more obvious and not so well heeled as Green Fedora--Tony-- but none the less the same type.

A disease of civilization, he thought. *The 'operators' provide the sport for the weak-kneed ones who don't have the guts to participate.*

He had watched and even participated in the icehouse fights back home but not so much as a spectator sport as a tool to learn and, if truth be told, an outlet for his tremendous energy that was not used up at his typewriter.

"I figure with you to watch my back I'll be able to take this German fella without breaking too much of a sweat, Boss Bob." He gave a playful punch at the Texan's shoulder and laughed. "I'd put down a bit on this brown boy to win!"

Howard joined him in the laugh. "I'll do that—and be your corner man. When is this fight gonna happen, Carney?"

"Next Friday night at midnight."

The Texan thought for a moment. "Well, I reckon even if I make some good connections with writers and such at that meeting," Howard said, "I'll be able to be back-to-back you up."

"Good," the big negro said. "Now I know I'll box this German fella's ears but good!"

The two friends went back to work in the main arena and put in another long night, but now the interior space was beginning to look like a circus.

That night the Texan had barely enough strength left for a few short letters he had to send out and made only half of his usual word quota.

The next days were sunup till midnight filled with hard labor so that each night the exhausted writer, after a reduced word quota, joined the other roustabouts in deep slumber. The buzz about the following week's fight had already begun and a lot of money was beginning to change hands.

The legend of 'The German' grew with each retelling; He had been a boxer in Chicago and killed a man, he was an enforcer for a California mob boss, and many other fanciful tales. All that was certain was that he had fought and won many bouts in Cincinnati and Kansas City and had a reputation for brutal wins.

Big Carney enjoyed his renewed celebrity status and, combined with the coming opening of the circus and the prospect of Howard finally meeting other writers the Texan felt like his first trip to the big city was a rip-roarin' success.

Then things changed...

Chapter Eight: Gone to Meetin'

Despite his exhaustion from the week of hard work Bob Howard felt like an excited kid on Friday when the circus opened.

Though the Texan had seen many of the rehearsals during the week, the dress rehearsal that the circus held for the roustabouts and a few invited guests to watch still knocked his socks off.

The acts were amazing displays of skill and everyone, even the formerly sulking Klaus seemed in a good mood. It seemed the magic spell of the big top had transformed the brick and stone building into a living dream for all who entered. Even the stagehands and roustabouts oohed and awed with everyone else as the trapeze artists, acrobats and riders went through their complex routines.

Julie was especially radiant and sent a special smile toward the Texan as she rode out into the arena for her show. Klaus' slightly sour glance did nothing to dull the effect of the blonde's smile.

Afterward Mr. Maxim held a feast for all the cast and crew and Bob truly felt as if he were at an extended family gathering. He had come to enjoy his time chatting with Bernie and Big Carney all week and Julie, who had often taken lunch near them.

The Texan learned she had grown up in a small town in Illinois, not unlike Cross Plains, and married Klaus when he had come through with a small circus. She had learned much and seen much since then and rose to a position in the circus world where she was a headliner. That rapid rise seemed to have affected Klaus and his gambling had gotten worse and his attentions violent.

She told Howard that she had begun thinking seriously about heading out on her own. And though Klaus had been 'minding his p's and q's' since Howard's talk with him it seemed as if her leaving the trainer was inevitable.

Some of the other roustabouts noticed the friendship of the writer and the rider but none seemed to take offense at it. Even Klaus seemed to be cordial when he saw the two talking, his expression modified to a slight scowl for most of the week.

Howard finished a novella for *Adventure* Magazine that night, feeling a tremendous sense of accomplishment. And excitement knowing that the next day he would fulfill his own lifelong dream, meeting other writers in person!

The American Fiction Guild met in the bar at a hotel on the east side of Manhattan and Howard hoped to find work from some of the agents or editors there. Even if he didn't find work, just being in a room with other wordsmiths had his scalp tingling with excitement.

"I just hope I don't go all goosefooted and make a laughingstock of myself," he said to Bernie as the two went back to the barracks after the opening Friday afternoon show.

"Ah, come on, Bob," the little man said. "Youse can talk as good as any guy I ever met when you want to and you sure got enough stories and stuff in magazines." He pointed to a *Weird Tales* on one of the bunks that had a cover illustration of a woman kneeling before a pagan god. In bold letters across the bottom of the cover were the words "A new Conan story by Robert E. Howard".

"That is one I wrote three years ago," the Texan said. "They are slow to print them sometimes."

"Still, it came out only last week. Bob, you'll do fine." He made a shooing motion with his hands. "Now get going. I got me a hot card game calling my name! See ya later!"

The Texan put on his good brown suit, shined his cowboy boots and brushed his Stetson as if he were heading on a date with Carole Lombard.

Several of the roustabouts whistled and razzed him good-naturedly as he left the Garden and after he blushed, he swept his hat off in a grand bow feeling like Gene Autry.

Bob consulted a little hardback guidebook with a map in it to find his path down to Gramercy Park to the hotel that housed the Author's Guild Meeting.

He did not notice the two men who fell into an easy step behind him the moment the Texan left the Garden.

Howard was still amazed by the sheer volume of humanity on the tiny island, the density of the population and the fact that everyone seemed to be hurrying somewhere. No one 'mosied' in the Big Apple and everyone seemed to take that all in stride.

The Texan's mind was on overload with the possibilities of life since leaving Cross Plains. Now he was actually going to meet other writers- and not just one or two. According to letters from his pal Howie Lovecraft there could be upwards of twenty or thirty authors at some of the bigger meetings. All in one place! And editors and agents as well.

Howard could not help but smile like a giddy bride-groom.

The wonders of the city continued to amaze and over-power the Texan's senses. Every face seemed to be a starting point for him to spin off into a wild story; how had that person gotten there, why was he or she smiling, frowning? What country were they from, were they going to? Were they chasing someone or was someone following them?

He turned down Fifth Avenue thrilled by the vista of the island above and below him that the wide boulevard presented.

As he was lost in his woolgathering looking up at the building, the first of the two men following him struck.

The thug swung a lead filled cosh hidden in a newspaper at Howard's head, directly at the crown of the Texan's hat.

That direct aim saved Howard's life. The sap crushed the crown of the stiffened Stetson hat and would have done the same for its wearer save for the guidebook that he had secreted under the hat!

The force of the blow stunned the Texan and drove him to his knees but did not incapacitate him as the attacker intended. Some instinct in Howard took over and as he dropped, he twisted and grabbed for the assailant. His vice-like grip latched onto the left pant leg just below the knee and yanked.

The attacker, surprised as much as his victim had been, pitched backward with a startled cry. Howard threw himself on the fallen man even though he was still not fully aware of what was going on.

"Get this hick off of me, Moe," the fallen man screamed.

The yell was like cold water on the Texan, and he snapped fully awake with the realization of the danger of a second man.

"Hold him, Mike," the unseen Moe called.

"I'm trying," Mike gasped.

Howard was completely on Mike now and found he was grappling with a man almost his size and bulk with strong hands that the man tried to fasten around the Texan's throat.

Howard was passed the stunned stage and full bore into frontier rage at the attack. As Mike tried to throttle him, Howard seized the thug by the shirt and heaved so that the two rolled over. Now the Texan was on the bottom where the second man could not get at him directly.

"For gosh sake, hold him, Mike, so I can bean him quick, we're drawing a crowd." Moe shuffled back and forth with his sap in hand trying to get at Howard.

At the same time the writer released his hold on Mike and threw a looping right cross that connected with the thug's temple. It was an awkward angle and a truncated swing, but it had all the Texan's anger behind it, so it did the job. Mike went limp.

Howard grabbed the unconscious attacker and shoved him into the legs of Moe.

Moe stumbled back which gave Howard the time to spring to his feet.

"All right, varmint," the Texan drawled, "Let's see how you do face to face!"

Moe was smaller than Mike and wiry with long arms and legs and a thin pale face. He took one look at the Texan's fighting stance and decided on the better part of valor.

"This ain't worth anything that Mueller could get for Red and not half what I'm gettin' paid!" The attacker squealed as he turned and raced off through the gathering crowd.

Howard started to chase the bandit, but the man was not only fleet of foot but knew the city well. The Texan could not keep up the pace with the assailant, who proved adept at darting in and out of the foot traffic well beyond Howard's ability. Moe outdistanced and evaded the Texan in less than two blocks.

"Dang!" Howard spat when he realized there was no hope of catching the footpad. He walked back to where he had left the unconscious Mike.

"Double dang!" The Texan exclaimed when he returned to the site of the attack and found nothing but his battered Stetson and the fortuitously placed guidebook.

Some fellas named Mueller and Red paid to have me ambushed, eh? Seems like I'm gonna have'ta make them fella's acquaintance real soon.

He looked down at his suit- noting that his trousers were ripped at the knee and grimy and shrugged with typical frontier cynicism. "Well, I guess I ain't goin' to no authors' meeting like this. Next time."

Chapter Nine: Big Top Mess

Howard made his way back to the circus with purposeful and angry strides, working to burn off his Celtic anger before he reached the Garden. The first person Howard encountered when he returned to the sleeping tent was Big Carney, sitting quietly in preparation for his fight later.

Even after his long walk the Texan was steaming mad.

"Wow, Boss Bob, you're back awfully early," the negro said without looking at Howard. When he did look up, he added, "You look a sight! Are them writers all that rough?"

The Texan laughed at the question and that evaporated most of the steam as he told the tale of the attack on him.

"That's powerful wrong," the African said. "You sure the names you heard them say were 'Mueller and Red?'"

"Yep," Howard said as he slipped out of his shirt and used a wet cloth to wipe grime off his face and hands. "It's what that bushwhacker Moe said."

The negro cursed softly. "Red has to be Red O'Bannon, the fella that is running my fight tonight."

"Any idea who this Mueller is?"

"I'm afraid I do, Bob," Big Carney said with a grim expression replacing his normal smile. "And you ain't gonna like it, I know I don't. Come with me."

He led the freshly redressed Texan out of the tent toward the performers' tents.

"What's the mystery?" Howard asked.

"That is the question, Boss," Big Carney said. "The Colossal Klaus is how he's billed, but his last name is Mueller!"

The Texan stopped in his tracks. "What? That varmint!" Howard's eyes narrowed and his jaw set. "You know I gotta do something about it, don't you, Big Hoss?"

"I know, Bob," the negro said. "But you gotta promise to go easy on this till we find out why Klaus would do such a stupid thing and how it hooks in with Red O'Bannon. That guy is a powerful bad fella!"

Howard looked into his friend's eyes and realized how serious the man was. "Alright," the writer said. "I'll follow your lead on this."

"Thanks," Big Carney said. "If this is true, he's gone too far this time to just let it ride." The two friends arrived outside the horse trainer's tent but there was already an argument in progress between Klaus and his wife.

"I can't believe you," Julie said. "After everything we discussed, after all the promises you made to me about stopping your gambling-"

"Shut up!" Klaus snapped. "It is my money as well."

"It was our money," the girl said. "Savings for our house, our future. You had no right to drain that account!"

"I had every right," the trainer answered. "I lost a lot of money bet on Big Carney's fight last week. And I saw what went on between you and that cowboy trying to make me seem weak. Well, I'll make it back when the German takes that shade tonight and as for the cowboy..." He laughed.

"You're sick, Klaus. This time I'm through with you. You've taken my youth and now you've taken our hope for a future with your gambling and insecurities. I'm leaving while I still have some self-respect."

"You can't leave me. Where would you go?"

"Maybe before last week I couldn't have left," she said. "But someone said only I could change my life and I'm not alone- as long as I have friends. And now I see you've always been using me. You don't love me, you love power and the gambling gives you an illusion of that power."

"You're my wife," Klaus screamed. "You're not leaving me."

"Yes, I am," Julie insisted.

Suddenly the sound of a slap exploded like a gunshot in the night.

Howard had heard enough. Despite his promise to his friend, his Gaelic nature took control and he barged into the tent. The scene was clear. Julie was on her knees, holding her swollen face. The blond Klaus stood above her and spun when the Texan entered.

"You!" the horse trainer yelled. "How?"

"You shoulda sent more men to bushwack me, ya skunk," Howard said. "Two to one ain't near good enough odds against a Texan."

Big Carney stepped beside Howard and snarled, "You can't be hittin' no woman, Boss."

"Get out!" Klaus yelled. "This is a family matter."

"Miss Julie is circus family," the negro said. "Keep your hands to yourself."

A mad light seemed to ignite in the trainer's eyes. He backed away from his wife to a dresser where he opened a drawer and pulled a silenced pistol.

"You stay away from me, you subhuman!" Klaus snarled. He waved the gun at Howard who had moved to help the woman to her feet.

"You, Cowboy," Klaus yelled. "You get away from my wife."

"I'm not your wife anymore," Julie said. "That last hit ended that. I'm done this time."

"No! No!" Klaus insisted. "You belong to me."

"Don't no one belong to no one no more, Boss," Big Carney said with a razor edge to his voice. "A lot of people died to make that a fact."

"Shut up!" Klaus snapped. Without warning he fired his pistol at the muscular Carney.

The impact of the bullet staggered the big man and spun him around.

Julie gasped.

Bob Howard sprang forward with speed that seemed beyond so burly a build. He slapped the gun from Klaus' hand then delivered a backhand slap that knocked the trainer off his feet.

Howard moved toward the gun but a harsh voice from the tent opening froze him. "Hold it, buddy!" the voice said. "Or I plug you."

All eyes turned to see Moe and Mike, guns drawn.

"You are a jerk, Mueller." A new player said as he entered. "I didn't tell you ta use my boys to run your errands just because you had problems with your dame."

The speaker wore a three-hundred dollar blue suit, hundred dollar handmade shoes and smoked an imported cigar, yet he wreaked of cheapness.

His face, beneath a bristle of orange-red hair, was a cartoon of an Irish thug. He had a button nose, freckles and a cruel fleshy mouth.

"Red," Klaus pleaded. "I had to stop the cowboy."

"Tony!" Red O'Bannon called out. "Check on Big Carney."

The green fedoraed Tony came in from the entrance and moved to the fallen negro, careful not to cross into the two gunmen's line of fire.

'Oh, geeze, Red," Tony said. "He shot Carney in the arm."

"I can see that, you idiot." O'Bannon said. "How bad is it?"

"Shot him through his left forearm. Looks like its broken. He ain't gonna box tonight."

"You done yourself in, Mueller." O'Bannon said. "I let you arrange this match so you could square it for the loss last week but you're gonna cost me more money this week." He nodded toward the quivering horse trainer. "Make it right, boys."

"No!" Klaus screamed. "It the cowboy's fault."

"Really?" Red said with a cold laugh. "You shot the local champ and you're gonna blame it on the hick?"

"If he hadn't messed things up last week calling Tony on the bet we wouldn't need this fight tonight," Klaus said.

"But we do, Mueller," Red said. "I brought in the German from Philly. That cost me money; and I put the word out and that is my reputation. And you shot the local draw!"

Moe cocked his pistol and pointed it at Klaus.

"Let the cowboy fight!" The horse trainer pleaded. "He thinks he's a tough guy."

"And he did take Mike out," Moe pointed out.

"He never got a chance to take you on, did he?" Mike snapped at his partner.

"Shut your traps, you two," Red snarled. He puffed on his cigar and looked the Texan over. "How about it, hick, can you fight?"

"If I have a reason," The Texan said. "But not to make you money."

O'Bannon laughed. It was an ugly sound. "A real tough guy, huh?"

Howard kept a stoic expression on his features, his eyes black coals.

"I got the lowdown on you, hick," Red said. "You're sweet on the frail."

"That's my wife," Klaus protested.

"She'll be your widow if you don't zip it," Red said.

"You have to get a doctor for Big Carney," Julie interjected. "He's bleeding badly."

Red ignored her request and nodded to Tony. "Get the dame."

When the tout moved toward the girl Howard started for him, but Moe and Mike shifted their guns to cover him.

"Tom Mix here will fight fine to keep the frail healthy."

Tony grabbed a stunned Julie. Big Carney made an attempt to stop Tony, but he was too weak from shock and loss of blood to do much.

The Texan started to move again but the two guns made it impossible to intervene.

"Help me!" Julie cried.

Klaus, stunned by the cascade of events made a whimpering sound and charged Tony screaming, "Get your hands off my wife!"

Red lashed out with blinding speed and smashed Klaus in the side of the head.

The horse trainer dropped like a sack of stones.

The gang boss held up the brass knuckles he used on Klaus and snorted. "You're in the right place here, you're a real clown, Mueller." He looked over at Julie, her mouth now gagged with a handkerchief, and struggling weakly in Tony's arms. "Losin' it over a dame? Jerk."

He made eye contact with Howard who was all but vibrating with impotent rage. "So, cowboy you be in that center ring at midnight, and you put on a good show till the fourth round- then you take a dive to the sawdust."

"Or?" Howard spat.

"Or that little lady has an accident."

The entourage of thugs left with the now quiet Julie in Tony's arms.

"Fourth round," O'Bannon said. "And make it good tough guy or the deal's off and so is the frail."

Then Howard was alone in the tent with the wounded negro.

The Texan raced to Big Carney's side, pulling off his belt to improvise a tourniquet for the man's arm.

"I gotta get you a doctor, Hoss," Howard said.

He moved next to the fallen Klaus but when he examined the fallen blond, he gave a deep sigh and shook his head. "He ain't gonna be hittin no more women," Howard said. "O'Bannon split his skull with those brass knuckles. He's dead."

"Get Doc Jason," Carney said with a new urgency, "He can keep his mouth shut; he's the show's vet. He can fix me up as good as any hospital. Can't get no regular doc anyway, they 'd have to report the gunshot. And we can't let them find Boss Klaus; if they do Red and them will just take off and there's no tellin' what they'll do to Miss Julie."

"I'll get Bernie too," the Texan said as he nodded in agreement. "We'll need him to know what is going on. You gonna be alright while I find the doc?"

Big Carney smiled. "Not one hundred percent, but I'll make it. What we gonna do about Miss Julie?"

"I don't know," Howard said, grinding his teeth in frustration. "But looks to me that like it or not, I got me a fight tonight."

Chapter Ten: Big Topsy Turvy

The crowd of over two hundred were all clustered in the first rows of the spectator seats of Madison Square Garden. Mixed among some of the circus folk who were 'in the know', the newcomers were not just the rowdy sort that Howard had first witnessed at Big Carney's fight on the Bowery. These new arrivals were some well-heeled types, even a number of couples were among the spectators as if the coming bout were a real sanctioned match.

The field of battle for the two gladiators was to be the center ring on the Garden floor.

Howard stood with Bernie in the entranceway to the arena, in sight, but out of earshot of Red O'Bannon's goons.

"That Schmidt has got a bad reputation," the muscular roustabout said in a hoarse whisper. "They say he done a guy in with his bare hands in Chicago-- he don't need to cheat to win."

The Texan focused on the center ring, his mind already on the battle to come. "Ain't no goin' back, Bernie; it's come down to this." He held up his fists. "It always has and always will; man is an animal pure and simple-- a barbarian to the core."

"I'm tellin' you, Bob," Bernie insisted. "That giant is not just gonna fight you, he's gonna try to kill you!"

"The word to highlight there, Hoss, is 'try," the Texan said with a wry smile. "And I ain't about to make it easy for him. In fact, I suspect he's in for a bit of a shock when I don't shake in my boots."

"But you still have to take that dive by the fourth round," Bernie said. "So maybe he won't try so hard to hurt you."

"Don't bet, Hoss," Howard said, "Big Carney and me are a burr under O'Bannon's saddle. He wants to make a public show of puttin' us down. Besides, he don't know he killed Klaus, but once he does he's gonna know we're the only eyewitnesses."

Schmidt entered the arena floor from the entrance across the ring. The German had short blond hair and glared out at the Garden as if everyone in it were his prey.

He was, like Howard, stripped to the waist, showing off a physique that seemed sculpted from ivory. His pale skin showed off a number of long healed scars that only served to make his aspect more fearsome. His jaw line was sharp, his cheekbones pronounced, and his blue eyes set deep beneath an overhanging brow.

The two men locked eyes across the distance and Howard knew just what kind of fight he was in for.

"You know, Bernie," the Texan said. "Society is glued together with a series of 'I shouldn'ts and 'you'll regrets'- as in 'I shouldn't slap down that loud mouthed kid 'cause I'll get in trouble,' or "you'll regret any violence against me when my lawyer gets through with you."

The shorter man looked puzzled but listened with rapt attention. "It promotes the illusion of a polite society. When, in fact it is a frightened society. It keeps most folks in check."

Howard stretched his neck and rolled his shoulders in preparation for the combat to come before he continued. "There are those who have none of that fear. They are a primal animal, the sort that chew at the glue that holds society together. Rats, who scurry through the dark corners, occasionally coming into the light. That fella, Schmidt there, is one of them. A real barbarian."

"You're scarin' me, Bob," Bernie said. "I know I said he's dangerous, but you make him sound like the devil."

"It's a devil I know, Bernie," Howard said with a cold smile. "You don't look for mercy from his sort, he feeds on fear and helplessness. I seen his type in Cross Plains before. He don't care that I'm supposed to kiss canvas in the fourth. He just wants to see fear and pain. I ain't gonna give him none of that."

"Are we gonna have a fight or what?" Red O'Bannon called as he walked out past his fighter. The Irish gangster led his entourage to just outside the chalked square where they all stopped. Moe and Mike on either side kept their eyes focused on the Texan.

O'Bannon continued to the center of the square, held up his arms and playing to the audience repeated in a loud voice, "We gonna have a fight?"

The audience cheered with more volume.

"Looks like most of Red's pug-uglies are with him," Bernie whispered.

"That'll make it easier for Big Carney," Howard said. "We know they didn't leave the Garden with Miss Julie-- so we just gotta keep all eyes here."

"You still gotta keep Schmidt occupied till Big Carney finds Julie or take that dive."

Howard grimaced. "I know. I'm gonna have ta take a whuppin'," he slammed his fist into his open palm, "-fer a while."

"Fighters!" O'Bannon called. "Toe your marks!"

Schmidt strode with the liquid grace of a stalking tiger. He stopped at a line drawn in the sawdust on the floor and stood stock still like some automaton with only the shallow rise and fall of his massive chest showing signs of life.

Howard walked with a buoyant step to a stop five feet from his opponent. He kept a poker face, his intelligent eyes locked with the lifeless orbs of the German.

The two men could not have been more different: Schmidt was several inches taller than the Texan, a perfect lean Aryan specimen from his blonde hair to his sky-blue eyes. Howard's muscularity was of a burly sort with his dark Gaelic coloring and fading Texas tan seeming even darker opposite Schmidt's pale flesh.

It was mostly the auras of the two men that contrasted even more notably. It was a Zoroastrian contrast, the difference between a creative force and a destructive one.

"Okay, gents," O'Bannon said. "You're here to have a fight not a dance so everything goes but biting and eye-gouging, got that?"

He tried his best to intimidate Howard with a hard look.

"Round's will be three minutes. The fight will continue until a fighter cannot make a ten count or the bell for the next round. Got that?"

Howard returned O'Bannon's stare with an openly contemptuous look but kept his mouth a grim, straight line.

He's so sure I'll dive, because he knows I'd never let anything happen to Miss Julie-- he thinks I'm stupid enough to think he'll let us go afterward; even not knowing he was a killer after Klaus, I'd be a fool to trust this sidewinder.

Howard suspected none of them, Bernie, Julie or Howard would ever leave the Garden alive once O'Bannon collected on his bets.

"Hey, where's the shade?" The Irish Gangster asked when he realized that only Bernie was accompanying the Texan to ringside. "And Mueller?"

"Big Carney is feelin' poorly," Howard said with enough disgust in his voice to make his statement credible. "Ain't got no stomach to watch another man take his place. And Klaus couldn't face this."

O'Bannon snorted a laugh. "Yah, likely it ain't gonna be pretty." He glanced over at Schmidt. "Not pretty at all."

The German stood impassive, eyes aimed at some unseen point in space.

"Alright," O'Bannon called, "fighters to their corners and when that bell rings come out fighting."

Both men went to their corner stools.

"Keep watch for Big Carney," Howard said while he loosened his shoulders. "He'll show up as soon as Miss Julie is safe."

"Sure thing, Bob," Bernie said. "Good luck."

Schmidt came forward in a standard boxer's crouch with a smooth shuffle step. Howard noticed a little light in the German's eyes, as if the prospect of the coming unbridled carnage had awakened a demon in him.

Something awakened in the Texan's soul as well, a tingling sensation that stood the hairs of his neck on end and sent blood coursing through his limbs. Howard recognized the atavistic urge, the savage at the core of the human animal coming to the surface.

I see it in his eyes, he's closer to that dark animal place all the time and he knows it. There are no limits for his kind.

The Texan grinned involuntarily. *But he's making a mistake if he thinks he's fightin' a civilized man; He don't know he's fixin' to tie into the man that lived in the head of Conan the Cimmerian.*

Chapter Eleven: Two Fisted Mayhem

Schmidt's first attack was little more than an exploration of Howard's defenses, being fast, light jabs. The Texan gave ground and deflected the blows with little effort, knowing that the blond was testing him.

It suited Howard's purpose to draw out the fight as long as possible yet he knew he could not just run the ring. He had to put up a fight to keep O'Bannon confident that all was according to the promoter's plan.

To that end the Texan suddenly stopped backpedaling and launched a hard right cross.

The abrupt reversal caught the blond off guard, slipping through his defenses to glance off Schmidt's ribs.

The taller man side slipped and shot back with a quick left jab that Howard took on his left forearm.

The men separated as explosively as they had clashed.

That'll teach you to mess with this bull, the Texan thought with more joy than he should have.

The exhilaration of combat was heady, and the writer had to remind himself there was a larger plan than just a simple fight. He had to stretch the combat as long as possible, making it seem as if he was going to take the dive in the fourth round to give Big Carney as much time as possible to find the girl.

Still, Howard thought wryly, *couldn't hurt anything to sting this son of a dog a little in the process.*

Schmidt retained his machine-like movement quality and the hunger for destruction still burned in his eyes but there was a slight change. He reassessed the 'yokel' he had obviously expected to be an easy victim. He would have to actually work to pommel Howard into submission.

"You figured I was just gonna take a beatin', huh?" Howard whispered. "But what kind of show would that be for the folks?" The Texan smiled. "I think I'm gonna make you work for it a bit."

A cold ghost of a smile flitted across Schmidt's thin lips. He tucked his chin, raised his guard and advanced.

This time the blond showed caution, his jabs calculated. He left no opening for a reply as he moved forward with the swift series of hits.

Howard knew his message had been received and the thought made him smile.

The two gladiators traded jabs to no effect until the bell sounded.

"Boy, you showed him!" Bernie effused when Howard took his stool.

The crowd in the stands was boisterous and the Texan could see Tony's green fedora collecting last minute bets.

"Gotta keep up a show," Howard said, sipping some water. "I'm supposed to take my dive in the fourth round but if they think I'm slacking or just running the ring--"

"I know," the bulky corner man said. "But you can't just let that sauerkraut eating statue just pound you." He looked over at O'Bannon and cursed. "That jerk ain't got a human bone in his body."

"I'll find out about his bones personally when this little tussle is over."

The two fighters exploded from their corners for Round Two like shells fired from a cannon. Both men were past testing the other, now their blows were powerfully intentioned.

The collision of knuckles on flesh was like thunderclaps in the arena, each fighter giving as good as they got. Both landed solid body shots.

As quickly as the explosion of violence occurred the two men separated and stepped back two paces.

He hits like a mule with a bad attitude, Howard thought.

It was hard for the Texan to tell if his blows had any effect until he saw the blond wince and stretch his left side where Howard knew he had landed at least one solid punch.

"There you go, Hoss," Howard whispered. "You are human after all."

The feral light was lambent in Schmidt's eyes, and he cocked his head to one side before he looked directly at Howard and smiled an evil grin. "It's usually just a job, cowboy, but this time I'm gonna enjoy pounding you to jelly," The German whispered.

Howard burst out laughing.

The reaction so startled the blond that the snake-quick left that scored a glancing blow on Schmidt's chin.

The German staggered back but threw two fast lefts to keep Howard from following up the hit.

The crowd cheered wildly.

Schmidt snarled and came at Howard with a rapid-fire power-house series of combinations. The Texan could do little but cover up and try to ride the trip-hammer blows.

Enough of the German's blows got through that Howard grunted in pain and his knees became rubbery. He almost went down as the bell ending the second round sounded.

"You got him angry," Bernie said when the Texan collapsed to the stool. "You think that's such a good idea?"

Howard had several scrapes where the German's fists had grazed him and was already beginning to bruise along his arms and his side.

"Seemed like a good idea at the time." Howard could see that the German also wore some badges of their battle and the sight gave the Texan reason to smile. "And I still think it is. You can't fight to your plan when you're angry or hurt."

Bernie looked at him with a jaundiced eye. "It's your head, Bob, but I'd hate to see him take it off your shoulders."

"I appreciate that, Bernie, but it's all our heads if Big Carney doesn't find the lady in time. Once this match is over, one way or the other, things is gonna get hot in here."

"I got my eye on those two gunsels with O'Bannon," Bernie said. "And a marlin spike in my pocket for when the time comes. And I know we can count on some of the guys in the bleachers when they see us in it. Wish we could have told them about Miss Julie."

"Couldn't take the chance word would get back to O'Bannon what we were doing," Howard said. "We're on our own on this."

The timekeeper looked to O'Bannon and then raised his hand to strike the bell.

"Sure hope Big Carney shows up soon," Howard said. "I think he's gonna lay into me heavy this round."

Howard was right, Schmidt started the third round with an aggressive attack that had the Texan on the defensive. Howard could see in the giant's eyes that it was now personal.

Good, the Texan thought while he did his best to dodge or deflect the onslaught of blows, *If he's off his game plan maybe I can get him to play mine.*

There was little more time for thought as the German threw combination after combination at the Texan, many of which slammed through Howard's defenses to land painfully.

Howard knew he had to stay on his feet no matter what until he knew the girl was safe, even if it meant going beyond the four rounds. He also knew that could mean a tremendous amount of punishment. He reasoned that if the fight were still ongoing O'Bannon would not dare leave the ringside to 'take care' of Julie. If he sent one of his stooges Howard hoped Big Carney could intercept him.

The Texan took some comfort in the fact that he knew that the German could be hurt, but as fist after fist smashed into Howard he began to doubt if he could stay on his feet to take advantage of his new knowledge.

I can't think that way, Howard thought just as a painful left slipped over his guard to slam into his left deltoid. Howard's whole arm went numb. He knew he could not keep it up in full guard.

Schmidt saw he had scored and pressed on hard with a right aimed at Howard's head. Just then the Texan did the unexpected and switched his feet so that he was suddenly in a southpaw stance. This protected his arm from the German's attack and was so unorthodox that Schmidt paused his attack momentarily.

The Texan used that momentary respite from the assault to attack with a powerful series of right jabs while he shook out his left.

Howard had seen a fighter do the same switcheroo move in an icehouse fight back in Cross Plains when the man had broken his hand on an opponent's elbow. The injured boxer went on to lose the fight, but he held out for another round.

Howard only hoped to do as well.

Schmidt recovered from his amazement and answered Howard's attack with a new barrage.

The Texan had a hard time countering and had to give ground at almost a run as the German pressed him.

I *can't take much more*, Howard thought just as the bell sounded to end the round.

Chapter Twelve: Three Ring Knockout

"How's the arm?" Bernie asked as Howard collapsed onto the stool. He was already working the muscle with rough but skilled hands.

Howard bled from an abrasion under his left eye and his lip, but he had a determined expression. "The arm's okay," he said. "But he's got my number; he's a better boxer than I am, more scientific. My only chance is to get 'im angry again."

"That didn't work out so well last time," Bernie noted.

Howard gave him a lopsided grin that turned into a wince. "Any idea worth anything is worth tryin' twice," the Texan said. "If it don't kill you the first time."

Bernie just shook his head. "You Texans are thicker than my mother's stew!"

"And proud of it!" Howard laughed.

Red O'Bannon appeared by the corner, smiling.

"Round four coming up, Cowboy," the gangster said. "A big round; lots of people's fates depend on it." He gave a crocodile smile, but his meaning was clear. He tipped his bowler hat and added, "Good luck."

The bell sounded.

Howard came out still in a southpaw stance as if to protect his arm, though it was fully recovered by now.

Schimdt charged with confidence, and it was clear from the cold light in his eyes that he had a calculated plan to win. Howard was sure the German would not wait for him to take any dive as it was no longer just about winning. Schmidt had a point to make and vengeance to wreak on the Texan for throwing him off his game. And for hurting him.

At least he'll try to put me down.

Howard had already decided that there was nothing to be gained by taking the dive. If Big Carney did not find Julie in time he decided to draw the fight out as long as possible on the chance that O'Bannon did not have a way to communicate with whomever was with the girl. If the gang boss had to send one of his men to actually carry out his threat perhaps it would give Big Carney someone to trail. If O'Bannon had a way to instantaneously tell the kidnapper the dive was not taken, if Howard fought all the way to the bell of the fourth round he was sealing the girl's death warrant.

All this weighed on the Texan's mind as he warded off the flying fists of the German.

Schmidt pulled out all stops trying, by bull force, to batter Howard's defenses down. He seemed as fresh as the first round and had the ghost of a smile on his chiseled features.

The Texan took several hard hits to his body and one glancing blow to his chin that all but 'rang his bell' but he managed to keep his guard up. He even managed to get in a couple of light hits to the German, though to little effect. He continued to be driven backward around the ring.

He's got more in his tank than me. He trains for this all the time, lives for this- I spend too much time behind a typewriter. He could feel himself tiring under the relentless onslaught. He realized he might not have the option of taking a dive, that Schimdt might just pound him into the promised jelly.

"You are gonna go down hard, Cowboy," Schmidt said with a wolf's grin. "You might as well just accept it and take your punishment."

Howard was about to reply when the Texan saw Big Carney.

The negro stood in the entranceway of the arena. He barely supported the figure of a semi-conscious Julie with his good arm. She looked frail and small against the muscular Carney.

Even across the arena Howard could see the bloody chaff marks on the girl's wrists and ankles where she had been bound. He could also see the bruises on her cheeks and the torn clothing that made it clear she had been roughly handled.

Something inside the Texan suddenly snapped.

A thunderhead of power coursed through his body like summer lightning on the prairie. Howard's blocks suddenly gained strength and his legs abruptly seemed to be rooted to the ring.

He would retreat no more!

The German did not know what had caused the sudden change in his opponent, as Big Carney was behind him, but Schmidt felt the change in the Texan's tactics.

The writer attacked. It was abrupt and furious, powered not by anger but by a deeper, darker, more elemental rage that boiled up from the Gaelic soul of the Texan. Howard no longer saw the Aryan fighting machine before him, instead the image of the abused girl hovered before his eyes.

Howard's fists were no longer fists; they were war hammers swung on the field of bloody battle. He was no longer a mere pugilist contending for something as simple as a win in the squared circle. He was an avenger!

The German was no longer an opponent, he was just an impediment to the real target of the Texan's rage, Red O'Bannon. Howard would not be stopped.

Some of the German's blows still made it through the Texan's guard but they were only flyspecks on a tank. Howard slammed his fists into any part of the German he could reach with no fear of his own injury, no fear of loss or thought to what would happen *when* he destroyed Schmidt except that he would take O'Bannon down.

Howard's combinations were reckless but relentless with the power of all his Gaelic fury behind them. Schmidt was suddenly overwhelmed by the cyclonic power of the onslaught.

No matter how many punches from the Texan that Schmidt countered there were always more powerhouse blows raining down on him. No matter how many of his own blows landed at full power on Howard there was no letup in the barrage of the Texan's flying fists.

The Texan was a force of nature unleashed. Beyond the red haze that swam before Howard he saw the cool calculation of the German melt into animal fear. He noted the change in Schmidt's eyes and felt a savage joy at it.

The German was the wall of a fortress that Howard was storming and each punch, every blow smashed another brick from that wall as Howard fought his way to O'Bannon.

Schmidt tried one last rally. He threw a jab-hook-hook combination that, at any other time, would have been devastating for all of its power and speed.

Now, however, it was like the Texan moved with the speed of thought. Howard actually counter punched both hooks and with the second smashed his right fist into Schmidt's right forearm with so much force that he broke the German's arm.

Schmidt screamed in pain.

Howard followed the strike with an explosive left uppercut to the German's breadbasket and a lightning quick right cross that dislocated Schmidt's jaw.

The Aryan pugilist dropped like an anchor and lie moaning in the sawdust of the floor.

"How's that for jelly?" Howard snarled as he leapt over the fallen man without a pause and raced toward O'Bannon.

The Irish gangster was on his feet as Schmidt fell. His bodyguards were also up, the two gunsels reaching under their jackets for their guns.

Howard reached the first bodyguard just as he cleared leather. The Texan didn't even break stride but barreled into the thug, felling him with a hard left at the same time he snatched the snub-nosed revolver from the man's hand.

The second bodyguard had his gun drawn and was just aiming at Howard when Bernie blindsided him with a dynamite right cross-aided by a marlin spike.

"Get Red!" The short roustabout called. Howard already was racing after the fleeing gangster as the bodyguard hit the floor.

The arena had erupted into pandemonium when Schmidt fell and went into panic when the guns appeared. Bettors screamed, cursed, tripped over each other and jammed the exits in their haste to escape. Several of the circus roustabouts ran toward Bernie and Big Carney to provide back up unbidden.

O'Bannon was trapped in the chaos, buffeted in the almost crazed crowd. "Get out of my way!" The redhaired gang boss screamed. He shoved a woman so she fell into other people. "Move!"

He kicked the prone woman, then jumped over her.

Suddenly O'Bannon was jerked backward by the steel grip of the furious Texan. "You can't leave yet, Red," Howard said. "I got a message for you from Miss Julie."

With that the Texan set about slapping the bookie.

"Didn't-"slap-"your-"slap,-"mother-"slap-"ever teach you manners?"

Slap, slap, slap, slap, slap!

Howard dropped the gibbering, near unconscious gangster at his feet. The Texan was a horrifying sight, bleeding from a dozen places, his lip split, his right eye all but swollen shut. He looked more an avatar of some pagan war god than a man. His breaths came in wheezing gasps as the adrenaline fatigue began to set in and he began to feel his injuries.

"I oughta stomp you like the snake you are," the Texan said with disgust, more at himself than at the Irish gangster. "But I guess I ain't as near a barbarian as I'd hoped. I'll let the law take care of you. I've been corrupted by civilization, after all."

Chapter Thirteen: The Hanged Man

The smoky corners of the London, East End pub were filled with a rogue's gallery of criminal types that all stopped talking briefly when the door opened. The half-seen faces turned as one to watch the entrance and survey the burly Texan as he walked in.

It was the very fact of the colorful clientele that had attracted the visitor to the Hanged Man Public House on Cable Road, north of the Thames.

The new arrival stood out from the rough characters that inhabited the public house not by being less imposing, for his height and bearing were in accord with a working-class establishment, but by virtue of his clothing. Bob Howard wore blue jeans, a denim shirt and worn brown cowboy boots with steel toes. His battered cowboy hat was pushed back to reveal a high forehead. In his right hand he held his black Underwood case.

Bob had come to England to see just such faces as were turned toward him. It was all grist for his writing mill. He had seen the sights like the tombs at Westminster and halls of Parliament, visited the bookshops and even stood for the changing of the guard at Buckingham Palace, but it was the faces of the common men and the stories that went with them that interested him more than the musty old buildings.

He'd had a good three weeks in New York, learning the ins and outs of Circus life and had gotten half a dozen assignments from publishers that would allow him to travel for a while. He even had a nice send-off party with Big Carney and some of the others he'd met under the big top. He smiled at the thought of the friends he'd made. *Gonna get writer's cramp sending letters.*

"A bit lost, ain't you, Guv?" The barkeep, who had a cauliflower ear and a scarred visage that was as frightening as any of his patrons', smiled to show an artistic dearth of teeth.

"Not if I can get a beer," Howard said with a warm smile in answer.

"A Yank, ain't you?" the pug ugly said as he drew a long tankard from the tap.

"Not by half," the visitor said in a soft drawl. "I'm from Texas!"

He'd grown tired of people calling him a Yank in the week he'd been wandering around London trying to get the lay of the land.

The bartender snorted and slid the drink across the splintered, stained wood of the bar. "That's what I said."

Now the Texan snorted, gave a salute with the tankard and took his warm beer to go sit in a corner table of the dingy room with his back to the wall.

Howard presented quite a sight for the legion of curious shadow-hidden faces; six foot two and a husky two hundred and fifty pounds of muscle, a plain but pleasant face and dark eyes that missed nothing. Bob leaned the chair back, slid the battered typewriter case beneath his chair and sipped the drink with a grimace.

"Uh, I'll never get used to this warm froth," he said aloud with humor. He nevertheless smacked his lips as he gulped down his first long drink of the day.

"It was hard to get used to again myself when I got back here." A lisping voice from the shadows beside him became a rough face with deep-set eyes and broad features. "I spent several years in the Canadian north woods and got a taste for cold beer like a Texan myself."

"I guess they got no choice but to like it that way," the Texan said. He was glad to have conversation though he knew enough from his time in boomtown bars in Texas to not let his guard down.

The new face and the lanky body that was connected with it slid his chair up beside the Texan. The speaker had broad shoulders and long arms and seemed a few decades older than the visitor.

"William Pratt," he said thrusting a long-fingered hand out.

"Bob Howard," the Texan said as he accepted a hearty handshake from the Englishman. "I'm a writer."

"A writer now? Of what sort?"

"I write for magazines," the Texan said as he sipped his warm brew. "Like *Weird Tales* and such. I just sold a story to *Argosy*."

Howard smiled and toasted by quoting one of his own poems, *"Within me lies a warrior, a savage killing ghost, of every Celtic ancestor, a fearsome shouting host, Of cattle raids and blood feuds, my cells are all composed, but life for me's no epic poem, just damn-ed, boring prose!"*

"Well, that's great," his new acquaintance laughed and toasted back. "A man should be creative; I did a little acting for a few years in Canada and Hollywood before I missed the lovely weather along the Thames."

He had a gentle laugh that seemed at odds with his coarse features. Howard joined him. "I have noticed the wonderful weather on arriving here; I haven't seen a fully dry day the whole week. I don't think we've had this much rain in Cross Plains in two decades total!"

The Texan sat in companionable silence with his new acquaintance for a time watching the room and enjoying the tableau of humanity that ebbed and flowed across the dark and smoky pub. Howard worked to memorize all the faces, his mind spinning tales of the lives that must have written the lines on them.

"You have an eye for characters, eh?" Pratt asked after a time. The Texan looked back at him with a quizzical expression.

"I told you, I used to be an actor; I still like to come to the likes of The Hanged Man and make my studies. I can see you doing the same."

"Why'd you get out of it?"

"Oh, the usual reasons," Pratt said. "I couldn't make a living at it working the Provinces playing Shakespeare in the lumber camps. I even went to Hollywood to try silent films. Changed my name to Boris to not shame the family if I got famous but I didn't, so not to worry."

He laughed. "I thought it sounded exotic when I heard some character in a play by that Tarzan writer, but I did some fair to middling films and even did a few major parts for Universal before that Lugosi fellow that played Varney in that film changed his mind and played the Frankenstein Monster. I decided at that point it was too hard and I really did miss home."

He spoke with frankness, but the Texan could see that there were some facts behind his tale that he was not telling and Howard didn't see any reason to press.

"I know missing that home turf," the Texan said. "Didn't think I'd miss the little dust hole so much when I took off on this across the world tour, but the soil of home does get in a man's boots."

"That it does," the Englishman said. "Dreams can distract from that sometimes."

"What are you doing here now?" Howard asked. "I see a whole passel of theatres here in the town to keep a dream alive."

Pratt laughed. "I still do some theatre to keep my hand in, but I have a regular job working in a stable and as a whipper-in. I got the job through my brother, sir John, for the Harkers outside of town in High Wycombe. I came in today to get some harness fittings for the Master of Horse."

"What's a whipper-in?"

"When they go foxhunting," Pratt said, "the dogs sometimes get a bit stroppy in the pack or lose focus; a whipper-in works the fringe and keeps the hounds in line."

The Texan shook his head. "That's the darndest thing I ever heard." He took another sip from his drink, minding the warmth less with each gulp. "You just shoo the hounds?"

"More or less, but it's a bit more complicated; it can be some hard riding."

"Sounds fun. I done a piece of riding back home."

"I should think so," the Englishman said, "don't all Texans ride like Gary Cooper and shoot like Annie Oakley?"

Howard laughed so hard he almost spilled his beer. "You are a very perceptive fella! Just like every Englishman is a lord."

"Lord of the stables." Pratt raised his beer to clink glasses with Howard. "Every stall is a castle!" His genial smile tightened a bit. "The job is not as hard as many I've had; ditch digging and such except that the Harkers, they are not easy folk to work for. They think of themselves as blooming lords for sure. Not their daughter Gwendolyn though; a wonder she's theirs. Just such a shame that she has been so rarely home from school abroad. A real angel she is with a sweet soul."

Somewhere out in the night, a foghorn sounded on the river, a low mournful sound muffled by the thick fog.

"Sounds like a soul lost in the night," the Texan said.

"You have quite an imagination alright," Pratt said. "I can see where that would serve you well in your profession."

"I imagine there are more than a few lost souls out there in the English fog, or over there in the Tower, waiting to make themselves known; maybe even some were-foxes ready to turn on you and your hunters."

The Englishman chuckled. "They are clever little beasts, I'll give you that," he said, "but I suspect none of them turn into monsters."

"Well," the Texan said with a smile, "not yet anyway."

Howard thought of his pen-pal, fellow writer H.P. 'Howie' Lovecraft, whom he hoped to meet when he returned home in the spring. The two kindred writers had written voluminously to each other often of such occult things, along with writings on philosophy, history, and mythology. Bob's New England friend wrote of secret things, in letters that Howie had often instructed him to 'burn this when you read it.'

Wish you could'a made this trip, Howie, Bob thought. *There is so much 'atmosphere' here it would give your New England a real run for the money for inspiration.*

But Howard knew that Lovecraft—though he had lived in New York for a time—was the opposite of the Texan in that he relished his small-town isolation and was anything but gregarious, as Howard was. The Texan had no doubt there was no chance of Lovecraft even deigning to talk to Big Carney, let alone sitting for a beer with him or with William Pratt. The thought made Howard a little sad, but he did not dwell on it.

Take each man as he comes and judge him on himself.

The two new pub friends sipped their beers and a second round, and sat, alternately chatting and silently observing the room till finally the Texan stood and stretched.

"I'd best be getting back to my bed and breakfast," the writer said. "I have a story to finish up for *Top-Notch* and want to take a train up to Scotland tomorrow. I plan to walk some of Hadrian's Wall and see if I can find some Romans to repel." He laughed at the image.

"A pleasure to meet you, Mister Howard—"

"Bob."

"Bob," Pratt said. "Hope you find some good local color for your stories. I'm only good for one more of these pints then I have to head back to my flat soon myself; I am not as young as I used to be."

"You have a good trip home, William," The Texan said, "enjoy the balmy weather." Bob Howard hefted his typewriter—he refused to leave it behind in the rented room—and headed out of the door.

Neither man noticed that several of the shadowy heads turned to follow the American's progress out of the pub. If they had they would have seen the eyes of those men shining with the hungry look of rabid wolves.

Chapter Fourteen: Out of the Fog

The husky Texan walked slowly from The Hanged Man feeling the stronger English beer more than he thought he would. The night air was heavy with moisture though it was not actually raining. Thick fog was rolling in off the river to the south and softened the edges of the brick buildings that were crowded one atop the other along the street. It had the effect of muffling the late-night sounds of the bustling city, but it was still more noise than the Texan was used to from his home.

The sleepy Texas town that Howard had grown up in was in the midst of a vast plain and though it had boom and bust times, was never more than a spot on the map barely worth stopping in. No library, one school and about as isolated as one could get; yet his mother had instilled in him a love of literature and he had been able to escape the dusty town through the pages of books.

Books had opened his eyes to the whole wide world beyond Texas and he had filled his writings with stories of far-off kingdoms, by-gone times, strange magicks and exotic locals. He had always been the outsider in his little town, the 'strange one' who actually made more money than most in the dusty crossroads, but whose ephemeral job confused many in the town. Yet there was the fact that the mere word-pusher could hold his own in icehouse boxing matches.

Howard patted the typewriter that was his constant companion and smiled. *You left me a greater inheritance than money, Mama, you left me the ability to dream.*

Howard became aware of muffled footsteps on the wet cobblestones behind him. There was more than one set. And, most disturbingly, they seemed to be matching his speed and direction. He slowed down and sped up several times to be sure, but the followers kept pace.

The Texan turned off Cable Street at the next corner and soon was in a warren-like maze of tiny East End streets. The footfalls behind him were constant and all doubt was gone.

Looks like I got me some suitors come-a-courtin' the Texan thought as he glanced behind him. He pulled his typewriter to his chest and reached under his coat to finger his grandfather's newly repaired Colt six-shooter he had in an inside pocket. After being jumped in New York he had started to mistrust cities as a matter of course.

Just as he reached for the butt of the revolver an object came out of the murky mist and slammed into the side of his head. The Texan dropped to his knees, the typewriter case slipping from his grasp to clatter on the cobbles of the pavement.

A shape stepped from the fog to reveal itself as a man. The new arrival was holding the board he'd hit the Texan with.

When Bob Howard tried to pull the gun out the figure swung the board again to smash into his side. The gun was knocked from Bob's palsied fingers and skittered into the darkness.

Suddenly three more shapes came from behind the Texan and moved in like a wolf pack on a fallen hind. They immediately begin kicking the fallen man.

"Don't let the blighter up," one of the shapes called to the others. "He's a brutish lookin' fellow!"

The Texan could do little while they put the boot to him but cover up and try to get his wits about him. He brought his arms up to cover his head trying to prevent them from striking him in the face or vital organs.

The heavy boots of the thugs slammed into him with practiced technique, each with the impact that jarred his teeth and made him sick to his stomach. All the while the men were laughing and joking as they worked.

Their laughter angered the Texan more than the pain of the boots or cowardice of their attack and gave him impetus to ignore that pain. He forced himself to roll violently to his left. This allowed him to collide with the legs of one of the attackers.

Howard latched onto the lower limbs he connected with, using both arms to pull the attacker off balance and bring the man down. The street thug Howard grabbed slammed into the cobbles with a colorful curse.

"Hell and brimstone!" the man screamed. "He's got me, Marty!"

The other three men angled to continue their boot attack, but the Texan clung tenaciously to the man he had grabbed and thwarted some of the kicks by using him as a shield.

"Get him off me!" the fallen man yelled. "You're kicking me!" but the three standing men continued the assault unabated, though the thrust of it was blunted with many of the kicks not landing solidly.

"Hold him fast, Charley," another one of the men called. "I'll hit him again with the stick."

They're gonna stomp my head lest I can get a breather, the Texan thought but he didn't dare slacken his grip to fight back.

Just then another figure came rocketing out of the roiling mist with a low war cry and slammed into the standing figures with force enough to carry two of them to the ground.

It was the break Howard needed and he squirmed free of the thug he had grabbed and rolled to his knees. Once up he threw a punch at the struggling Charley that connected with the thug's jaw. The ruffian fell back semiconscious.

This allowed the Texan to make it all the way to his feet and confront the last standing attacker face to face.

The man Howard faced was as tall as he but built along rougher lines. He had a face that proclaimed his participation in many fights with a nose that was barely a lump of gristle. His left eyelid drooped with an almost sleepy tilt and from beneath it a muddy brown eye glared at the Texan.

"All right, you bloody Yank, time to take you to school." The man exploded at the Texan with a flurry of punches.

Howard was not, however, a mere armchair adventurer. Here his experience in the many icehouse bouts back home came into play. More than one opponent had found him no shrinking violet wordsmith. Now he accepted the charge with forearm blocks, moving smoothly backward to be clear of the fallen Charley.

The Texan let the English thug drive him back five steps until he knew he had room to move. Then, with a war cry that would do any Comanche proud, the Texan lowered his head, hunched his shoulders and counterpunched.

Hard.

Howard let all his Celtic blood boil to the surface and launched a series of trip-hammer combinations at the thug that all but overwhelmed the English ruffian who was barely able to block.

The thug was taken completely by surprise by the fury and the skill of the counterattack. He barely blocked several strikes but could not backpedal fast enough to avoid a hard right cross. The blow staggered him, and Howard pressed his sudden advantage.

The writer followed the right cross with a series of body shots that slammed into the mugger to elicit a sharp wheezing cough from the thug. The English rough had clearly never fought anyone on an even field and his defense melted against the ferocious onslaught.

Howard stepped inside the man's weakened guard and sent one last one-two combination into the criminal's breadbasket. The trip-hammer fists sank deep into the diaphragm of the mugger so that the thug dropped unconscious at the Texan's feet. At the same moment, the three figures rolling nearby on the ground broke apart.

Marty rose out of the mass of bodies. The two figures left on the ground were still locked in a violent struggle. One was one of the attacking thugs and the other, William Pratt!

Marty looked around the two on the pavement then bent to grope for the board he had used as a cudgel.

Howard searched for his six-shooter but when he saw the gang leader swing the board into Pratt's back, he knew he could not wait to find it.

The Texan charged across the street, spotting and picking up his typewriter on the run. When he got close enough, he swung the hard leather case and smashed it into the side of Marty's head with a satisfying 'thunk.' The thug dropped as if poleaxed.

Pratt was groaning and obviously hurt but still held onto the cutpurse he was wrestling with.

Howard reached past his rescuer and bounced his knuckles off the criminal's chin—that took the last of the fight out of him and he sagged in Pratt's arms.

As suddenly as the violence had begun all was quiet again.

Pratt rolled over, his features contorted in pain. He looked up at the looming shape of the Texan, squinting in agony, not sure if he was being attacked again. He tried to raise his arms in defense.

"William," Howard said. "It's me, Bob."

"Oh," the fallen man said, "are you alright?"

"Am I alright?" the Texan said. "I just saw him smack you with that tree." He bent to gingerly help the Englishman to his feet.

"I thought you were a goner," Pratt said as he painfully found his footing. "I saw these blokes leave the pub just after you did and got suspicious they were up to no good. I followed them for a few blocks and then saw them give chase when you darted off."

Howard located his six-gun and hefted it with a satisfied grunt, glad that he always took the frontier precaution of having the hammer rest on an empty chamber. He turned to survey the chaos of the street with the four thugs strewn around unconscious. "Looks like a dang Apache attack," he said.

"I arrived just in time to see that fellow hit you with the board," Pratt continued. He stood with his right hand on the small of his back, slightly stooped over, his face contorted in contained agony.

"I'm darn glad you did," the Texan said. "I ain't ashamed to admit that I was not doing all that well when you happened along." He grinned and picked up his typewriter case then noticed how badly Pratt was injured.

"Will," he said, "are you gonna be okay?"

"It's an old injury from my time in Canada digging ditches." Pratt took a tentative step and winced.

"Come on, Hoss," Howard said. "Lean on me." He stepped up and let the Englishman put a hand on the taller man's shoulder.

"I'll have your guts for garters," Marty hissed from his place on the pavement. Blood was trickling down his forehead and there was virulent hate in his eyes.

"You just better stay down, varmint," Howard said quietly. "Elst I'll weigh you down with a couple of chunks of lead from Grandpa's gun to keep you there." His grin was wolfish, and it was clear he would relish using his grandfather's bequest. Marty froze where he was and just glared in venomous hate.

The other thugs began to moan and slowly come to consciousness, but none were in any shape to rise and offer danger to the two friends.

"Let's get out of here," Howard said to Pratt. "I think I could use one or two more of them warm English beers to finish out this night."

Chapter Fifteen: Keeping up with the Harkers

"You really do not have to do this, Robert," William Pratt said in protest. "You really don't owe me—"

"Now stop that," the Texan said as he tried buttoning the red riding jacket. "First off, it's Bob and secondly, you saved my hide, true enough in that alley the other day—it's the least I could do."

The two men were in the small cottage where Pratt lived when he was working on the Harker estate in High Wycombe. Pratt was propped up on his bed, a board slid behind him to allow him to rest on an angle. The mugger's club blow to his back had inflamed his old injury and his entire back was in painful spasm.

After the night attack, the Texan had returned with his rescuer to his bed and breakfast to fetch his belongings and then insisted on accompanying Pratt back to High Wycombe on the train.

"I ain't got nowhere in particular to go on any schedule, Will; Scotland will still be there in a couple of days. This is just another way to collect me some local color for my writing." The cowboy spoke as he helped the Englishman to the train. "I came to see the sights. Might as well see the sights in the country as the city."

The Englishman's protests had little strength when the seriousness of his back injury made it clear he did need help to get home.

"The worst thing is that I was bringing these harnesses back for the hunt on Thursday," Pratt confided to Howard as the train rumbled up the tracks out of London. "We are short-handed on the estate, and they will need me to ride with the hounds."

"Well if you can't do it by then," the Texan had said with no doubt, "I'll just ride for you."

Though Pratt's back was improved somewhat it became clear by Wednesday that he would not be able to ride. But by then the genial Texan had made himself welcome around the stables of the estate with his 'I can help with that' attitude and gentle wit.

He had also proven that he was more than capable in the saddle though his inability to post in proper English fashion was a source of considerable amusement to the grooms.

Now Howard was dressed in one of Pratt's riding outfits, the jacket long enough but not quite fitting across the chest.

"I'll stay at the outside of the pack away from the patrons," Howard said. He looked at himself in the full-length mirror and smiled. "My Ma would bust a gut laughing if she could see me now, all gussied up and looking like a duke."

Pratt laughed. "Any duke that looked like that would be exiled from the castle most certainly, my friend." His voice was still a little strained; it really did hurt only when he laughed.

Howard pouted and then laughed at himself in a deep, hearty belly laugh. "Well," he said, "at least I'm all Texan from the shins down." He had not been able to fit into Pratt's boots so he still wore his cowboy boots, albeit polished like they had not been for a long time.

"You are a good friend, Bob, I will not forget it."

Howard blushed. "It's what you do for friends, Will. You didn't ask me if I needed help, you just gave it." He picked up the black top hat and fit it to his head. "We're both lucky you have a head as full of dreams as mine; else I'd have to go out there with my head exposed to your lovely weather."

The Texan went to the door and tapped the rim of the hat in salute. "Have a nice day, my lord," he said in a horribly bad British accent, "and rest your back."

The foxhunt was in celebration of the Harkers' daughter's return from a private school abroad. It was not, by peer standards, a massive affair but it was close enough to her birthday that the lord and lady of the manor had a tea set out for the twenty guests to enjoy after the ride.

The cowboy whipper-in took his place with the other riders, mostly avoiding any notice except for Alfie, the head rider giving a gentle chuckle at seeing his boots.

"At least we'll be safe from red Indians on our ride," Alfie said, with good humor.

"We aim to please," Howard smiled back. "But I'll keep an eye out for any Comanche, just in case."

The Texan got his first look at the lord and lady as they rode up, side by side with their son, Quincy. All three were handsome figures of English aristocracy and were everything that the Texan expected minor English nobility would look like.

The father, Jonathon, was an even-featured older man with graying hair and a classically square jaw. The mother, Wilhelmina, was a pale-skinned beauty with wide blue, intelligent eyes and auburn hair that had just a hint of gray. Their twenty-seven-year-old son Quincy was a perfect blend of both parent's features but with a cruel cast to his downturned mouth and a shadow of selfishness in his gaze.

"He's going off again," Alfie hissed when he saw the younger Harker ride up to the lunch pavilion and immediately begin to yell at one of the maids.

"You stupid bint," Harker snarled at the girl, "you've put the wine out too soon; the sun will warm that Madeira and make it undrinkable." He raised his riding crop like a sword and aimed it at her and for a moment the Texan tensed thinking the Englishman was going to strike the girl.

"Yes, sir, sorry sir," the girl cowered and moved the wine back into the shade of the tent, taking herself out of the crop's reach.

"Easy, Yank," the older Alfie whispered when he saw the Texan's body tense. "The young master can be loud, lad, but he never gets too bad when the lady is around; she holds him on a tight rein."

Indeed, when the younger Harker continued to berate the girl, his mother rode up beside him. "Let us move on to the starting area, dear," she said quietly, but forcefully. The lady's voice was lower-pitched than the Texan would have thought from looking at the delicate line of her neck but had the full force of aristocratic history behind it.

The Harker scion's eyes flashed with fire at his mother's rebuke, but he quickly doused it with a contrite "Yes, Mother."

The two nobles rode off ahead of the group to meet and mingle with their guests and await the start of the hunt.

"I ain't got much stomach for seein' women folk yelled at," the muscular writer said as he moved to mount his horse.

"Not much we can do about it, lad," Alfie said. "Them's the nobles, lad, they are different from you and me."

"Guess that explains why we asked you folks to politely leave the continent back in '76," the Texan said. "'Cause any man that yelled at a servant girl like that in Texas would lose the ability to do it fast as I could draw."

The older groom shook his head. "Cowboys!" he muttered.

The two men joined the other whipper-ins, most of whom were on foot, in the form-up area by the pen where the hounds were waiting noisily. The four who were on horseback would range ahead with the dog-pack to make sure the nobles got their sport with a minimum of disruption and the men on foot would keep the hounds from becoming distracted.

The master of hounds pointedly did not look at the Texan too closely and for his part, Howard moved as far back in the group of riding whipper-ins as he could, keeping behind the others to hide the irregularities of his riding costume.

From this position, Bob was able to observe the interactions of the strange breed of people called nobility as they chatted amongst themselves. He found himself staring and occasionally shaking his head as they fretted about their mounts or gave terse orders to some lackey.

"Civilization's finest," he muttered quietly to himself, "not a single one of them peacocks would last a day along the Pecos."

"But then would you be able to navigate Lady Wyckor's spring teas without creating a scandal?" A female voice drew the Texan's attention to a pretty young woman in a cream-colored riding habit who had appeared behind him. She was a few years younger than Quincy, but Howard could see Harker features.

Her skin was pale and her eyes a translucent sky blue. She had her mother's long neck and her father's square jaw, yet softened and feminine. Around her neck he saw a lovely choker with a pendant cameo image of a pretty woman against an intricate pattern of swirls and lines. It seemed a delicate and somehow regal decoration for the young girl to wear.

"I expect I'd be quite the clown at such a gathering, Miss," the Texan said as he took his eyes from her necklace, "but then, rattlesnakes along the Pecos pack a bit of poison."

"Oh, so does Lady Wyckor and her circle, I can assure you, Mister Howard."

"You know me, ma'am?"

She gave a gentle giggle at his obvious discomfort. "I assure you I have no special powers: I stopped by Master Pratt's cottage when I heard he had been injured and he informed me of the circumstances of his injury. I knew you had to be his western friend."

He followed her gaze and answered her with a shy smile. "The boots give me away, huh?"

"They helped, but I would have recognized you in any event, sir, as you stand out like a wolf among the hinds by your carriage."

He didn't know whether to take that statement as compliment or critique until he saw the playful light in her eyes.

"If I am that wolf, Miss Harker, then you are a greyhound."

This made the girl giggle again. "I see William did not exaggerate when he said you were a teller of tall tales, Mister Howard."

"Call me Bob, please, ma'am. My dad is Mister Howard."

The girl was about to say something more when the master of the hunt sounded the horn to assemble everyone, and she pulled her horse out ahead of the pack.

"Have a good ride, Miss Harker."

"Gwendolyn," she said and added, with a tittering laugh, "I shall endeavor to, Bob. You keep an eye out for peacocks and rattlesnakes." Then she was off to lead the hunt at a full gallop.

Now that, he thought as he watched her course away, *gives even a fella like me hope for civilization!*

Chapter Sixteen: Life on the Edge

The horses of the fox hunters flew through the woods drawn by the howling of the hounds as they chased their prey. A light drizzle grayed the greens of the woods and made the grass slick and treacherous for the racing equines.

Bob Howard, who had grown up riding the rough back-country of his home state, raced along at the fringe of it all with a breathless excitement coursing through him. He was sure that his blood was pumping as swiftly as the blue bloods he was flanking, and the thought made him smile.

His nature and long practice drew him back to riding western style though the hunting saddle forced him into an ungraceful hybrid of both western and English styles. The horse didn't seem to care which way he rode, for the animal glided over the terrain with surefootedness and with a wild joy at the chance to run. It was a spirited hunter that Howard suspected had some common heritage with the wild mustangs of the plains he was used to riding. In any case, he and the animal had no problem forming a rapport so that they flew over the uneven ground with ease.

Howard felt that same savage joy as his mount. The primal sense of the hunt sent his blood to a boil, and he suddenly began to understand some of the appeal of the fox-hunt to the upper classes; it allowed them to feel the keen sense of the primitive that the Texan believed was the natural state of all mankind and its ultimate end. A state their elevated position in the world, insulated from many of the realities of actual survival, was denied to the 'upper classes.'

Barbarism was the beginning and the end of things to the Texan, a savage purity of being unhampered by the artificiality of civilization. Now he clearly saw that even those who lived perfumed lives that purported to be distanced from the primal urges had a sense that such a state was the truth of the universe and had to invent a way to satisfy that primal desire.

The volume of the hounds barking increased as they caught the trace of the fox ahead of them. They surged forward at the new scent and exploded through the underbrush so that the following horsemen had to work to keep up.

Even with the fox out front, some of the dogs ranged out of the pack and Howard proved he was as adept as any of the other whipper-ins at sending them back into the main body and keeping the animals in a tight grouping.

The chase went on for a half-hour, out of the fields and over gently rolling hills into and through stands of trees. The fox even led them across a shallow stream.

A clever vixen, trying to throw the dogs off the scent. His natural frontier sense of justice had his sympathies with the object of the hunt, always with the underdog in any fight. It appealed to the racial memory part of him that remembered the primordial struggle against the forces of chaos at the very beginning of time, when it was the lone human against a pack of dire wolves or herd of mastodons.

I could see this if it were for food, he thought as he dodged a low tree branch at a full gallop, *but this is about pretending to be superior; the fox is the hero here.*

The chase broke from the tree line and moved out across a broad rolling field that bordered on an old stone quarry. The edge of the quarry created an abrupt cliff.

Most of the riders lagged behind the two Harker siblings by a considerable distance, having slowed going through the dense underbrush. The brother and sister showed superb horsemanship maneuvering through the rough country and forged ahead.

The lead rider was Quincy Harker, his mount almost on the heels of the hounds, but his sister was not behind by much. The Texan was able to appreciate the girl's ability even from a distance as he ranged the terrain guiding the dogs.

Howard was almost parallel with Quincy and the two exchanged a gleeful grin as they came abreast, both reveling in the sheer excitement of the racing mounts.

Then the young noble's horse slipped on a muddy patch crossing a shallow pond. It was little more than a large puddle, but it was enough to make the footing treacherous. The animal went down before the nobleman could jump clear of the saddle and slammed full on Harker's leg. The horse pinned him as the animal rolled and Quincy was left hanging from the stirrup.

The horse whinnied in fright but regained its footing, eyes wide with terror. Spooked, the animal took off at a mad run across the open field dragging the semi-conscious nobleman with it.

"Quincy!" Gwendolyn screamed. She wheeled her own horse about and spurred her mount to ride after her brother, attempting to overtake the fleeing animal.

Howard reined his own mount off chasing the hounds and rocketed straight for Quincy's frightened horse. He realized immediately he could not overtake the beast directly, so he rode at an angle to the racing animal, not trying to catch it but to cut it off in its mad dash as it headed inexorably toward the open quarry pit.

The panicked horse ran full tilt, and it was clear in its frantic flight it was blindly heading toward the precipitous edge of the quarry. The helpless, disoriented Quincy was bounced along the rough ground and screamed as he was dragged. He was so stunned he could not even make an attempt to grab for the ankle trapped in the stirrup.

Dang I wish I had a lasso, Howard thought but he had only a short whip, the snap of which would not even be heard by the maddened runaway. He leaned forward in his saddle and urged his own mount to greater speed, his mind hatching a desperate and outrageous plan.

If Howard could not turn the galloping rogue he had to stop it, or the trapped nobleman would be dragged over the cliff. That fate was only seconds away unless the Texan took a mad chance.

There was no time to ride alongside or try to turn the horse with shouts or by gestures, so Howard would have to turn the animal forcibly.

The Texan whipped his own horse to a frothing frenzy and angled it to collide with the racing stallion on the cliff side of the animal. He had to time it exactly, to shoulder his horse into the runaway so that both did not tumble over the edge.

Howard could see that Quincy was conscious but still so disoriented that he could do nothing to help himself.

"Sorry, fellow," Howard whispered to his horse at the moment the two galloping equines smashed shoulder to shoulder. Both animals lost gait and the runaway stumbled but did not fall.

The Texan leaped from his saddle and clamped his arms around the neck of the still-moving runaway. He bore down and exerted his full body weight to torque the horse's head. This had the effect of bulldogging the animal so that it fell over toward him and away from the dragging noble.

Horse and men were enveloped in a cloud of dirt as they slid forward on the wet grass.

Howard dug his heels into the ground to slow the slide, but the momentum of the stallion's weight kept the whole mass moving toward the cliff edge. He screamed at the top of his lungs to the rapidly approaching Gwendolyn. "Get him loose before we go over!"

The mass of man and beast continued sliding toward the edge of the quarry cliff, propelled by the momentum from the frantic run. At the same time, the maddened horse was violently kicking and trying to get on his feet, but he was held down by the husky cowboy.

The girl raced up and jumped from her own horse as nimbly as an acrobat and landed at a full run. She raced to her brother's tangled leg and began to frantically pull on the boot that was trapped in the stirrup.

"I can't get it out!" she yelled as she tugged on the leg.

"You have to!" Howard yelled. "I can't hold it!"

The edge of the precipice was less than a yard away and the momentum of the horse on the slick grass was pulling them all toward the soft soil of the lip.

Gwendolyn yanked at the boot and began to work it off her brother's foot.

"Gwen!" the nobleman managed to utter, his confusion and fear clearing.

"She's going over!" the Texan yelled as his feet felt air over the quarry lip.

At that moment the boot came free from Quincy's foot and the girl screamed, "He's free!"

Quincy's horse went over the cliff in horrific slow motion, still whinnying in an agony of confusion and fear, all its legs kicking wildly.

Howard's own legs went over the edge as well and he had to spin in place to press his chest down and clutch at the ground to keep from certain death. He grabbed the soil, digging his fingers into the soft loam to hold himself from following the animal over. His feet dangled in the air, and he still slid slowly over till he drove his fingers into the ground to clamp on.

The horse screamed all the fifty feet to the bottom of the quarry, its terrified yells echoing off the stonewalls until, with a sickening thud, it was silenced.

After a horrible, eternal moment when his legs dangled free over empty space and his fingers dug knuckle deep into the wet soil gripping the earth, Howard managed to claw his way far enough to crawl onto the grass. He kept crawling until he was lying flat on his stomach on the sodden grass. All his strength went out of him then, his breath coming in huge gulps.

The Texan turned his head to look over at the two Hark-ers and saw the siblings in a heartfelt embrace. The girl held her brother's head in her lap, comforting him with soft words. The still-stunned Quincy was staring blankly up at her, his right hand holding one of hers while he gulped air.

Gwendolyn looked up from her brother and, seeing the Texan's gaze, smiled a radiant smile.

"At least there ain't no rattlesnakes," he said when he saw her looking at him.

"But that always leaves peacocks to watch out for," she said.

The two of them were still laughing when the others rode up.

Chapter Seventeen: Caste and Castigation

The lead hunt riders had been at the edge of the forest when Quincy's horse had gone down and many of them had helplessly watched the entire headlong chase. It had only taken a few minutes but to Howard, Gwendolyn and especially Quincy, it had seemed to go on forever.

"My boy!" Wilhelmina Harker yelled as she jumped from her horse and slid down beside her son.

Several of the men had already come to Quincy's side and were administering aid to him. Others had gone to his sister and to Howard.

"I am quite fine," Gwendolyn protested as she was helped to her feet, "see to Quincy and Mister Howard."

"I'm just a bit singed around the edges," the Texan said as he stood and brushed some of the mud off himself, "but I'm afraid I pretty thoroughly ruined Will's outfit for sure."

"That was the bravest thing I have ever seen," Jonathon Harker said as he stepped up beside the Texan. "And damn fine riding, sir."

"I learned from the best in Cross Plains," Howard said with a shrug, "and I was just doing what anyone would have done." As he spoke his shrug caused him to realize that he'd split the jacket across the shoulders as well as covered it in dirt.

"Darn it all, I owe Will a jacket!" he mumbled absent-mindedly. His hands began to suddenly shake from adrenaline fatigue, and he became a little light-headed. He reached out to steady himself and his hand contacted a shoulder.

"Easy, Mister Howard," Gwendolyn said. "It seems you are not a man of iron after all."

"Excuse me, ma'am," he said. He pulled his hand back and blushed at the contact; the girl years younger than her brother seemed suddenly very more mature than the Texan.

"I never claimed to be more than flesh and blood," Howard said as he rubbed a hand along an oozing scrape he discovered along his cheek, "and at some times more blood than at others."

Some of the riders wanted to go back for a trap but Quincy stood and waved them off. "I am fine," he said in a shaky voice, "just a game ankle." He limped over to Howard with the help of two of the men and stood eye to eye with the Texan.

"A bally good ride, sir," he said. He extended his hand to the Texan and they shook. Howard noted that it was a limp grasp on the nobleman's part but chalked it up to the man's recent experience.

"My pleasure, sir, glad I could be of service," Howard said with a genial smile. It was clear he was a little embarrassed by the compliments and did not regard what he had done as anything more than what needed to be done.

Quincy Harker looked at the Texan and a strange expression flashed across his features as if he wished to say something more, but the words stuck in his throat. Then he moved off to be helped up to a borrowed horse.

Gwendolyn had no such reluctance, however.

"Thank you, Mister Howard—I mean Bob," she said with a warm smile. "I am rather fond of my brother, thank you for returning him to me."

Howard had a hard time looking her in the eyes, his gaze drifting away and downward where he noticed a tear in the knee of his riding britches. "Dang," he whispered out loud as he touched the tear.

She saw his expression and the direction of his gaze and reached up to lift his chin with a finger.

"You have saved my brother in a singular act of skill and bravery; learn to accept your accolades, my Galahad. And fear not, I will see that William has a full replacement wardrobe."

"I 'preciate that, ma'am, I hate to ruin his Sunday clothes on him." He found himself enjoying her pale blue eyes. A ghost of a smile slid along his lips.

"Yet you want nothing for yourself?" the girl said.

"Fer what?" he said with a little confusion.

This made her laugh, a wild musical sound that was primal and real as the lightning and tingled his skin the same way.

"I will explain it to you when we get back to the pavilion," she said as she linked her arm through his, "right now I am very hungry!"

Neither one saw the eyes of Wilhelmina Harker narrow as she watched the two of them walk off in conversation.

The visitor from Texas was the center of attention at the afternoon's tea with many of the nobles both impressed by his riding and fascinated by his background and profession, not to mention his 'quaint' accent.

He was not comfortable with the attention and endured it because it seemed to be a source of amusement to the effervescent Gwendolyn. She stood by his side the entire time accepting compliments and deflecting inquiries for information from the Texan. He found her company more than a little pleasant and her amusement at his predicament fair compensation for the discomfort of the public attention.

Quincy sat, his ankle wrapped and elevated, in a chair near the head of the lunch table and drank copious amounts of wine. He accepted well-wishes from all but observed the crowd that swirled around the Texan with jaundiced glances. Quincy's mood seemed to darken the longer the Texan endured the attention of the crowd and the focused company of his sister.

The hero of the day even began to relax and respond to questions from the partygoers about his home state and his profession with witty stories and humorous anecdotes. Soon Howard's natural storytelling ability and simple manners had drawn a larger group than the Harker scion.

"You will bore a hole in the cowboy's back if you stare any harder, Quincy," the Harker matriarch said quietly to her son. She stood by his side and pointedly took his half-empty goblet of wine from his hand and set it on the table. "And you are drinking too much in public."

The young nobleman shook himself and turned to look up into her eyes. "It is not I who you should be speaking to about propriety. Our darling Gwen is making a fool of herself with that barbarian."

"It is unbecoming for you to appear ungrateful to the man who saved your life," his mother said. "You need to be more jovial for the sake of those watching."

"I don't feel very jovial," Quincy said. "Give the peasant a gold cup and let him be on his way; he only did his duty."

The woman leaned in as if to give a motherly peck to his temple and quietly hissed, "You will get up and express proper magnanimous gratitude or I will cut off your allowance for the next year. The White Glove has plans for you and The Master would be disappointed if you did not achieve your full potential. You will be all hail and well met; you have to be seen to be egalitarian if you are to gather any political support for your future Parliamentary position."

The younger Harker shuddered at the fire in his mother's eyes and sat up straighter. "Yes, Mother," he said. "As you say, I should be magnanimous." He pushed himself up on the arms of his chair and put on a public smile.

"I was amazed you knew so much about the Crusades," Gwendolyn said to Howard when the two of them were alone for a moment while the party guests sat down for scones. "You fairly made Major Higgen's head spin. He's usually such a bore about it."

"Shucks," the Texan said. "It's sort of my business to know such stuff. And reading on history and cultures is my hobby as well."

"Do you come from a family of writers?"

He gave a gentle, dark laugh. "I am a pioneer in my profession, just as my grandfathers were in theirs, in that I am the first man in my section to earn his living as a writer. But I have to admit that to most where I come from the idea of a man making his living by writing seems, in that hardy environment, so fantastic that even today I am sometimes myself assailed by a feeling of unreality."

"Stop doing that," she chided him.

"Doing what?"

"You always make less of yourself, be proud of who you are and what you have accomplished."

"You seem to think more of me than—"

"Now stop that," she scolded him. "I have had all the advantages, as have many of those I know, of education, secure income and all that comes with that, yet none of them—or myself, have done so much with our opportunities or are so well-read as you are."

"Now you are being over-modest, ma'am," Howard said. "You were keeping up with the conversation just fine with a fair knowledge of things from Carthage to Constantinople and you've done a darn fine job of protecting my flank against some sneak attacks from some of those 'rattlesnake' guests."

She blushed. "I didn't—"

"Oh yes you did. You were as skillful deflecting rude questions and uncomfortable statements made by your friends as a sheepdog working a flock."

Gwendolyn laughed. "Oh my, that is the first time I have been compared to a sheepdog in a complimentary way."

Now it was the Texan's turn to blush.

"I didn't mean..." he stammered. "I meant that—"

"I know what you meant, Mister Howard, and I am very complimented indeed by the observation. Woof!"

"Then please call me Bob, okay? I know we ain't exactly had a proper introduction, but you're making me feel downright elderly with that 'Mister Howard' stuff."

"Alright, I'll call you Bob if you stop backtracking on yourself." She stuck out her pinky and he smiled when he recognized the schoolyard gesture. He extended his own and they locked them and shook.

"Done!" He found a strange electric thrill from the contact of the digits and tried to ignore it.

"Done!" she replied with a broad grin that danced all the way to her eyes.

"And just what is being done?" A smiling Quincy hobbled over to the two.

"Quincy!" the girl exclaimed. "You shouldn't be walking!"

"Pish!" he said with a wave of his hand. "My ankle is sprained but Doctor Armond said no ligaments were torn. I've taken more of a beating on the football pitch. Besides," he chuckled, "I have enough wine in me to dull any pain and mitigate my normally brusque manner."

He extended his hand to Howard and smiled. "I want to thank you again, chap, for the life of the wretch who stands somewhat shakily before you."

The handshake between the two was firm this time.

"It was my pleasure, Mister Harker," Howard said with genuine joy in his tone.

"Quincy, please," the Harker scion said, "let's drop all the formality. And I hope you will stay to supper with us; I want to quiz you on how to ride like Tom Mix!"

Everyone in the pavilion laughed at that except Gwendolyn who regarded her newly emotive brother with a quizzical expression.

Chapter Eighteen: The Dark Veil

"I can barely believe what you've told me," William Pratt said repeatedly when Bob Howard returned to the cottage and recounted what had occurred on the foxhunt. The invalid had the soiled clothes and the word of all the other grooms who had already stopped by to tell Pratt what had happened, but still the Englishman shook his head in wonder at the tale.

"It's not like I planned it," Howard said with a laugh, "far as heck from it; but I got me an invite to the big house for victles!" He produced his one good suit from the closet where he'd hung it and borrowed a clean dress shirt from Pratt.

"I promise not to ruin this," the Texan said holding up the shirt to check that the sleeves were long enough. It would be tight across the chest but would fit him.

"Oh, think nothing of it, chap," the Englishman said with a genial laugh. "Lady Gwen also stopped by and told me all about you and your adventure and promised a whole replacement riding suit for me. She also told me I had good taste in friends." He took great delight when the Texan colored pink.

"How is your back feeling?" Howard deflected any further compliments with his question.

"Much better after another day of rest," Pratt walked slowly across the room to demonstrate. It was the first time the Texan noticed he was very bowlegged.

"Here," the Englishman said, producing a necktie from a dresser. "This will bring you luck." He slipped the tie around his friend's neck and tied it in a four-in-hand knot.

"I look right the dude," the Texan said as he admired himself in the mirror. "Thanks, Will."

"Just mind your Ps and Qs with that crowd, Bob," Pratt said. "They may seem like members of the gentility, but I was raised among that class, and—despite where I have fallen to because of my love affair with Thespis—they can be a vicious bunch."

he Texan grinned. "That's almost what Gwen said." He paused with the thought of the girl fixed in his expression and recited, "*What do I know of cultured ways, the gilt, the craft, and the lie? I, who was born in a naked land and bred in the open sky.*" And laughed at his own state.

"I often wonder how they ended up with an angel like Gwendolyn," Pratt said, "in that...that pit of vipers."

"That's been on my mind as well," the burly Texan said, distractedly admiring his reflection in the mirror. "The fact that she is an angel."

The supper at the Harker house was a boisterous affair, not nearly as 'stuffy' as Bob Howard had anticipated. The guests from the hunt had remained and dressed for dinner so the meal was set in the main dining room.

Bob was still the subject of many odd and intrusive questions, but once again, as with the afternoon's tea, Gwendolyn Harker was at his side and acted as both shield for him to deflect the most obnoxious of the inquiries and cheerleader to steer the conversation to topics at which he was adept.

Howard enjoyed watching her deftly maneuver through the perils of society's rattlesnakes as skillfully as a matador dodging a herd of charging bulls. She noticed him enjoying her skill and often flashed him a secret smile when there was a quiet moment.

The two new friends sat next to each other at dinner and spent much of the time chatting on every topic imaginable, a fact that delighted both of them. Each time that one thought they had a topic the other was coming up short on, they were surprised with a new revelation and a new direction of the dialogue.

"You say you never traveled from Texas before, yet you know more about Paris—which I have been to many times—than I do!"

"Not much else to do back home in Cross Plains but to read, write stories and letters, and to dream," he said with a touch of wistfulness. "Where I come from there weren't but a handful of folks that had ever read a book, I reckon, other than The Good Book." He laughed at a memory.

"There was this library in the next town and when it was closed for the summer, I'd sneak in and take out a bunch of books, read them, bring them back and then do it again. I did it all summer. I'm pretty sure they knew but didn't all mind that much."

"Did you not have anyone to talk to?" She sipped from a glass of punch, and he did his best not to notice how coyly she glanced at him over the rim.

He blushed, taking his eyes from her to focus again on the choker she wore. "I had friends like Tevis Smith and a couple of others, and, a…a…girl fer a bit, Novalyne who I thought really understood what I was trying to do but…"

"But?" the blue-eyed girl regarded him with no prurient curiosity, but rather real interest, so he continued.

"But I guess it just wasn't a strong enough connection." His voice dropped and his brows knit with the pained memory. "We sort of grew apart and then with Ma getting sick and all…"

The sadness in his voice caused the girl to reach out and touch his forearm with gentle fingers.

Her touch was cool, but he felt a hot flash of energy shoot up his arm from it, even more powerful than the touch of their fingers from their pinky swear. He felt himself amazed that it was so easy to talk to her.

He had all but no experience talking with women and felt his own awkwardness, yet it seemed the most natural thing in the world to talk to her, the words flowing out as easily as if he were writing one of his tales.

"I have never had a boyfriend, Bob," she suddenly said quietly. "Not since middle form where Rodney Echart pulled my pigtails. And after university, my parents sent me to boarding school so I have never felt that special connection either." She looked directly into his eyes. "But I have dreamed as well."

"Near misses hurt the most," he said as he tried to tear himself away from her eyes, *"Dreams half-formed, Plans that don't quite gel, Life's the pits, And loving's hell…"*

He saw her eyes widen and the line of her mouth hovered between smile and frown. "That is beautiful and so dark as well. Who wrote it?"

"I did. I write a lot of poetry in between my boxing and crusader stories."

She shook her head and laughed. "You are a deep well, Mister Robert Ervin Howard. One from which I think I would like to drink deeply for a long time."

He blushed again and she answered his blush with one of her own.

He tried to deflect her comments and asked, "I noticed your lovely necklace; where did you get it?"

She reached up a delicate hand to touch it. "This choker, I've had it since I can remember; the cameo was actually a brooch, but I had it refashioned into this pendant to hang from the choker. I like to wear it this way."

"Is it an ancestor's image?"

"I do not know," she said with a shrug and a smile. "Mother said only that I should always keep it with me but won't tell me any more about it. I often imagined it was given to my great-grandmother, or such by some dark-haired, blue-eyed prince from far away as a token of love."

"You are a true romantic, Miss Gwendolyn Harker."

"And you have very dark blue eyes, Mister Howard," she said and made him blush again.

The delight that the two opposites had in each other's company was not lost on the elder Harkers or Quincy.

"I cannot take much more of this, Mother," Quincy whispered to his matriarch. "She is almost slobbering on that heathen." He kept up his smiling front and even appeared jovial as he made jests with some of the other dinner guests. He had confined himself to soda water since the afternoon, at his mother's insistence, but it had not helped his mood.

"Patience, dear," the Lady Harker said with a cold undertone to her whisper. "Your father and I will make sure this does not go on much longer, but it must be handled delicately."

"Yes, Mina dear," the elder Harker said, leaning in to pat his wife on the shoulder, "I will take care of it directly after dessert." His voice was quiet and reserved with none of the steel of his wife's pronouncement, but his son knew he was every bit as capable as his wife in enforcing an iron policy.

When the meal ended the guests retired to a drawing room and some of them gathered around a piano to sing songs. They even persuaded their hero of the day, much to Gwendolyn's delight, to join them in a chorus of "Deep in the Heart of Texas."

The jocularity continued for a time with various show tunes and old school songs all around. True to his word, however, Jonathon Harker found himself near the Texan after a time.

"I hope you don't mind if I borrow your hero for a bit, dear?" The elder Harker said to his daughter, "I think a smoke and some brandy are in order."

"Of course, Papa," she said with a sparkling laugh. "But don't get talking real estate law with Mister Howard or I shall never see him again."

The two men left the group of guests as Gwendolyn was pressed into singing at the piano and walked back toward the elder Harker's study.

"I have always been fascinated with both writers and your Texas wild west," Harker said, "and believe it or not, my son was named for a Texan acquaintance that passed on some years ago."

"Really?"

The two men entered the book-lined study and Harker slid the doors closed, closing off the sounds of conviviality from the drawing room. The study was a warm space, sober but appealing to the Texan for the depth of the books along its walls and the substantial stone fireplace. The large desk was neat but full and there were several chairs set before the fire.

"You have quite a book collection, sir," the Texan said. He was drawn directly to the wall of books and ran his fingers along the spine of some of them, pausing at the oddly textured spine of one. "I see that a bunch of them are...uh...occult subjects." The book his finger had stopped on was titled *Nameless Cults.*

"Yes," the elder Harker said, "I do have some interest in that direction. You have an affinity for such things?"

"Only as reference for some stories I've written and even then, more in a historical context. My buddy Howie Lovecraft ~~was~~ is more the expert in it; we corresponded a good deal and he gave me quite an education. I've never met him but his letters—some I suppose I shouldn't talk about much—talk deeply about such things." His tone shifted as the Texan recalled the friend he hoped to meet in person upon returning from his world trip. "You sure have enough books on the subject to qualify as an expert like him though."

"Numbers alone hardly qualify one for expert status, but I do try to keep up. Sit, lad," Harker said, "you will accept a cigar and a cognac?"

"Yes, sir, to both," Howard said. He looked around the room, taking note of a glass case on the mantle that held a bone-handled Bowie knife in it. "Though I am more a beer or whiskey drinker, usually, I see the charm of cognac right now."

When both had lit their cigars and settled into the over-stuffed chairs to sip their drinks, the older man spoke again. "There are a great many things here that I am sure seem...strange...to you."

Howard took a puff on the cigar and regarded the noble-man though the cloud of smoke. "Right you are there, sir; I ain't but seen a tiny piece of the big wide world before this trip. At least not in the real; I done read up on it, though."

"Yes," Harker said, his tone still genial, "I was listening to much of your elucidations outside; you remind me again of my friend Quincy Morris of so long ago. That was his Bowie knife you were admiring."

"It's a fine blade."

"Indeed; and storied. But then, Quincy was a teller of tales as well," Harker chuckled. "It seems everyone from Texas is a bit of a talker."

Howard answered his chuckle with his own. "Yes sir, my mom used to remark that a Texan could talk the wings off St. Peter and never once touch on the truth but not quite lie outright either."

"Well, you will hopefully land close to the truth here, sir," Harker said, "for I have a question for you." The older man's tone was now serious enough that the Texan turned in his chair from staring at the fire and looked the peer in the eyes.

Howard had a suspicion what 'truth' the patriarch was alluding to, and he would not have even thought he would ever be in such a conversation before that day. He knew what the subject of the man's question would be: Gwendolyn.

He knew she was, as his mother might have said, 'above him' but he also knew, as the girl had also taught him in less time than he could have imagined, to be ashamed of nothing in his life and no part of his heritage. His mother had often said he carried his grandfather William Benjamin Howard's temperament, he who had settled first in Texas. Bob had pride in his family's background and humility in himself.

Maybe too much humility according to Gwendolyn.

"You impressed my daughter today," The elder Harker said. "She has come to regard you as something of a Sir Lancelot, Mister Howard."

Now it's out in the open.

"I just did what needed to be done," the Texan said honestly, "I weren't trying to impress anyone."

"She is an impressionable girl."

"She is a remarkable girl," the Texan pointed out. He had leaned forward in his chair now and he held the cigar without taking a puff.

"Hmm, yes," Harker had to admit with a father's pride. "And as such Gwendolyn deserves a remarkable man."

He really does think I'm rustling in his corral. But with that realization Howard found himself pondering just what was happening. Gwendolyn was a charming, intelligent girl and, though she bore no physical resemblance to his mother, there was a quality about her that did remind him of the artistic temperament and intelligence of Hester Howard. He realized that the light in Gwendolyn's eyes when she looked at him sparked a warmth in him he had not experienced before. And he found himself thinking that he wanted to see more of her. A lot more.

"Yes, sir. She certainly does deserve the best."

"I am glad you agree, Mister Howard. So, you will have no objection then to leaving our estate tomorrow, with no prejudice, of course, and with my profound thanks for your truly heroic rescue of my son."

Howard saw red and felt his blood boil. It was all he could do not to rise with clenched fists and fiery eyes. His ancestors' ferocity bubbled to the surface, but he restrained himself and spoke quietly, though forcefully, through clenched teeth.

"Excuse me, sir," The Texan said doing his best to hold his Irish down. "Maybe I'm just a simple country bumpkin; did you just tell me to get off your ranch?"

Harker glared at him over the rim of his snifter. "I suppose I did, sir. Is that not clear enough for you? Or must I be more blunt?"

Howard slowly stood. He set down the snifter very deliberately on a side table and tossed his cigar in the fireplace. "Mister Harker, I am a guest in your house, have eaten your food, drunk your liquor and you have been gracious. I am grateful for that. And I do think your daughter is one of the finest people I have ever met. But sir, I am not about to let *anyone* tell me a Howard ain't good enough fer anybody."

"The truth is, Mister Howard," Harker said with no rise in the volume but with a sharpness coming into his tone, "you are *not* good enough. Gwendolyn is young and impressionable and what you did today has intrigued her but that will pass. You are a near-penniless vagabond, a writer of low penny dreadful trash and not even suitable to be seen with her at all, let alone as any sort of companion. It is just not done."

Howard felt his blood pressure rise and flow to the surface. His color rose and his teeth ground together. His fists vibrated and he knew that he was a single word away from physical violence.

"I am in your home, Mister Harker," the Texan forced out the words through his teeth, "but if we run into each other anywhere else you better be carrying that Bowie knife, 'cause by the soul of my dear departed mother, sir, I swear you will need it."

Howard turned abruptly to leave but suddenly the room seemed to swim around him, and he felt dizzy. He reached out a hand and grabbed on the back of the chair to steady himself. His temperature spiked and he felt sick to his stomach.

His vision began to swirl into kaleidoscopes of color.

I didn't drink that much.

He noticed that Harker was holding a handkerchief over his mouth and had stepped up to the fire. The Englishman used a poker to spear the discarded cigar and he pulled it out of the flame to drop into the ash bucket.

"You drugged me!" the Texan managed.

"I was fairly certain you would be recalcitrant about this."

"You sidewinding son of a—" Howard began. The room spun and then with no chance to even cry out, Howard fell forward into darkness.

Chapter Nineteen: The Power from Beyond

"But I just don't understand, Quincy," Gwendolyn Harker said to her brother. "Why would Mister Howard leave without at least saying goodbye to me?" The two were seated in the breakfast room the morning after the foxhunt and the girl was clearly distraught.

"I really don't know, Gwen," Quincy said, his voice dripping with sincerity, "but if I would venture a guess, I would say that he just couldn't handle the attention; seemed a modest sort of chap, you know." The sibling grinned while he spoke and made a show of spreading marmalade on his toast.

"It is just that…that I thought…" she began. "I mean…we had a certain…uh…connection." She was dressed for horseback, having expected to see the Texan for a promised morning ride. "Last night I assumed he retired early but was sure he would be here at breakfast." Her pretty features were cast in a dark expression.

"Come now, dear," her brother said, "it's your first full day back, cheer up. He was a vagabond, after all."

"He is a writer. I shall find some of his writings to show you." Then quietly she said as if almost to herself, "I know they will be good."

The elder Harker entered the breakfast room at that moment wearing his lounging jacket and looking tired. "Good morning, dears," he said. He sat at the head of the table and accepted a hot cup of tea from a maid.

"'Morning, Father," both siblings responded.

"Your mother will be eating in her room," the elder Harker said as he set about consuming his hearty breakfast; his wife always joked that he ate like a peasant for all his breeding.

"I hope Mother is not feeling badly?" Gwendolyn asked. "Not one of her spells?"

"Not really, dear. It was just the excitement of the day and then the guests last night tired her out. She hopes you will understand."

"Of course," Gwendolyn said, "I hope she will be rested by lunch."

"I'm sure she will, Gwen." Her father said. He studied his daughter's features and made a 'tsking' sound. "You are the one that seems down at the edges, dear...are you feeling well?"

"I...uh...well I am physically fine, Father, but..."

"Our little Gwen is heartsick that her cowboy has taken to the prairies without saying goodbye to her." Quincy's features lit with a smug smile.

The girl shot her brother a withering look.

"Quincy!" the elder Harker said in a sharp tone. He softened his voice when he addressed his daughter again.

"When I spoke to Mister Howard last evening he expressed some apprehension," he said, "and well...he was at least gentleman enough to not want to confront you with his misgivings."

"What do you mean?" she asked with fear in her voice. "What misgivings?"

"Quincy," the patriarch said softly, "don't you have something to do?"

"Of course, Father," the sibling said rising. "I have to head into town to meet the fellows for cribbage; I plan to fleece old McQueen again. Fellow can't bluff worth a tinker's—"

"Good luck, then." His father hurried him along with an arched eyebrow.

The boy stooped to kiss his sister on the forehead and then left the two of them alone.

The atmosphere in the room became electric once Quincy left, with the young girl staring at her father. "What is so terrible you had to speak to me alone?" Her cheeks pale with apprehension. "Has Bob...I mean Mister Howard been injured?"

Harker smiled gently. "No, dear, he just...well...he just felt that you were getting the wrong impression about him and his feelings toward you."

"Wrong impression? Whatever do you mean?"

"This is not easy for me to say, dear." The elder Harker rose to stand beside his daughter and put a hand on her shoulder. "He...well he said he might have given you the impression that he was thinking of you...eh...romantically. He, in fact, has some woman back in his little hamlet in Texas."

"But he told me about the girl, Novalyne." She shook her head in confusion. "It was over years ago. He was honest with me. Open. Truthful. He is not a coward. Why would he leave without at least—"

"I know dear, but some men have more courage with a runaway horse than in seeing disappointment on a pretty woman's face."

The girl did her best to keep tears from her eyes but had to turn her face away from her father. "I thought he was different from—"

"I am sorry to be the bearer of this sort of news, dearest, but I am afraid the lower classes just don't have the same sensitivities as we."

"He is sensitive!"

"I am sure, but well...let us just say he feels...uh...differently. Not at all the sort of match a girl of your station deserves. But come." He pulled his daughter to her feet. "I see you're ready to ride and I have something to show you in the stable."

"What?"

"Come now," the Elder Harker said, taking her hand to help her stand. "I've gotten you a present that is just at the right time to cheer you up." He led her unprotestingly from the house along the path to the stable. He refused to answer her inquiries as to what the surprise was but just smiled cryptically.

When they arrived at the stable, he signaled to a groom who disappeared into the barn with a cryptic smile of his own.

"What is this?" Gwendolyn asked again.

"You will see." Harker's smile turned broad and even when she playfully pulled at his arm—a gesture from her childhood where she pleaded, "Papa, Papa what?"

Finally, the groom brought out an impressive white stallion, a broad-chested hunter, fully appointed with saddle and tack.

"He's lovely," she gasped when she saw the animal.

Her father gestured for her to approach the horse and she did. The horse gave a snort and whinny and moved to nuzzle her.

"He's sweet-tempered as well. Who does he belong to?"

"You."

She looked at her father, stunned, and he laughed. "He's yours."

"Really?" her eyes went wide, and she giggled which made the animal nudge her again to her great delight.

"He was the pick of Lord Wentworth's stable," the elder Harker said. "I knew when I first saw him last winter that he was the perfect mount for you. Do you like him?"

"Of course I do," her voice filled with joy. "What is his name?"

"I thought it appropriate that you name him since you will be calling him by it from this point forth." The man smiled at his daughter's delight.

The auburn-haired girl petted the muzzle of the horse and stared into the eyes of the magnificent beast.

"You're sweet," she said aloud, "but I sense you have a wild side, eh boy? Ready to throw off the shackles of civilization, eh?" The horse snorted and pawed the earth, anxious to leave the barn and run.

"That's it then," she said with a touch of wistful sadness, "I shall call you 'Tex.'"

The swirling mists pushed into the darkness that enveloped Bob Howard. The writer felt as if he was swimming upward through a viscous sea of blackness to the dim light of consciousness. Then sounds, dull at first, began to intrude in the darkness and formed themselves into a recognizable sound, a human voice.

"The bumpkin is coming around, Mother," Quincy Harker said.

"You may leave now, son," the matriarch said. "Get along to those friends of yours in the village, dear; it will look better if you have a presence there today. Your father by now has told Gwen that this fellow was not feeling up to the rigors of courting a Harker." She laughed a chilling, crystalline laugh.

Howard heard her words, but distantly, as if he were at the bottom of a well. He forced his heavy lids to part and was presented with the sight of Wilhelmina Harker standing in the center of a bare stone room. Her green gown was highlighted in golden tones from the dancing flame of a wall torch. Her pretty features were now cast in haughty lines that seemed to have been carved from wood.

"I know you are awake now and can hear me, Mister Howard, so listen well. I think it is important you understand your new circumstances and how they came about…some say it will…uh…sweeten the experiences to come." She had a sinister smile on her pretty face.

"My husband and I had an experience thirty years ago that left me with certain abilities that my children barely suspect, and knowledge of Transylvanian magicks that have served us well. They have allowed me to help elevate my solicitor husband to a peerage and by my judicious use of them our son is destined for great things as well. This has put us in contact with those who understand the true meaning and means of occult power."

The lady stared down at the Texan and waited for the full import of her words to sink in.

"That also means that Gwendolyn must marry well. And that can only occur if no stain is even implied on her reputation. You are a stain. You have come into her life at exactly the wrong time for many reasons."

The groggy writer attempted to speak to her in protest, willing his heavy limbs to move but to no avail. She saw the effort and gave her chilling laugh again.

"A vagabond like you could never bring anything to her but amusement and even that for only a blink of the eye. Most certainly not respectability or position advancement. Your sort serves no useful purpose so will not be missed; your belongings will be gathered and shipped to your imaginary next stop. Gwen will soon forget you and be amenable to the 'alliances' I will arrange for her this next season." The woman leaned down to let him see the swirling evil that lived in her eyes.

"She'all ain't got none of you in her," Howard forced a whisper from his cracked lips. "No taint of your evil at all is in her soul."

The statement seemed to infuriate the matriarch and she snarled and slapped the Texan across the face. "You have no idea what true evil is, Mister Howard, but I assure you, tonight you will. Unfortunately, you will not have very much time afterward to contemplate your discovery. Not very much time at all."

She passed her hand before his eyes and in an eyeblink all was oblivion.

Gwendolyn Harker had a spirited ride that almost drove the melancholy of Bob Howard's departure from her, but whenever the horse slowed or if she saw any of the trail

features from the wild ride the day before her features darkened with memory.

When she put the horse away after feeding him an apple
in reward, she found her mood still not buoyed and her mind
lingering on the Texan's smile and his soft words. She went
to the house and changed for lunch but found she was not
hungry.

The rest of the day dragged on for the girl, her thoughts
preoccupied with the conversations she had with the Texan
the night before. She found herself little interested in reading
Bryon or her tatting, or any of her usual activities until she
was inspired to ride into the town's free library. She went in
search of magazines with Howard's work in them. She was
lucky enough to find two issues of *Weird Tales* and one each
of *Argosy*, *Fight Stories* and *Oriental Tales*.

She took the magazines to her favorite reading spot in a
summerhouse on the grounds and spent the afternoon im-
mersing herself in the worlds created by the Texas writer.
She read each tale several times, marveling at the depth and
vividness of the realities he created.

She was especially delighted when she found two of his
poems in *Weird Tales* and *Oriental Tales* as well as stories.
The poems were melancholy things, one lament about a crusader and one calling to ancestors from before time. She
could picture him reciting it.

"This man did not just leave me with no word," she concluded as the evening shadows settled over the grounds and
made reading difficult. "No matter what fears he might have
had, if he had anything to say he would say it to my face;
there is no cowardice in Mister Howard of Texas' bones!"

She walked around the estate trying to make some sort
of plan, to decide what to do about finding out where Howard had gone until she happened to see the cottage that
William Pratt occupied. She moved to the door and knocked.

"Come in," Pratt's voice sounded.

She entered the cottage, pausing at the doorway to let her eyes adjust.

Pratt was seated at a table in the center of the main room working on some tack. He looked up and for a moment she could see that the low light made it difficult to see who she was. Once he did Pratt sprang to his feet.

"Miss Harker," he said. "Please come in."

"Good evening, William," she said as she entered the room. He pulled a chair out from the table for her to sit. "How is your back doing?"

"Much better, Miss Gwendolyn, I'll be back to full duty in the stable this week. I've been catching up on some of this work. How are you after your adventure yesterday?"

"I'm fully fit, and even wiser for the adventure," she laughed then she noticed a battered suitcase and a smaller leather case she knew held the Texan's typewriter. Pratt noticed her gaze.

"Mister Howard's things. Your father came by this morning and told me that the Yank would send for them."

She frowned. "I just don't understand any of this," she said. "Bob said nothing about leaving and what is more he did not say farewell to me."

Pratt gave her a troubled grimace. "Nor to me. Bob seems to not have been the sort to be so rude; anything but."

"I know," she said as if having him agree with her confirmed her fears. "I know he would never leave his typewriter behind no matter what." A hint of a mischievous smile touched her lips. "He joked that it was his wife and any woman in his life would be only a mistress to his muse."

"He's a poet of the Pecos for sure, and I agree, Miss, he—well I don't think he would have just disappeared like this without some sort of reason."

She walked over to the typewriter and touched it as if it were the talisman of the Texan. There was a silence between the two for a long moment.

Finally, she said, "In none of his statements nor in all the spaces between his words, did Bob give me any hint that he had lied to me about his friend Novalyne or that there was any other woman in Texas or anywhere else." She ran her fingers over the typewriter case. "I think my father was not truthful with me when he implied it." There was so much pain in her voice that the stableman walked over to her to place a comforting hand on her shoulder.

"Perhaps the master was just...mistaken about the Texan's intentions, or misinterpreted Robert's words—he does speak 'Texan' and you know they are sometimes hard to understand."

This made the noblewoman smile. "Thank you, William, but I—"

At that moment a serving boy knocked on the cottage's open door. "Excuse me, Miss," he said, "Mister Pratt; but the master sent me to fetch the Yank's belongings up to his study."

"His study?" Gwen asked.

"Yes, ma'am." The tow-headed boy said.

"I'll bring the things up, boy," Pratt said. "You run along."

The boy stood with a confused look on his face for a moment until the girl added, "That's alright, Toby. William and I will see to it."

"Yes, Miss," he said and raced off.

The girl stood and picked up the typewriter case. "Come, William," she said with her jaw set in a determined expression. "We must have answers. Let us talk to my father."

Chapter Twenty: Sacrifice Redux

Bob Howard did not expect to wake up, let alone in one piece.

Therefore, it was a pleasant surprise when he came to consciousness and discovered he was alone and essentially unhurt. He felt a throbbing pain in his head and his stomach hurt so much that he thought he might have been beaten or stabbed but otherwise he was whole.

The Texan was unbound and lying on a hard, flat surface of damp stone, certainly wasn't the carpeted floor of the study. He felt around his stomach for blood or a wound and was surprised to feel that he was shirtless. He was relieved to find no obvious wound. It encouraged him to explore further with his hand and discovered he was stripped of his shoes and socks as well.

He risked opening his eyes just enough to confirm that he really was alone before opening them fully to explore his surroundings. He was still in a stone-walled room but found that it was a different, small cell-like space. A torch on a wall sconce flickered violently, sending eerie shadows around the room.

He sat up and looked down to see where he was hurting, once again reassured that there was no blood.

Howard could not guess how long he had been unconscious, but a hand along his chin found no beard growth, so proved to him it had not, at least, been a full day.

"Dang!" His voice echoed off the walls, muted but still telling him that the space was larger than it appeared. He started to rise and had trouble standing so that he had to lean against the wall.

He felt a cold, unreasoning spike of fear up his spine, a primordial terror that his rational mind knew was unfounded. *Whatever drug Harker gave me is still in my system.*

He felt a bit wool-headed, and simply because he was shirtless and shoeless felt more vulnerable, the same sense of exposure that had compelled his ancestors to fashion garments from animal skins.

Get ahold of yourself, Texan. Heck of a barbarian you'd be if you cared about a bit of nakedness. He laughed at his own initial reaction, a short sharp laugh that held all his contempt for the 'civilized' world. "Practice what you preach," he admonished himself out loud.

The floor of the cell was slippery and cold as was the wall he felt his way along. He searched for a door or other opening to get out of the space but found none. He decided by the dampness on the walls that his prison had to be subterranean. The shadowed ceiling was vaulted and so he thought perhaps it was the cellar of the manor house. The stonework was certainly old enough to be part of the manor's original foundations.

Why? he kept asking himself. *Why would they leave me down here; do they think I'm so darn charming that Gwendolyn would run away with me?*

He grinned at that thought for he had never thought of himself as anything but a bulky, rough sort of fellow, not at all the sort to appeal to women at all. He was sure his one and only continuing female friend, Novalyne, had only spent time with him because he was the only guy in Cross Plains who could spell and punctuate worth a darn! Still, the thought that the Harkers were so afraid of his romantic power over the delightful, strong-willed girl he'd met—only that day?—made him smile broadly.

Not the most horrible idea at all.

Howard finally came to a door, hidden in the shadows across the room from the torch. It was a wooden portal, banded with iron and flush with the stonework of the walls. There was an iron ring suspended from the center of it. The Texan summoned his strength to grip the rough metal in both hands, took a deep breath and strained his muscles to pull.

The door, though heavy, swung easily on the hinges that seemed to have been recently oiled. That caught him off guard, so much so that he almost fell back. He regained his balance, all the more cautious for it meant he was moving into an inhabited area. He crept down a short corridor that ended in another door, much like the one he had come through.

There was light beyond that door but no sound to tell him what he might expect, so he moved forward cautiously. There was a smell coming from ahead of him, a stale-air scent that caused him to cough.

He pushed through the doorway and found himself in a large circular room with a ceiling high enough that it faded into darkness above. Ahead of him was a ten-foot wall that circled the entire football field-sized room and above the wall was a void of blackness that faded into indefinite space.

Far above in the center of the room was a circular shape, little more than a lighter patch of black that might have been some sort of window or skylight.

He concluded that he was in an amphitheater of some sort.

The floor was, unlike the room he had come from, hard-packed sand and dirt. There was a line of torches stuck into the ground and placed at six-foot intervals around the entire circumference of the space, forming a circle within the stone circle. The air above the flaming markers was thick with smoke that smelled vaguely of incense and added to the miasma of age that permeated the space.

Howard stood where he was, flattened against the wall beside the doorway, trying to see behind the torchlight and smoke. Above the wall was darkness and beyond the opposite echelon of torches were only vague shapes.

He stared hard and spotted what might have been another door, similar to the one he had come through, across the open area. Howard took one more look behind him and then scanned the blackness above the wall before he moved across the open space.

He felt a deep vulnerability because of his near-nakedness and the fact that he could not see who might be lurking in the darkness above the wall. In his mind's eye he felt exposed and imagined archers somewhere up in the darkness of the arena drawing a bead on him.

He was only halfway across the open space when the door behind him suddenly slammed shut. He snapped his head around just as he heard the sound of a bar being slipped into place on the other side of the door through which he had entered the amphitheater.

He fought the impulse to race back to the door, knowing it would be a futile gesture; he had been maneuvered into the space for some specific purpose. He was not going to give whoever did it the satisfaction of seeing him panic.

He took a deep breath and studied the area around him with new eyes, noting with macabre interest that there was a dark stain in the sand in the center of the space. *That might well have been dried blood.* The whole structure was old, he could see, the stonework possibly predating the manor house.

"An old Roman arena I'll bet?" he said aloud.

"Exactly right, old fellow." The harsh voice caused the Texan to turn his head. A figure materialized out of the darkness above the stone wall. By squinting Howard could now see there were stone seats rising into the black.

The voice that spoke and the figure to whom it belonged was Quincy Harker. "We discovered this structure when digging the new well and decided it was just too nice to pass up so we found a way into it from the house through the wine cellar; a very short tunnel." He smiled with self-satisfied delight. "Makes a wonderful...eh...diversion from time to time. And very private."

"Why are you doing this? I saved your life." He tried to move toward the side of the arena, slowly and as casually as he could, his eyes fixed on the figure descending the seats toward the wall.

"Yes," the nobleman said as he jumped nimbly from the stone seats to the edge of the surrounding wall over the floor of the arena. "And that is the only reason why you are not dead outright, you savage."

"But I helped you!"

"You only showed off to impress my sister, and to make me look a complete fool."

"I can't improve on nature's work, boy," Howard shot back. "You *are* a fool." His anger was blunted as a new paroxysm of pain wracked his body. "Come down here and I'll varnish this floor with your brains!"

This made young Harker laugh. "Spoken like the true savage you are."

The drug they gave me still hasn't worn off all the way, but why not just kill me that way?

The Harker scion stood on the edge of the arena with his smirk barely registering the insult from the Texan. He waved a riding crop at the prisoner like a pointer and laughed.

"We Harkers are destined for great things, old chap, I will sit in the House when the White Glove Society has established its world government, and Gwen is going to marry well, so you have just got to disappear to remove any distractions from her."

"You're the second Harker male to worry about me walking off with your little sister. You must be pretty sure there ain't much in the way of real manhood on this little sceptered isle to compete with this poor old country writer."

Howard eyed the edge of the arena with a thought to racing for it and vaulting up but he could see that there was a pistol butt protruding from Harker's belt. *I have to keep him talking, Get him distracted.*

Harker's expression twisted to a cruel snarl. "Blood will out, savage, and Gwen will ultimately choose the right match when distractions, like you, are removed from her sight. Mama and Papa will make sure to *help* her along with that."

"What is it to be, Quincy? Going to have me shanghaied to far Cathay or take a coward's way out and kill an unarmed man, just shoot me down?" Howard took a defiant posture. "Or will you face me on equal ground like a man and prove your 'genetics' are up to the challenge?"

Harker laughed. "Momsy learned so many wonderful things from her time in that little area between Romania and Hungry so long ago," Quincy said as he moved along the wall. He stopped above the door opposite Howard which the Texan now saw was different than the one he had come out of; it was more of a gate with hinges on the top of the portal. "One of them was the ability to take base materials and transform them into something else."

He laughed again, a cold and merciless sound. "Though I doubt she could do much with you, she can make some amazing changes in things. And people. Father has since met like-minded individuals and they are working to improve the breed, so to speak. Still, there are costs for everything; now and then we in the family who know help to pay for the powers she has gained. Everything must be paid for eventually, you know."

He began to work the release of the gate and for the first time Howard noticed that there was movement beyond the barrier. He could hear a growling sound. It was some large animal. "And you are tonight's payment, bumpkin."

Howard jumped backward to stand in the center of the arena. The skylight above showed a gibbous moon as the cloud that had obscured it cleared and the blue light added more of an unreal touch to the whole scene.

"Don't be concerned, Yank. When I open this gate, you will be giving your power to help the Harkers' star ascend. Think of it as helping Gwen progress in life, in your own small way, if it will make it easier." He giggled like a schoolboy.

Howard was about to make his move for the wall before the gate was opened when another voice from the shadows of the gallery above drove all hope from his heart.

"Don't pamper him, son," Jonathon Harker said. The older nobleman stepped down to the edge of the arena and sat in one of the first-row seats. "She is getting restless, let her out."

"I will, Father," Quincy said, "I just thought the sacrifice would have more value if he had some knowledge of his fate."

"You have your mother's cruel streak in you, boy," the elder Harker said. "Just open the gate and get it done. The moon is close enough to its apex to give the best result. The Elder Ones will be ready for their soul-feast."

The boy seemed annoyed by his father's admonition, shooting the older man a dour look, but then redoubled his efforts to work the gate upward.

Howard knew the time was now or never for any chance to escape so he raced for the edge of the pit. He had waited too long, however, for before the writer had moved five feet forward the gate gave way with a crack and groan and flew upward. Out of the dark maw of the opening charged a beast from hell and it came straight at the Texan with a snarl of defiance.

Chapter Twenty-One: With Fang and Spear

The moon was near its zenith when Gwendolyn Harker and William Pratt reached her father's study. They had encountered no one else in the family upon entering the house, which in itself was unusual. The girl knocked at the door but received no answer. Gwen tried the handle but found it locked.

"We had better leave the bags here, Miss," Pratt said. "I will ask some of the servants if perhaps they have seen the Yank."

"No," the girl said. "I want to find out what is really going on here and there might be some clue to where Bob has gone in this room." She set the typewriter down and produced a hatpin that she slipped into the lock. When she saw the shocked expression on Pratt's face she grinned.

"There are many things for one to learn at an exclusive Swiss girl's school besides Latin and Greek," she said with a smile. "The matrons thought they had us all securely sealed in at night. They did not."

The lock clicked and she slipped the door open. She realized that the servant was hesitant to follow her. "I realize this is not above board, William, and it could very likely bring the wrath of my father, so I understand if—"

Pratt gave a soft smile. "Mister Howard is my friend, Miss. I can find other employment; true friends are harder to come by."

She touched his forearm and nodded with understanding as she pushed the door open. The two of them looked at one another then entered the study.

Moonlight streamed through the French windows across the large room and gave the interior a ghostly blue tint. The mantelpiece with its Bowie knife and other items was illuminated in stark relief in the silent room.

"I don't know what we're really looking for," Gwendolyn admitted when she stood in the doorway surveying the room. "I've seldom been in this room, never alone and not for years; it has always been Daddy's sanctum sanctorum."

Pratt felt for an electric light switch in the wall and the room assumed a more normal appearance. "I'm not sure either, Miss. How would we begin to find where Mister Howard went? What shall we look for?"

"Paperwork," she remarked and went to her father's desk. "He can't banish me any further away for rifling his desk than he can for picking the lock and my father is one for documenting everything; he was a barrister." She set about looking for some clue to the Texan's whereabouts.

"Do you think your father might have written down what happened to Mister Howard?"

"Yes, my father has also always been an avid diarist. When I was a little girl before they sent me away to school the first time, I came upon him in here writing in it and he was furious when I peeked at what he had written. It was something about 'full red moon!' He punished me and yelled at me to never enter his study again. I have only been in here half a dozen times since then, and then only at his invitation and in his presence."

She searched several drawers until she discovered a locked journal in the bottom one. She placed it on the desk and gathered her courage. "In for a pence..." she whispered then performed her hatpin magic on the lock. She quickly flipped to the most recent entries with barely contained apprehension.

"Any help, Miss?" Pratt was nervously casting glances back toward the open door, ready to bolt at any sound.

"Oh my God!" she murmured. She stared at the tome as if it were a serpent, but kept turning pages, her eyes filling with tears as she did.

After a few silent minutes, she stepped away from the desk as if the book had sunk its fangs into her. Her blanched skin proclaimed her horror even more than the silent tears that coursed down her cheeks. "How could they?"

"Miss Gwendolyn?" Pratt moved beside her and when her shocked expression told him she could not speak he read the pages she indicated himself.

"Heavens!" he gasped as the words burned themselves into his mind. "I…uh…I am so sorry."

The girl recovered in a few moments, with color returning to her cheeks. "The past is neither here nor there, now, William." She took a deep breath and squared her shoulders. "We are here to locate Mister Howard. It says, '*take him down to the arena*' in the diary. What could he mean? The wine cellar?"

"It seems likely, Miss, but if what is written there is true I cannot imagine they would feel free to act. Too many servants enter the cellar at regular intervals."

The girl drifted away from the desk to stand beside the mantle, leaning on it for strength. She was clearly fighting the emotions that were welling up within her, but she worked hard not to give in to more tears. She sniffed them back.

"William," she said, turning abruptly, "do you smell that?" She sniffed again, but with deliberation. "Smoke!"

The whipper-in stepped beside her and smelled. "Yes." He knelt and touched the ashes in the fireplace, but they were cold. "It is not from here."

"Could something be on fire?"

The two followed the faint scent of smoke to a bookcase across the room. The odor was strongest by the case.

"There might be a fire in the wiring for the electric lights," Pratt said, but then he peered closely at the end of the case. "Look. There is an opening behind here, a deliberate one." He sniffed again. "And it isn't an electrical smell, nor is it just charcoal smoke; it smells much more like church incense."

He applied himself to prying the case away from the wall, assuming there was a hidden door behind it to open but it would not budge.

"There must be some sort of catch but I cannot find it," Pratt said. "We need something to pry it open."

They both looked around for something to use to wedge behind the bookcase and the girl's eyes lit on a fireplace poker but as she moved to grab it, she noticed the Bowie knife on the mantle. She removed the broad blade from its glass case and brought it back to Pratt.

"Here, this might be better. Try this, William." He took the blade from her and was able to slip the edge into the crack behind the case. He slid it down until, with a click, he found a catch that it released.

There was a sharp sound and the bookcase slid into a recess in the wall. The strong cloud of incense smoke came from the dark space behind the case.

And the sound of growls.

"They must have Bob down there," she said with fear in her voice, but not fear for herself. She started to move through the opening, but Pratt stopped her.

Wait," he said and went to the Texan's luggage and opened one case. "I packed this when he did not come back." He removed the single action six-gun that the Texan had brought with him. "I suspect we may have need of it."

The dark shape that moved out of the open gate at Bob Howard was a thing from nightmares; neither wolf nor human but a horrid combination of both. It shambled forth on two hind legs, it's front ones intermediate things between arms and legs.

The beast's face had a short lupine snout and wide, savage eyes with yellow pupils but strangely enough, blue irises.

Saliva dripped from the slavering jaws, which were open to reveal white, curved fangs that seemed oversized from what might have been on a normal canine.

The smell from the space behind the creature, even across the open space of the arena, was fetid and reminded the Texan of the smell of a bear's den. The beast seemed to pant with anticipation of a meal, its eyes fixed on Howard as it slowly slunk out of the dark space behind the gate.

It must be some sort of illusion, Howard thought at first but then remembered many of the letters back and forth with his friend Howie Lovecraft about the possibility of such occult monsters being real.

Guess I'm gonna find out, Howie; but I guess it don't really matter if it is real or not, Bob chided himself. He remembered a quote from a letter he himself had written to his friend:

Let philosophers brood over questions of reality and illusion. If life is illusion, then I am no less an illusion, and being thus, the illusion is real to me. If it can hurt me I can hurt it.

The Texan backed to the center of the arena looking right and left for anything he could use as a weapon to 'hurt' the apparition. He decided on one of the upright torches and moved toward it, but the snarling beast noted his movement. It growled again, more fiercely, as if to warn him to submit.

"Don't make it worse on yourself, Yank," Jonathon Harker called, "Just stand and it will be quick."

"You may kill me," Howard called, "but you don't have to insult me and keep calling me a Yank. "

"I hope he puts up a fight, Father," Quincy said. "I like it when they fight a bit. After all, a feast is better when one works for it; when they surrender it is so boring."

Surrender was not in the Texan's nature. He darted for the upright torch and grabbed for it with both hands. It refused to come out of the ground on his first tug and the wolf-creature that had been poised to spring, stopped. The creature let loose a howl that was almost a laugh.

Howard watched the monster over his shoulder and applied his whole bodyweight to dislodging the torch. Then with a roar of his own Bob wrenched the iron-banded wooden pole from the earth of the arena floor just as the beast leaped.

The Texan whirled his whole body and swung the flaming rod like a stickball bat. The body of the torch, below the flames, slammed into the side of the airborne animal with the full torque of his turn.

"No!" the elder Harker screamed as if he himself had been struck by the pole. He raced to the edge of the seating area and for a moment it looked like he might leap down.

The wolf creature roared and fell to the ring from the swat, rolling nimbly to its feet. It shook its head and hissed, snake-like, in annoyance.

The Texan was disappointed to see that the flame had not touched it. He switched the torch to use like a spear holding the flame between him and the now cautious beast.

Howard formed a plan.

He surmised that the beast had some sort of den behind the gate, and he hoped there might be a gate or means of the keepers feeding it in that den. If he could get past the creature, he hoped to find a way out of its den that way. It would at least get him away from the pistol that Quincy held.

Howard prodded the beast with the dancing flame and maneuvered it at an angle so that he was steps away from the gate.

"Not so clever, Yank!" Quincy said with emphasis as he slammed the gate closed from his position on the top of the wall and cut off any chance of retreat. "There, that should remove any temptation to spoil our little bit of sporting fun!"

The Texan could do little more than cast the Harker scion a quick, dirty glance—he needed all his attention focused on keeping the flame between himself and the stalking animal.

Howard's mind worked furiously trying to find another avenue of escape but the beast in front of him seemed to have frozen his thought process. He could conceive of no other path to freedom.

The monster began to slowly advance on him again, this time moving its head from side to side as it looked for a way past the flaming lance. Its huge jaws opened and closed with anticipation while it licked its chops.

"Shoot him now, Quincy! Hurry," the elder Harker called with concern, "before he has a chance to injure her."

The boy moved to comply, pulling his pistol from his waistband and taking deliberate aim at the Texan. "I'll just wing him, Father. I don't want to take all the fight out of him so this sacrifice will have full power. Besides, if I seriously wound him this will be boring."

"Don't do that, sir," William Pratt called from the shadows at the top of the arena. "Or I shall be forced to shoot you as well."

"Who dares?" Quincy called, his head snapping around to peer up into the seats.

"Bob!" Gwendolyn yelled out as she raced down the tiers toward the arena wall.

Howard and the wolf creature both reacted to her voice, turning as one to look up into the shadows.

"Gwendolyn!" the elder Harker said as he turned away from the action in the arena. "Leave here this minute!"

The girl ran directly up to her father. "No!" she cried, "I read your diary; I...I saw what you are." She screamed angrily, the words all but unintelligible for that anger. "I saw in that horrid book who I am!"

The elder Harker's face darkened and there was a sudden great sadness in his features that seemed to age him. "Gwen, you have to understand we didn't want to keep the truth from you but—"

"But you were so squeamish," Quincy added, "weak. Mother was for putting you out of your misery right then and there, but Father—"

"That is enough, Quincy," Jonathon Harker snapped. "Gwen, when your parents died—they were such good friends we felt compelled to raise you as our own."

"Oh, tell her the truth, Father," Quincy said. "You felt guilty for the way her parents died."

The wolf creature, apparently fascinated by the human speech above it, now snapped its jaws with annoyance and howled in anger. In a moment it turned its attention back to the Texan. Before Howard could react, the monster jumped forward to fasten its jaws on the shaft of the torch.

Bob gave a half-hearted tug on the torch but knew the animal would outmatch him for strength and so he hopped back, releasing the shaft. The monster took it and shook its head like a terrier with a rat.

Howard turned and ran for a second torch even as the beast threw the first one down and came for him.

"No!" Gwendolyn yelled. She pushed past her father and jumped down from the arena's lip, landing with a stumble and a cry of pain as she turned her ankle. "Bob!"

"Gwendolyn, stop!" the elder Harker screamed too late.

The wolf beast veered from stalking the Texan to head for the girl.

"No you don't, you varmint!" Howard yelled at the animal and launched himself onto the back of the monstrosity. His over two hundred pounds slammed down on the hairy back of the creature and he wrapped his legs around its waist. He clamped his fingers into the fur along its back and dug in.

The wolf beast went mad as a loco mustang with the contact of the man on its back, spinning in place to try and dislodge the Texan from behind it. It snapped its jaws and roared its disapproval.

"Get up and run, Gwen!" Howard yelled.

"I can't stand. I've hurt my ankle."

The wolf beast renewed its snarls and redoubled efforts to shake the man from her back, spinning wildly in place and bucking like a rodeo bronc.

Howard dug his fingers into the animal's back till he drew blood and squeezed his powerful legs with all his might to hold fast.

"Gwendolyn, grab my hand," her father called down from the arena wall. He leaned over the edge of the stone-wall.

"Get off her!" Quincy screamed at Howard. He raised his gun to aim at the wildly gyrating figures in the arena. He cocked the hammer on the pistol and started to squeeze the trigger but the gunshot that echoed off the walls of the arena chamber did not come from Quincy's gun. The shot came from the six-shooter in William Pratt's hands.

The Harker scion twitched once and fell forward over the arena wall to smash to the floor of the pit with a wet thud.

Chapter Twenty-Two: The Thankful Dead

When young Harker's body hit the ground the wolf creature's attention was drawn to it. It froze for a long moment, its head down, the blue eyes of the monster fixed on the still form of the nobleman, then with a new, haunted howl the beast abruptly went mad.

The monster bucked like a horse so violently that it crashed over onto its back slamming the Texan into the sandy dirt of the arena. The fall was so hard that it jarred Howard loose.

Rather than turning on him, however, the beast raced across the arena to the still body of Quincy. The animal sniffed at the body and nudged it with its great head then pawed at it.

Howard scrambled across the space to Gwendolyn's side, grabbing her to him in a heartfelt hug.

"I knew you wouldn't leave me," she whispered.

There was no time for Howard to say anything for the wolf beast howled a cry that was the most agonized wail of pain anyone in the room had ever heard and turned to charge at full speed across the arena at Howard and the girl.

The Texan stepped in front of Gwen to block the attack with his own body, prepared to defend her with his bare hands but she pressed the Bowie knife into his grip. Howard felt the comforting weight of the wooden and ivory handle and took a fighting stance.

"No, stop!" Jonathon Harker jumped from the lip of the arena wall and landed in front of the wolf-monster. "You have to stop! Gwen is all we—" he began but the animal pounced on him and savaged him with a quick bite that tore his chest open. The beast shook him like a dog's chew toy and then tossed him aside.

"Papa!" Gwendolyn screamed.

As the beast flung Jonathon aside Pratt fired twice into the body of the animal.

The monster ignored the shots and resumed its charge at the Texan and the girl.

Howard took the charge of the wolf-beast straight on, his powerful legs bent, and the knife held at his right hip. When the great furry body slammed into him, he drove the blade in and pulled up hard. He yelled a savage war cry that matched the monster's howl as the hairy body knocked him backward.

Bob jerked up and back on the Bowie, ripping a gash up the belly of the carnivore. The monster howled a long last mournful cry and then slid down the Texan's body to the ground at his feet, great founts of gore and blood pouring from its ruptured belly.

There was a sudden hard silence in the dark chamber save for the sobs from Gwendolyn, and Howard's own ragged breathing.

Pratt let himself down from the edge of the wall and sprinted over to the Texan.

"Bob," he called, "are you alright?"

The Texan was covered with gore from the beast and for a moment his adrenaline spike made him dizzy from fatigue. He looked at his friend with momentarily blank eyes and just nodded.

The young Harker girl hobbled to her father's side.

"Papa!" she sobbed.

"Gwen," the fallen man murmured. "Don't cry. Perhaps it's better this way."

"Why, Papa?" she sobbed. Howard came to stand beside her and placed a hand on the kneeling girl's shoulder. She reached up and squeezed his hand in hers as an anchor to some sanity.

"My word!" Pratt exclaimed. "Look!" He pointed to the body of the wolf beast and as they all stared at it the form began to shimmer and change before their eyes. It grew smaller and the texture of the flesh changed until in moments it was the bloodied corpse of Wilhelmina Harker that lay on the sand of the arena floor.

Gwendolyn, already stunned by the horror she had witnessed, still found new depths to her agony and gasped at the sight.

"It was Mina's first transformation many years ago," the Elder Harker whispered as he lay bleeding on the arena floor. "We were traveling in the Carpathians, trying to deal with the aftermath of events from what that monster Count Dracula did to me keeping me prisoner in his castle and then what he did to her here in England. It all left her-- changed. She had been investigating secrets of the powers she had gleaned while under his sway, obsessed with controlling the same forces that had led him down so horrid a path and she changed." He looked up into the eyes of the girl and there was apology in his expression.

"Your real parents were one of her first kills before we learned to anticipate the changes. I found you in the morning by their side crying. I could not leave you. Your parents were good English stock and your mother even looked like Mina so a deception was easy; we brought you back and told everyone you were our own child. Even Quincy, who was already five, knew and accepted you as a member of the family. But you were always so curious, and we came to fear you would discover the truth. So we sent you to schools—"

"I always thought you hated me." The girl who had thought all her life to have been his unwanted daughter sobbed.

"No." He coughed up blood as a paroxysm of pain passed through his broken form. "Far from it, dearest. Even as Mina changed, became more ferocious and found others who shared her obsession with the dark arts—I saw more and more of her as she had once been, pure and sweet in *your* smile. I often forgot myself how you came to be with us. I loved Mina with all my heart, no matter how her appetites grew more extreme as time progressed. But I have always loved you too."

He looked up at the Texan and tried to extend his hand to him. "You are a good man, Yank," Harker said. "It is better this way. Find a way to help her."

"I will, sir," Howard said fighting back tears, despite his revulsion at what Harker had been part of. "I promise."

"You are the Harker legacy now, Gwen," the dying man said, "try to do better with it than we did."

Then the last of the Harkers closed his eyes for the last time and all was darkness.

The horrible events of the Harker tragedy were never made public. The authorities were led to believe—after the weapons had been arranged to support the story the three survivors told—that Quincy and Jonathon had fought, and the boy had gone mad and killed both his parents over inheritance issues. With the English desire to think their nobles better—and to keep any such scandal quiet—the events were accepted as presented and no great outcry resulted.

Bob Howard stayed for weeks at the country house in one of the guest cottages while the girl tried to absorb all the terrible changes in her life. His experience with his own mother's passing made him a sympathetic ear and he did his best to be the friend she needed. Often during that time, she made him read to her, old and new tales that made her smile in the midst of her grief.

She particularly loved his tales of Dark Agnes and Belit, and she was sad when he said he had only written the one story with the pirate queen. He promised to think about a Grace O'Malley tale for her, already casting her as the Western Ireland pirate in his mind.

Gwendolyn could not bear to read any more of her father's diary and, along with a promise from William to never discuss it, tried her best to put the whole contents of it out of her mind even though she knew that when all things were settled, she would have to deal with it. The fact was that a whole new world of dark forces and deception had challenged everything she had ever believed in. If not for the caring and positive attitude of Howard, she might well have crumbled or gone mad.

When all the last of the official affairs were concluded Gwendolyn decided to go abroad to friends near her school in Switzerland and spend some time in meditation and reflection.

"I would ask you to come, dear Robert, but you have your own adventures to pursue and as wonderful as it has been to be with you, I feel I must look inward for a time."

"I think it's a good idea, Gwen," Howard said reluctantly. He, of all people, knew the value of traveling to new places to help distance one from dark thoughts.

"Yes, ma'am," William agreed. Despite their difference in background and station, the three had been drawn together by their common horrific experience into a deep and real friendship. "The time away will help."

"I had always thought, always on holidays how much I wanted to come home but now, now this doesn't feel like home anymore. I want to go to the Carpathians and find out who my real parents were."

"But later. There will be time for that, Gwen. Now rest and heal; when you decide to go I'll ride shotgun for you on that trip," Howard said.

"What will you do now?" she asked him, doing her best to ignore his advice.

"I'll keep on my trip. There's a whole lot of this wide world I ain't seen or written about yet." He took her hand in his. "But I will be ready to come to you any time you want me to, no matter where I am."

"My cowboy," she smiled. "And you, William? Will you stay on here?"

"No, ma'am," he said. "I think I'll go back to the theatre and take another try at it so watch out for my stage name, Boris Karloff. I'll see you both get an invitation when I open at the Royal Albert Hall."

The three friends laughed. Then Gwendolyn's face got serious. She removed the choker from her neck and held it out before the Texan's eyes.

"In my fath—Mister Harker's diary he said this had been my real mother's," she said. "It is hard to keep this and not know…is it an image of my mother? Her mother? An old family heirloom? Somehow, I cannot bear to not know. Yet it means so much more to me at the same time as it is my only link to my real parents."

"Keep it close to your heart, Gwen," Howard said. "I'm sure it will one day help you to find out about your real folks when the time is right." The two stared into each other's eyes intensely.

"Memories are strong things," he continued, "and you may find your childhood memories of your real folks may come back. In the meantime, you'll have good ones to crowd out the dark ones and there will be more, many more good ones to come."

"You will write to me, Bob?" she asked, "from wherever you are? Long, wonderful letters; with poems in them?"

He grinned broadly looking like a giant mischievous elf. "That I can guarantee, my lady," he said. "That I can guarantee."

Chapter Twenty-Three: See Paris and Die

The low winter fog off the Seine crept along the wharfs and gave the whole of the city of Paris a dreamlike quality in the early evening light. It was the city of lights, after all, and of romance to most, but to the tall Texan, Bob Howard, it was a place of mystery and of history.

He walked the city, his cowboy boots clicking on the ancient cobbles, feeling a little conspicuous, not because of his battered Stetson, rather because of the tailored jacket he wore.

Gwendolyn Harker had insisted he have the suit made by her family's local tailor at 22 *rue Saint Lazare* while in the French capital and even though he felt the fool—after all how many suits did a pulp writer need?—he could not refuse even the slightest wish of the delicate but strong-willed girl.

He smiled, remembering the expression on the little French tailor's face when Bob handed the man a letter of introduction from the girl that asked the craftsman to fashion a wardrobe for the burly Texan.

It was a tossup which of the two, the Texan or the Parisian, was more perplexed by the clash of cultures in the hour that followed, as the craftsman poked and pinned the writer to fit him in the latest style. Howard returned twice over three days to be fit and have the suit adjusted before the little tailor proclaimed the suit 'perfection!' The Texan had to dissuade the man from throwing out his old clothes and took them with him. The small bundle took the place of his typewriter that he had taken to leaving in his hotel room after his first days of carrying it around the city with him. He realized he had missed the comforting weight at his side.

When Bob left the shop, the writer could not deny that the new blue suit looked exceptional on him and fit like a second skin. He tapped Gwendolyn's letters in his inner breast pocket in a gesture of thanks to her.

I sure feel all fancied up and self-conscious; like I'm heading off to church or a funeral. A regular fancy lord! No one seemed to notice his change in status, however, so the fact that his cowboy boots and hat did not quite match the European cut of his suit seemed not worth bothering about. If anyone took note of him it was because of his wide shoulders and easy smile, not his attire.

Bob walked the cobbled streets of the fabled city with no purpose or destination, seeing not the motorcars, radio aerials and phone cables, but rather the places where the past still lived, unaltered.

Here was where a barricade had been made of cobbles in a student riot. There was the Bastille with its formidable gates, which personified history. Down that alley was where the Musketeers clashed steel with the Cardinal's guards!

Bob could see in his mind's eye the Viking hordes attacking the medieval city, the noblemen dueling in the streets, the revolutionaries swarming the barricades, all of it in a single sweeping look, like a super-imposed motion picture. He saw his Celtic ancestors—the Parisi—when they settled on the river and made the town that grew to be the metropolis it was.

He saw the warriors and the wastrels, the wantons and the woe-begotten of all the ages as he listened to the Seine lapping at the riverbank. It was the ancient background song of the city waking from its day of activity for the even more active night of revelry.

The Texan eventually made his way to the narrow streets of Montmartre, the Mount of Martyrs district, where all of the city was laid out below him. He stood for a long moment, almost holding his breath with the beauty and mystery of it. He felt a strange sense of calm as he wandered with no distinct destination. The very age of the place filled him with awe.

Every stone, every edifice spoke of times past, of great age but it was a sleepy age, a long-ago activity beneath the surface of the modern, living city. It made him conscious of how young the edifices in his home were, his Texas, his America, all of it merely a mewling babe in the world, still raw and closer to a wild frontier. There was a vitality to the land of *his* Texas, a vibrancy that many sensed in Howard himself when they met him. Both had a wildness, still untamed—a sharp stone in the river of time whose edges had not yet been worn smooth by the warping passage of civilization.

But there is still some rawness here, still some essence of the bloody hordes that raged across it. It makes me wonder what I'll find when I get to places like Turkey or Egypt!

The prospect of moving backward in time by visiting those exotic places sparked the writer's imagination. He had walked Hadrian's Wall, stood in the center of Stonehenge, seen the White Cliffs of Dover and the port of Calais in the two months since he had seen Gwen off at the airport in London and felt the same primal 'I am returning home' sense in each of those places.

It was all completely thrilling and world-shaking for the Texan, save for the absence of Gwen, off in Zurich. He had not had a letter from her in two weeks and even that seemed longer.

"Tarnation," he whispered out loud. "Sure didn't think I'd miss you so much, gal. Wish I could share all this with you."

He looked around and said, "Well, I guess I have to write you a heck of a letter about Paris, like the others I wrote from the other places, won't I, eh? Gonna have to work my adjectives overtime to even come close to describing my feelings about this place, for sure. And maybe how I feel about you not being here. Maybe a poem."

He smiled at that and set about composing some verses in his mind's eye, spinning off to those long-ago locals and thinking about how they might have reacted to a fellow from Cross Plains. His attention was not on his immediate surroundings at all that moment—which is why he was taken by surprise when the two street thugs set upon him.

"This must be the *Gadje* American, Maurice," the wider of the two men said as they stepped out of the darkness ten feet from him. The speaker seemed completely unconcerned that the Texan heard. "Look at his Tim McCoy hat."

"A buffoon," the second man sneered. "But then all Americans are, Luc. Indeed, all *Gadje* are." Both men were swarthy complexioned, with rough features, mustaches, and coarse clothes.

The one called Maurice had an earring in his right ear and this, with the other clues from his appearance, seemed to mark him as a Romany. They came up the narrow street from a side alley straight at the writer, obviously speaking in English to make him aware of them. It was clearly a challenge to him.

When Howard turned to face them, his frontier senses aflame, the two men produced Navarro knives, the oversized folding blades of the Romany.

"I keep his hat," Maurice said with a cruel smile as he lunged for Howard's stomach with his eight-inch blade.

The Texan dodged the straight-in attack with a grace that belied his bulk, using his clothes bundle as a shield, and replied with an equally straight right punch to Maurice's jaw. The blow rocked the attacker back on his heels.

Luc came around his compatriot's back and slashed at Bob's left side with the naked blade barely missing the Texan's jacket.

"Easy there, Hoss," Howard snarled with a very angry voice. "My lady got me this getup."

The Romany slashed at him again, but Bob dodged back, then lunged in to pin the slashing arm against Luc's chest with his right shoulder. Howard reached his left hand around the attacker's head to Luc's left ear and pulled back to bulldog the thug.

Howard took Luc all the way to the ground in a spinning corkscrew. The Texan gave a quick boot to the fallen man's hand to disarm him then jumped over him to spin and place the fallen man between him and Maurice, who had recovered his feet.

The second attacker tried again to stab at the writer by slashing over the fallen Luc.

Bob slipped away from the thrust by a fraction of an inch and grabbed the over-extended arm with a vice grip at the wrist. "You're got, boy!" the Texan said, then yanked hard so that there was an audible pop from the Gypsy's elbow.

"Merde!" Maurice yelled as he dropped his knife.

Bob did not let go of the arm, however, but added his second hand to it and pulled down so that the yelling footpad was toppled onto his own compatriot.

Bob stepped back, tipped his Stetson and said, "Sorry gents, I hate to fight and run, but I don't want to mess up my fancy duds. Maybe we can play pin the tail on the Texan another time!" He moved off down the street at a relaxed but brisk walk while the two fallen men cursed him with adjectives as only a romance language allowed them.

Bob Howard made his way to his small hotel on a quiet side street without further incident, stopping at a café to steady his nerves and pick up a small snack. After he calmed down he dismissed the attack as just 'one of those things' with his new suit having attracted the local opportunists. He went back to mentally working on composing a poem to Gwendolyn as he walked. He smiled when he stopped at the front desk and found he had not just a letter from Gwen— dated over two weeks before—but a separate small package as well that had been sent five days before that.

Now that is a little bit of early Christmas! He was giddy with his discovery and all but skipped up the three flights of narrow stairs. His spirits were buoyed by the mail. All thoughts of his earlier encounter with the Romany street-thugs were pushed completely out of his mind.

When he got upstairs, however, he noticed the door to his room was open. The Texan paused in the hall and listened for a moment, his nerves newly raw with fresh memory of the alley fight so that he was suddenly ready for combat again.

He slipped off his jacket to protect it, then rushed forward to push the door open. He discovered the room within was empty and in a disordered mess. He found himself a little disappointed that there was no one on whom he could take out his annoyance for the state of the room.

The mattress had been removed from the bed frame, the drawers pulled out from the dresser and dumped on the floor. The closet's contents were strewn about the floor like a wild animal had ravaged the room. The Texan stood in the doorway and gave a deep sigh. *Somebody was searching for something.* He looked around and a sudden, panicked thought stuck him, *My typewriter!*

He raced to the chaotic pile of bedclothes and papers to search for his treasured word machine. After a few moments, he excavated his typewriter case with a cry of triumph. The case had been opened, but the machine had not been damaged.

"That's better, but sure as heck ain't my day," he said aloud as he began to straighten the overturned chairs and pick up the drawers that had been pulled from the dressers.

His next thought after his typewriter was to locate his Grandfather's Colt 45. He found it in its holster under a pile of scattered clothes then spent fifteen minutes reassembling pages from a current story he had been working on that he hoped to sell to *Adventure* Magazine. The pages and the carbons were all there with only a few of them so torn or crumpled beyond repair that he would be required to retype them.

"Makes a fellow wonder at being so popular all of a sudden," he said aloud as he closed his typewriter case. He glanced at the now-closed and locked door and put a hand on his six-gun—now on his belt—wondering what other danger might be lurking beyond it. *Like I had something somebody wanted.*

He began to think of the attack on him in a different light. He put his hand on the packet of Gwen's letters in the breast pocket of his new jacket—he always kept the packet with him when he went out. Aside from his typewriter, he considered them the only things of value he had, even more precious.

The gesture made him remember the new letter that he had thrust into the jacket's hip pocket in his shock and all but forgotten. Bob sat on the edge of the bed frame and opened the scented envelope.

> *"Dearest Robert,*
> *I hope this letter finds you well. I enjoyed your last letter and look forward to reading that story you sold to Sport Stories, though I must admit I enjoy your Breckenridge stories more than your boxing ones. And I hope you are enjoying your time in Paris. I hope someday we can see it together."*

He smiled at that.

> *"I also hope you will not think me impulsive or mad, but these last weeks in Geneva have left me much time to reflect and I realize that I must know from whence I have come—who my parents were and how I came to be with the Harkers. By now you will have read my adoptive father's diary that I sent you before this and will understand why the events of those months ago cannot be allowed to rest—will not allow me to rest until I know for certain.*

To that end, by the time you read this letter, I will already be at Borgho Pass deep in the Carpathian Mountains.

I know, it is mad, but I must know, my cowboy poet, so please do not think badly of me. It is a journey I must undertake myself. I will go to the village mentioned in the diary to try and follow the trail of my faux-parents' visit there, in hopes of finding out about my real parents. If you will not be too angry with me, write me. I may even be able to give you a plot for one of your darling tales. I hope you will forgive me. I will write in a few days when I reach the village whether or not I learn anything.

Yours in hope, Gwendolyn."

Howard stared at the note for a long time, his mind working to absorb the enormity of what it said. "Well gal," he finally said aloud, "you sure know how to keep a fella off balance. I know you gotta make your own way, but, running off like that...wow, I would'a gone with you if you really wanted to go. I know how much roots matter to a person. Mama taught me that."

He looked at the note again then opened the companion package with deliberate care. It contained a battered leather journal with a bookmark on a single page in the center of the diary. It was written in an almost delicate, precise script.

"20 November, 1918

Dear Diary,

Now that hostilities are concluded, Wilhelmina and I have finally been able to get passage to Transylvania and to return to the place where our lives were changed forever. She had begun having episodes more frequently, unexplained anger, headaches and the urges again for such things as red meat. I know it goes back to...to...that experience I had in the mountains, and she had at Carfax Abby. She feels she has to know exactly why. I concur which is why I agreed to this trip as soon as it was safe to travel. The compulsion returns to her regularly, as if she were being called by…by…Him…even though he is really dead this last ten years. She says it is strong now and almost constant.

It is hard to believe it was nearly twenty years ago when I was imprisoned here and it was then that the incidents happened to her.

We were able to charter the last coach available at the port to take us to the Tihuta Pass that the locals call The Borgho Pass but have had to share it with a young couple. The man is an architect from Swansea who has been working in Budapest and had come to the port to meet his wife and child and is taking them on a tour before they return to his work. It turns out both were on the same ship with us. It is remarkable that the mother looks as if she could almost be a relative of Mina's and her toddler is a darling girl named Gwendolyn. It makes me miss Quincy terribly, but it was necessary to leave him with his grandmother while this problem of his mother's is addressed. When we reach Stregga I hope we will find out what direction our quest will take.

Will I find a way to end these spells of hers? Will this strange compelling voice in her head cease? It is my hope that all of this will be resolved so we may move forward with my membership in the White Glove group and we may take our true position in the scheme of things."

The Texan put the diary down and looked at the dates of the letter and did some quick math. "She sent the diary from Geneva, but the letter was sent from Vienna more than a full week ago. That would put her in this Borgho place at least five days before. And no letter from her since then. That has to mean she is in trouble."

Without hesitation he set about packing up his belongings for his trip to the far-away town of Stregga.

"Little lady," he spoke as he packed, "you sure are an impulsive thing, and sure enough I admire you for it, but I just hope you can hold on till I get there."

He tried not to think about what might happen before he could reach her, but he was cursed with a writer's imagination that hurried him to pack with greater speed.

Chapter Twenty-Four: Rails of Death

Bob Howard was able to find a plane that was scheduled to fly to Bucharest the next morning and paid an exorbitant fee to board it. By the following night, he was halfway across the continent from the City of Lights in another small hotel in the Romanian capital, on a quiet back street. And feeling helpless.

The entire trip he worried that the attack on him had been motivated by the message from Gwendolyn and that if they found him once they could find him again. He spent the time not only worried about what trouble she could be in but about being bushwhacked a second time as well. If the attack and the searching of his room were not robberies, as nothing had been taken, then they had been looking for something. And the only thing he had that was new was the diary that Gwendolyn had sent him. To that end, he poured over the book looking for some reason it might be important to attackers.

The book told a strange tale of a trip to the interior of the mountain country where Gwen's faux mother found no answers about her transformation—at least none her husband recorded. Only cryptically on the last page it stated, "*Wilhelmina says The Master's very essence is here, yet it escapes her. I fear this trip was fruitless—save for the foundling Gwendolyn, we return empty-handed.*"

There was no way for Howard to leave the city late at night and head up toward the village of Stregga. The destination was 'up country' and isolated with no easy way to reach it.

Howard sat in that small hotel room with a chair braced against the door and slept with his Grandpa's Colt under his pillow. His dreams were troubled. He was glad when he woke that he could not remember them clearly, but the sense of helplessness that marched through them in shades of red lingered with him.

At an hour past dawn, Howard was able to take a train partway north toward the Borgho Pass but found he would have to leave it by late afternoon at a small hamlet along the line when the train swung west, away from his destination. It was a small town that was little more than a whistle-stop but apparently a departure point for areas to the direct north of the country on a regular basis.

The train was an old-style steam engine and belched smoke and steam that all but obscured it as the writer climbed aboard amid a hearty early-morning crowd.

It was a pleasant trip back in time for Howard, with the elegant, old-style coach cars with rich wood and brass fittings. He found a seat in the general car, placed his typewriter and valise in the rack overhead and settled in to attempt to rest.

He found the rolling clack of the wheels soothing and, knowing he had hours before the upcountry stop, settled back and tried to doze. He worried that his sleep would mirror the troubled sleep of the night before, but the regular rhythm of the wheels was balm to his nerves, and he slept deeply.

The Texan abruptly jerked awake when the train came to a stop. He jumped up, prepared to grab his gear but the uniformed conductor pointed to a pocket watch dial and managed to relate to him that it was just a watering stop for the locomotive to refill the boiler and they were still three hours away from Howard's actual stop.

The Texan laughed. "Thanks, Hoss," he said. "I think I lost a few years with that start!" He realized he was stiff from trying to fit his bulk into the cramped railroad seat. He stretched. "I think I'll step out on the rear platform and stretch my legs while we're stopped."

He moved down between the row of dozing or reading passengers. He noted with some amusement that one of the passengers was reading a two-year-old copy of *Weird Tales* in Cyrillic with his Conan tale 'Red Nails' on the cover and it made him smile. Across the way a teenage boy was reading a German pulp western with someone called '*Sohn Von Shatterhand*' who looked like a stalwart copy of General Custer.

Well, I'll keep having work as long as people are reading. He also saw a newspaper headline in French that he understood to be about the rise of Heinrich Himmler and his Nazi party in Germany. It was something that the Texan had all but ignored back home in the States, but which he had been increasingly and alarmingly hearing about since he came to Europe.

All the more reason to keep writing to give people escape, Howard thought. *But only proof of what I've always said, the savage nature of man, in the end will win.*

He made his way to the platform at the back of the car where two other passengers had stepped out to have a smoke and stretch their own legs.

The Texan smiled and tipped his hat to them, and they both nodded. All three said nothing but stood looking at the rugged countryside and keeping their own council.

The smoke from the old steam engine was drifting past as they fired up the boiler again and it made him think of the trains he had been on the last months, from the ramshackle local leaving home to the one he took cross-country to New York, then the strange underground trains, the subway in Manhattan that Big Carney had taken him on *"to broaden your mind a bit more, Boss Bob!"* and even the London Underground that he had taken a trip on with Gwendolyn and William during an excursion into London. So much change, so many miles from his start.

And so many miles to go!

Howard stood at the rail, thinking about Gwendolyn, praying to all the dark gods of his soul that he was not too late to save her. He leaned his weight on the rail, his hands gripping the smooth wood. He looked down and was surprised that there was a small plaque on the rail that read "Property of The San Antonio & Gulf Coast Railroad Company."

"I'll be darned," he said aloud. "I guess they had to sell the rolling stock when it got old. No stranger, I guess, than this old Texas boy out here in the middle of nowhere!"

He looked up and watched the thick woods. The steam from the 'drinking' engine hissed and crawled along the side of the train and even in the daylight imparted a dreamlike quality to the dense forest on either side of the right of way. The trees were different woods than back home, with a sense of mystery to them and his 'barbarian soul' called for him to climb off the train and just go exploring.

After the artificial clacking of the train, the natural, quiet sounds of the forest were refreshing as was the crisp Carpathian air. The passenger car's observation platform faced the blank wall of a boxcar, and the Texan knew there was a second boxcar then a caboose beyond that to complete the short train.

Howard let his eyes unfocus and found his mind returning to all he'd read in the diary Gwen had sent him. The monstrous Carpathian nobleman who had held Jonathon Harker captive in his castle and the horrible aftermath with Mina Harker's occult transformations. The Texan knew he was going to be facing something more in the realm of his friend Howie Lovecraft, whose knowledge of the dark and otherworldly was deeper than any realized.

Whatever it is, I'll find her, I'll fight it and we'll win.

He tried not to dwell on how long it was taking. *I will find you, Gwen, I swear. Just hold on.*

There was a sudden burst of steam, and he felt the train jerk. He realized he was alone on the platform and the train was moving again.

"Gotta stop wool-gathering," he admonished himself aloud. "Gotta be sharp to save the-"

Suddenly a phantom horse snorted out in the white and a blur of a man launched itself from the steam. The intruder slammed into Howard driving him back against the wall of the train car. Arms like corded cables wrapped around the writer pinning Howard's arms to his side. The attacker squeezed so hard Howard felt the air driven out of his lungs.

A second attacker leaped onto the observation platform from a horse just as the train picked up speed and began to accelerate down the rails. The Texan was vaguely aware of this second man, but most of his consciousness was occupied with trying to resist the crushing grip of the man who was holding him.

The first assailant was bearded and dark and smelled of wine and spices. He was even wider than Howard and his arms massive. But he was also shorter than the Texan and Howard used that fact to slam his chin down on the bridge of the man's nose repeatedly. The attacker grunted then yelled in pain as the nose broke and blood fountained freely from it.

The vice grip of the man's clinch released just enough for Howard to shove with all his might and propel the man away from him. The second attacker, a slim, mustachioed man, had to dodge around him to come at Howard at an angle. He was brandishing a knife.

Howard had not worn his pistol so only had his bare hands to react with; he did so by slapping at the knife hand of the off-balance assailant. The Texan hit the forearm of the man and deflected the knife, but the attacker pulled back to attempt a second thrust.

Howard slapped the knifeman in the face with his Stetson and then flew at him using the wall of the train car as a springboard. The Texan put his full body weight behind the punch. It connected.

The knifeman lifted up off the platform and flew backward to slam into the railing.

The first attacker had recovered enough to come at the Texan again; his bulky form was not agile, and the narrow space of the platform hampered him. When he tried to swing it was a wide one and Howard moved inside the slugger's reach to launch a fusillade of jabs. The hits were solid on the bearded man's jaw and backed him up.

When Howard had rocked the bruiser on his heels at the edge of the platform he stepped in and threw all he had into a right uppercut that sent the thug tumbling off the moving train with a grunt and a yell.

That left the knifeman and Howard spun to face him but the man had no heart for a solo assault without his knife. When the Texan advanced the man yelled, "*Gadja Meesh!*" and threw himself off the speeding train.

Howard watched the attempted assassin roll down the grade and limp away, then stooped and picked up his Stetson. "Well damn, sure seems like somebody connected to Gypsies is dead set on stopping me." He dusted his jacket off, donned his hat and reentered the train trying to look as if nothing had happened.

Chapter Twenty-Five: The Carpathian Cowboy

No one on the train had noticed Howard's skirmish with the two men that he took to be Romany so he returned directly to his seat. The first thing he did before sitting down, however, was quietly get his grandfather's six-gun out of his suitcase and slip it under his coat.

He sat hyperalert the rest of the train trip, suddenly suspicious of his fellow passengers. The remainder of the trip was uneventful. The Texan studied a map of the region and determined that the easiest way— and the quickest—to reach the fairly isolated village of Stregga was by carriage, the same way the Harkers had so long ago.

His guess was confirmed when the train stopped to let him and some others off in a small town that reminded Howard of the ramshackle whistle-stop towns in Texas.

The roads Howard saw from the open platform of the 'station' were rudimentary. The small town was comprised of little more than two dozen buildings. Several other passengers detrained as well for the trip northeast of the country, and he learned they also planned to travel by coach.

He followed the others to locate the local livery stable that consisted of two large ramshackle buildings with a large corral between. It seemed to be one of the larger businesses in the tiny town.

The four who had debarked with Howard had obviously done this before. They went straight to a bent-backed silver-hair who was seated out front of one of the buildings. They exchanged a few words in Hungarian and then the old man called out to a stable boy.

The young boy led the two couples to a carriage inside the stable building and began to tack a team to the coach.

Bob watched them while keeping his eyes alert for any more attackers. He reassured himself by feeling the six-gun under his jacket—now in a shoulder holster—and wondered if any of those fellow passengers might be in league with the forces that were menacing Gwendolyn.

Nonetheless, Howard was about to ask if some of the passengers that were renting a coach were going toward Stregga and he might ride with them when he sighted a McClellen Cavalry saddle on a peg just inside the barn door and had a better idea.

He walked up to the saddle and ran a hand along the butt-polished leather of the seat. Bob had ridden using one in Texas and it was like seeing a little piece of home in the stable.

I suppose it ain't so much of a reach to find one here, seein' how Capt. George McClellen said he based it on a Hungarian model used in the Prussian service. With the plaque he had seen on the train he was beginning to feel like he would find a frontier palisade fort around any turn at any moment.

The old man out front saw the Texan's interest and tottered into the barn to him. The silver-hair questioned Bob in his native tongue but when the writer just shrugged and smiled the old man tried halting English.

"You want horse?"

"Sure, I do, Hoss, and I think this here saddle is sure the one I want."

"Cowboy!" the old man said, slapping the worn leather of the saddle. He smiled to show a gap-toothed smile.

"Not quite," Howard said with a laugh, "but close enough, I suppose."

After that by gesture and a few halting words from each man the Texan negotiated for a horse, bedroll, some saddle-bags, and tack to go along with the saddle, and confirmed his route on the map. In short order, Bob had changed into rough-out clothes, repacked his belongings into the saddle-bags and was on his way upcountry.

With the exception of his typewriter strapped behind him, the Texan—his Stetson pulled down tight, his trousers tucked into his boots and his grandpa's gun snuggly holstered under his left arm— looked like one of his own ancestors riding to chase horse thieves into the badlands.

Well, I am going to head'er off at the pass, he thought with a laugh. *I guess it sorta applies.*

He looked at the wild winter landscape ahead and thought about the Ottoman invaders that had once ridden across that land and thought, *I'm beginning to believe that the old, old theory of Turkish-Gaelic affinity is well borne out. The races have so much in common: cruelty, treachery, loyalty, fatalism, spend-thriftiness, berserk fighting rage, a love of music and poetry.*

He soon passed the slow-moving carriage of his fellow train passengers and was reassured he had made the right decision when he saw the state of the poorly maintained main 'road.' The thoroughfare was little more than a muddy, rutted path between heavy forest growth.

"Near as I can figure from this here kilometer thing, Seabiscuit," Howard said to his horse—whose name actually was '*Sebesseg*,' "I know that ain't yer name, quite, but I can't pronounce it, so Seabiscuit will have to do. I figure we need to chat to pass the time." The horse gave a snort, and the Texan took it as a 'yes.' "We got about a hundred or so corkscrew miles till we get to this village. I figure we can make it in four long days if we keep at it and go straight."

He had taken the precaution of getting a full meal at a small restaurant at the train stop and purchased a handful of sandwiches and a thermos of coffee for the trip. It was not much for the days ahead, but he had been hungry before—it was almost an occupational necessity with a writer—and he had never had a better cause.

Seabiscuit proved a steady and reliable mount so that by nightfall when the Texan had taken the right fork off the main road, he knew he had covered even more than he'd hoped to the first day. And he was well ahead of the carriage that had left just before him from the train stop.

There were no inns along the rough road, at least not in the direction that Howard was going; the left fork would have taken him to an old Roman road and to a further pass through the mountains than the Borgho Pass. The Texan made camp by the side of the road as the sun oranged the horizon over the distant peaks.

"Well, fella," Howard said after he had unsaddled the horse, fed him some of the oats he'd brought from the stable and tethered the beast in a makeshift *remuda,* "I appreciate the effort today. Keep that up tomorrow and we'll stay real good friends."

He made a small fire in a cleared space near a fallen tree that lay beside a small trickle of water. It was a tepid little stream, but the babble was soothing, and Howard stretched out gratefully, sure he was going to be very sore at the end of the ride.

I guess I ain't near as tough as I make out to be, he thought with a chuckle. He laid out his bedroll, set his head against the saddle and sighed. *I might be of good stock but I ain't no barbarian for sure.*

He thought about kicking off his boots but realized he didn't know if there were snakes in Carpathia, and if so, if they were poisonous. *I guess there are gaps in my education I had better rectify as soon as I get me near a library. 'Course I know there are two-legged snakes, so it is better to be ready to get-a-goin' just in case.*

The night sounds of the forest were beginning as the dark replaced the light, still hours away from moonrise. Howard stared up at the stars beginning to dot the sky and thought about how many more there were to see than over Manhattan at night.

Almost as many as from Cross Plains, he thought with a grin. *Big Carney would love this amount of sky. A man can really feel free looking at this display.*

Then he thought of Gwendolyn. He tried not to think about how long it was taking him to get to her, tried to 'starve his imagination' about what danger she might be in. And his mind went to poetry; *"By night dark pass, To hunt a lass, From dangers all uncertain, As she assails to lift the veils, From black mysterious curtains, Of long ago progenitors and recent red predators, But will my journey be in time, And make this all a Pointless rhyme?"*

As he finished composing the poem there was a sudden, long, low howl from the darkness. In a few moments, an answering howl sounded from somewhere further up the trail. Seabiscuit whinnied and kicked restlessly at the dirt in the *remuda.*

"Easy, boy," he said. "Well, ain't no doubt there are wolves here." He touched the handle of his grandfather's gun beside him and checked to make sure the hammer was still on the empty chamber—that gave him five shots to discourage any animal visitors.

He rose and stoked the fire higher, setting more firewood beside it before he laid back down. Despite new apprehension about animals in the night, his exhaustion claimed him and in minutes he was deeply asleep.

Chapter Twenty-Six: New Gun in Town

The village of Stregga was on the southern branch of the Roman road that led to the Borgho Pass through a low, wide valley. It had an ominous castle that loomed above it at the far end—an old stone building that clung to the side of the far hill, a dark shape even in the bright light of the afternoon sun.

The main rutted dirt road leading through the town twisted away from the old paved Roman path that went toward the castle as if the founders of the town had wished to avoid any and all discourse with the castle and its inhabitants.

The Texan realized he was riding into the village on market day, so what was probably a normally empty street was bustling with stalls and farm folk come to hawk their wares or buy supplies and just generally to exchange news and gossip.

The village was what would be described in a tourist brochure—should there have been one for the isolated town—as 'picturesque' with old-style waddle and daub structures above stone-foundation first floors. All clearly handmade and with the aura of great age about it all.

Bob Howard's arrival at the village of Stregga caused little reaction at first as folks went about their own business and he was just another person come to market. But as his unusual appearance, Stetson, and worn cowboy boots were noticed the whispers about him began. In short time he might as well have been heralded. And from the looks he was as welcome as the black plague making a reappearance from its dark ages outbreak.

Soon old women pulled their shawls tighter and children pointed chubby fingers at the stranger with numerous signs and hand gestures launched in his direction, some of which he recognized as wards against the 'evil eye.' In no time at all the occupants of the hamlet stared at him as if he were Poe's Red Death himself.

These folks ain't never seen a real live writer I suspect, he smiled. He looked back at the stone faces with as genial a grin as he could summon knowing well it was the 'it is an outsider' mindset all small-town folk had.

The Cross Plains folk all had it. "Who is this, why are they in *our* town, and what bad thing does it portend?" they would wonder, with an inner resentment for all that was different. Sometimes it was not even from those outside of the town, but from any element that could disrupt the normal, even boring, course of their lives. The sameness that they embraced as comforting. Anything else was frightening.

He had seen that very look all his life from his own people. They feared what they did not understand and a fellow making a living from 'mere words'—more money, in fact than even his country doctor father—was 'not right' in their minds. It tilted their worldview and they felt threatened. It was why he had grown up so isolated, with few friends and even those friends did not fully understand him. Only Howie Lovecraft, the writer friend he had only met through letter, seemed to really grasp who he was.

At least until Gwendolyn Harker came into his life.

It all once more reminded Howard of how little 'civilized' man had progressed from his cave-dwelling barbarian ancestors; starting at shadows and lashing out at anything or anyone who would bring disruptive influences—or information—into their comfortable ignorance.

Why you're such a treasure, Gwen, Your open mind, your questing for new knowledge; dang girl, I am gonna find you!

Howard maneuvered his mount through the crowd to the town's center, aware already of the differences even in the villagers—he could differentiate the farmers from the towns-folk from the slight differences in their clothing and by their posture and looking at the calloused—or un-calloused--hands of the men and women.

And there were other outsiders among the Transylvani-ans. They were standing at several impromptu *remuda* and booths, darker folk, dressed more colorfully and watching all from behind hooded eyes—Romany! He found his hackles raised with new caution, wondering if any of the Gypsies were allied with those that had attacked him in Paris and on the train.

The Romany stood out with even more wary looks than the Stregga villagers yet they dickered with the locals about the horses with an enthusiasm that would have put Arab trad-ers to shame. The Roma women, their hair hidden beneath colorful scarves, sold jams, flowers, and cloth from booths. Many of them moved through the crowd in tight groups with the locals stepping out of their way with wary looks.

The local men cast covetous glances at the 'outsider' women, who returned the look from half-closed eyes and with sly smiles. The local women crossed themselves and elbowed their men or pulled on their arm to hurry them along.

Bob laughed at the interaction but then the Texan re-membered those who had jumped him and he was glad for the comfortable weight of his Grandfather's six-shooter un-der his left arm. It also made him realize how hard it might be to find Gwendolyn.

Just where do I start looking for you, gal? The enormity of searching for and finding her in this strange country seemed overwhelming.

Howard's horse snorted, making a slight misstep on a slick paving stone in the street. It snapped Bob back to his present. "Sorry, boy," he said, patting the horse's neck. "I'll get you bedded down and fed, then I'll go looking for Gwen."

It was not hard to locate the town's stable; it was just beyond the main square, where several wooden and stone structures had attached corrals.

Half a dozen of the Romany were loitering around the horses in the corral when the Texan dismounted and walked Seabiscuit to the front of the stable. There was an old local sitting out front who looked almost a twin of the fellow he had rented his horse from at the train stop. The old fellow was keeping a wary eye on the Romany but let his gaze wander to take in the writer.

"Cowboy?" the old man said.

Howard shrugged. "Ain't no hiding it, I guess." When it was clear the old man did not actually know what the American was saying Howard tried the combination of pantomime and broken English that had gotten him the horse, but this hostler did not seem as quick as his 'twin.'

"May I help?" A voice speaking in English from behind Howard startled him. He turned to see an old woman. She was dressed like a local with a heavy shawl pulled over her gray locks.

She was barely over five feet tall but was so stooped over it was hard to tell what her true height had been. Her face had strong cheekbones and parchment-like yellow skin stretched tightly over it with both age and worry. Her eyes, however, were bright and seemed younger than her features.

"You speak English?" Bob asked. The woman's face creased into a smile.

"After a fashion," she said in a soft voice. "You are American?"

"Guilty, ma'am, I just want to stable my horse and get him some oats."

The woman spoke in Hungarian to the stable owner who looked dubious until Howard produced local currency he had picked up in Bucharest and paid for a few days stabling and food for his mount.

While the transaction went on the Romany hung about watching with wolfish eyes. When Howard shouldered his saddlebags and lifted off his typewriter case, he thought he saw the eyes of the Gypsies go wide with interest. He was once again glad for the comforting weight of the gun under his arm.

"I sure appreciate your help, ma'am," the Texan said. He walked back toward the town square and the crowd there with the stooped woman tottering beside him. "I didn't give no proper introduction. My name's Bob Howard and I'm right glad for your assistance."

"You are welcome. I am Magda. It is only right to be hospitable, something many seem to have forgotten in Stregga."

"Oh, I don't blame them none, I come from a small town myself. Folks tend to be clannish. I get that. Can I ask you where a fella can rent a room around here, though?"

"There is only the tavern, the Boar's Tooth, they have a few rooms upstairs they rent from time to time. Not often though, few outsiders come to Stregga."

The two had almost reached the town center now, at the outer edge of the market crowd but Howard noticed that two of the earringed Romany had followed them, lingering at a distance to appear casual. The writer kept one eye on them while he asked the old woman, "Do you know of an English girl that came through here this last week or so? She's named Gwendolyn Harker."

The old woman arched an eyebrow. "I did not see her, but I did hear that someone from outside came here last week. She was British, yes?"

"Yes." The Texan's heart raced and he stopped dead in his tracks to face the little woman. "Really, you heard about her?"

"Talk from some of the others of my tribe. The young ones."

"You're a Gypsy then?"

"You did not know?"

"Sometimes I ain't so quick on the uptake, ma'am," he said. He noticed now that her long skirts, though shabby, had the same colorful stitching as the vests of the other Romany.

The two of them had turned off the main thoroughfare to cut through a smaller cobbled side street heading toward the inn the old woman suggested but stopped abruptly when two figures emerged from the shadows ahead.

"It is bad enough you make yourself *gadji* by keeping that fake holy man, Magda," said one of the Gypsies that stepped before the pair. He snapped out a knife and held it up and smiled. "Now you pick up this stray *gadjo* to defile our valley?"

"I just ain't got no luck with alleys," Howard said in disgust. He set down his typewriter case and waved at the men. "Come on, boys, let's get this over with. I'm tired."

Chapter Twenty-Seven: Secret of the Town

The two Gypsies advanced, their knives catching sunlight to look like slivers of silver. "Our blades are thirsty, *gadjo*," the taller of the two hissed. "When it is learned later that you have murdered one of our tribe, there will be none to question our justice." The two turned their attention to the old woman and began to advance on her.

"You would shame our people to rid yourself of me, Dimitri?" The old woman spat back at the two.

"What is the shame if none know of it?" the second Romany said. "The Dragon will reward us for flicking this fly off his flank. First the old priest, now this trash. You are the one who should have shame, you baggage."

"Hate to interrupt a family quarrel," the Texan said, "but that ain't no way to talk to a lady."

Dimitri did not hesitate but lunged forward with his blade, the point aimed at Howard's heart.

The Texan was ready for him and drew his pistol with old-west speed, the barrel actually slapping the knife blade so hard it drove the knife out of Dimitri's hand.

Howard cocked the hammer of the six-gun and put the barrel against the startled Gypsy's forehead.

"Now I 'spect the bullet from this will go straight through with no brains to impede it," the writer said. "But in case there is any thinking ability left in you, think twice about speaking to this woman that way again. Got that?"

The Romany's dark eyes widened with fear.

"Now apologize to the lady!"

Dimitri's features fought to show anger under his façade of fear. Howard prodded him with the gun barrel, all the while keeping the second Gypsy in his periphery.

"You heard me, Dimitri."

"I apologize," the attacker said through clenched teeth. "But know this, Magda. You cannot defy The Dragon."

"Need work on that apology, Hoss," Howard said, "but it will do for now. Git!"

The Romany backed up but when he made a move to pick up his discarded knife Howard barked, "Leave it."

"We will meet again, *gadjo*," Dimitri threatened.

"If we do," Howard said, "Grandpa's equalizer will do my talking for me. Now, git!"

The two men left to a string of Romany curses from the old woman. When they were gone, she turned to the Texan with tears in her eyes.

"What did that fella mean, about the shame, ma'am?" He holstered his pistol and picked up his typewriter while keeping the two fleeing men in sight.

"I do have shame, Mister Bob, but it is for my people." She pulled her shawl tighter about her as if from a chill, but it was clearly of the soul. She glanced up the village to the looming shape of the ancient castle overlooking the valley. "That place is evil. It has cast a shadow on my people."

"Sure is a spooky place. But I don't understand. What did that fella mean about—"

"Not here. And now it will not be safe for you to stay at the inn. You must come with me; my home is humble, but none dare cross its threshold to do harm."

Howard arched an eyebrow, his writer's mind wondering if the whole circumstance was an elaborate means to get him out of town to be bushwhacked. Yet his cowboy sense of honor could not let him abandon a lady in distress, even if that lady was a member of a tribe that had tried to kill him. He resolved to keep his hand close to his six-gun and his eyes open.

The old woman led Howard out of the bustle of the town up the road in the direction of the imposing fortress. Half a mile from the outer edge of the village they turned off into a small side path.

She spoke softly, and vaguely of 'the shadow' that had fallen her people decades before. "A corruption from the Dragon who ruled here, who died and yet did not die."

When Howard questioned her about it, she lapsed into mysterious silence again as they approached her home.

Howard's senses were keenly alert, but he could detect no traps as they moved to a ramshackle *vardo,* a Romany wagon, that was parked off the path near a small stream. It was a poor thing, with a roof that needed patching, shutters that seemed to barely be hanging on and with peeling paint all around. There was a small lean-to shed nearby where a skinny cow and an old horse were standing desultorily in the shade of a large oak.

The shadows were lengthening when they reached the site but there was still enough light for the Texan to note a number of symbols carved into the trees around the little clearing with the encampment, and little bits of cloth tied on bushes, and they were obviously not there by accident.

Magda saw the Texan's interest. "They are wards, my friend," she said. "Even the young ones such as we met in the alley fear the place which is the home of a *taltos.*"

"I know that word," the Texan said. "My friend Howie wrote me about it; a *táltos* was supposed to be hand-picked by God before they were even born to take care of folks, cure both body and soul. They was born with some sort of special mark—"

The old woman smiled to reveal gapped teeth. "You are smart for a *gadjo,*" which brought a laugh from the burly Texan.

"I've heard that before," he said. "I apparently do not present well."

She continued, "Janos was born with a full set of teeth. In his childhood, he was taught by the wise ones, shown the ancient knowledge of the shaman even before he took his

Christian vows." She led Howard to the door of the vardo and knocked a rhythm and waited.

"Janos?" Howard asked but before she could answer a weak voice came from within.

"Magda?"

"*Igen,*" she said then followed it with a string of words in Hungarian. She turned to the Texan.

"My friend may be frightened by you, as you are a stranger, Mister Bob. Also, he cannot see, so do not approach him 'til you speak."

The Texan had given up on trying to get her to say 'just Bob' on the walk from town so he just followed her into the surprisingly spacious Romany wagon.

The interior was a study in effective space usage, with the walls and cabinets painted in bright colors. Everything was clean and orderly and belied the worn appearance of the outside of the wagon.

Seated on a wicker chair in the center of the space was a man. His manner said he was a broken old man, with a beard, thin white hair, drawn features and blind, staring eyes. His lower body was covered with a quilt, but it was clear from how the covering fell that his legs were missing.

Magda spoke softly to the man in Hungarian and then took an apple from her bag and placed it into the man's hand. His smile was warm and he thanked her in that language.

"Father Janos. The friend with me is an American."

It was then that the Texan noticed that the old man wore the clerical collar of an Eastern Orthodox Priest.

"American?" the old priest said in English. "You have traveled far."

"Miles to go a'fore I sleep," Howard paraphrased. "Call me Bob."

The old man smiled. "As do we all." He brought the apple up to his face but only inhaled the scent of it. "You are a searcher, Bob. This I sense, but for what?"

"Whom. I'm searching for a gal."

Magda spoke as she put the few food items she had brought from the village into a cabinet. "He searches for the English girl we heard tell of."

"Then you have heard of Gwen?"

The old priest nodded. "There was word that came to me over a week hence," he said. "A girl with dark red hair?"

"Yes!" Howard almost jumped forward to grab the old priest and shake him. "That's her; auburn-haired and dang pretty."

"*Sarkany Kastely!*" the old priest said.

Magda hissed and crossed herself. When Howard looked at her in confusion she explained, "The Castle of the Dragon, that which casts its shadow over this valley and my people."

"That is where word came to us that she had gone," the priest said.

Howard felt a chill up his spine at their tone. It was what he had feared, that she had gone to the very castle where her adoptive father had been kept prisoner. "When was this?"

"I heard the rumor ten days ago when some of the young ones stopped by for me to bless their new lamb," Father Janos said. "People here notice outsiders. She had inquired in the village and it was said she found someone to lead her to the cursed place. That is all I know."

"Cursed place," the Texan whispered with a hiss. "She sure would go to such a place if she was looking for her parents' truth." He started to turn for the door, but Magda put a hand on his arm.

"It is not right to go near that place at night—the forces of evil dwell there."

Howard touched the butt of the six-gun under his jacket. "I got no fear of evil, ma'am, not while I got my brain and a righteous equalizer."

"Righteousness has fled this valley," the priest said. "When I was young I fought it, tried to bring Magda's people to the light. It was my mission as *taltos* as well as a priest of God to tell all the Hungarian nation when there was a time of danger, to warn against invading armies or worse." The old man's voice was stronger than his shattered body. "I fought The Dragon in my youth, he who came out of the past, rising to grip the young of this valley with temptations of greed."

"Was this 'bout forty or more years ago?" the Texan asked.

"Yes," Janos said. "An Englishman came and his coming seemed to embolden The Dark One to come down from the castle. It was in the final battle with that monster—or so we thought—when my legs were destroyed by a wagon over-turning on me. But it did not end then. Somehow, he returned not long ago. Weakened, it is true, but like a festering wound he squatted in that castle and waited, feeding on the evil he had infected Magda's people with."

"Greed and a desire for the Romany to have power," the old woman said, "such as they imagined they once had in the past. That and a desire to take revenge on those who they feel have shunned them."

"And Gwen went up to that castle?" Howard moved for the door of the vardo again, but the power of the priest's voice stopped him this time.

"We *táltos* are able to go into a deep meditation. What you would call a trance and in such a state can cure sickness of almost any kind. But though I pray every day I have not been able to bring a savior to this valley."

Howard pushed his Stetson up on his head and grinned. "Well, Padre, you got a Texan now, and there's them that say that's often been near enough."

Chapter Twenty-Eight: The Voivode

The girl who had grown up as Gwendolyn Harker woke with a gasp and a start. She was confused at first, disoriented until she realized she was lying on her back looking up at an arched stone ceiling.

Where is this place? She was cold but the shiver that ran through her was not from that; it was from fear.

She was in a dark room that seemed a cell, with a flickering torch on the damp stone wall and no other illumination. Gwen realized she was on a rough bed of straw on a shelf carved into the naked stone of the wall.

How did I get here? She rose shakily to her feet, her legs stiff and her balance precarious so she had to hold onto the edge of the stone ledge. She forced herself to stagger across the room to the roughhewn door.

The door had a small square window in it with iron bars. She pulled at the door handle, but the portal had no give. Gwendolyn pressed her face to the window, but some instinct told her not to call out—instead she tried to see into the gloom beyond the door.

All that was visible was a dark stone corridor, with the same hewn stone construction as her cell.

Still, she hesitated to call out.

Her last memories were of riding up the narrow defile that led to the Castle of the Dragon, her horse walking tentatively along the long-neglected trail. Ahead was the Gypsy who had agreed to guide her.

The sheer walls that rose from the narrow path loomed menacingly on both sides, winding up the rocky crag on which the ancient fortress sat. She knew the legend, that the ruler had made his own nobles work as slave labor till they dropped from exhaustion, in revenge for their not backing him in an earlier time.

The landscape was bleak and lifeless. She noticed that even the birds were silent for the last mile as the horses trudged along the winding path, as if all living things eschewed the area. The castle was no longer visible though the path continued to angle upward.

"Are you sure this is safe?" she called to the Romany named Dimitri, ahead of her.

"This is the only way to the castle, English lady," the guide said. "We will reach the plain before the hold soon."

Almost as he spoke they rounded a curve and the brooding edifice of the Castle of the Dragon came into view. It was dark stone and its darker windows looked so much like a skull's empty eye sockets that she shuddered. Her hand went to the brooch she wore on her choker—the one thing she knew had been her true mother's—and she stroked it.

"Protect me Mother," she said softly inside the stone cell. "And help me find the truth."

Suddenly Gwendolyn's hand went to her neck for the choker she always wore, and she jumped back from the cell door with a gasp. "My brooch!" She turned from the door, her confinement forgotten as she searched the bare cell for the missing jewelry.

After a cursory search she dropped to her hands and knees and felt around the damp floor, thrusting her hands into the shadows in hopes of finding her keepsake, but to no avail.

This, more than her incarceration, brought her to the verge of tears. "No, no, no!" she sobbed. "I have to find it."

"You have not yet begun to despair, Miss Harker," a deep voice boomed into the room. The voice spoke in accented English and seemed to come from all around her at once.

Gwendolyn whirled to see a pale face at the barred window in the door.

She rushed to the portal. "This is an outrage! I am a British citizen. Release me!"

The figure on the other side of the door had piercing, dark eyes beneath thick white brows. He laughed in a deep, resonant tone then said, "Always you English call upon your heritage as if it were both sword and shield." He spoke clear English but with strange accenting.

The speaker backed away from the viewing window as if inviting Gwendolyn to bring herself to press against the tiny aperture. Despite the fact that the speaker beyond the door terrified her and made her skin crawl she moved to the window to observe him as he stood in the middle of the corridor outside.

Gwendolyn's captor was a thin, older man, yet he stood upright and projected an animal vitality despite his long, white hair. He had a narrow, sharp-cheekboned face with a long white mustache, pointed ears and displayed sharp teeth when he smiled. He had a hooked nose and a pointed salt and pepper beard with a clear streak of white in it. His whole image was one of a creature that was 'other than' and different from common men. A predator.

"Where is my property?" She drew herself to her full height, fighting her unreasoning and unexplained revulsion at the sight of her captor to stare directly into his feral eyes.

"You demand nothing!" the man hissed. He was dressed in an old-fashioned long black frock coat and his extraordinary pallor made the long scar on his forehead stand out like an ugly brand. "It is I who rule here."

The power of his statement was such that the girl stepped back away from the door as if physically assaulted.

"It was I who drove back the Turkomans, who brought the arrogant aristocrats of Wallachia to heel. I am a *voivode*, a prince of my people and you will give me deference, English intruder!"

Gwendolyn felt the savage energy of the man through the door, but her fear gave way to indignation, so she fell back on her upbringing among nobility. "Why have you incarcerated me, 'Prince'?"

Again, the laugh that was more a wolf howl than human-sounding utterance, and the figure in the hall smiled to reveal his long canine teeth that were almost fangs. "I will ask the questions," he said. "You will tell me why you have come to my homeland—were you sent by my agent Wilhelmina, your mother?"

"She was not my mother," Gwendolyn shot back with more anger than she thought herself capable. "She raised me but she was not my mother—she killed my mother and my father, my real parents!"

The pallid jailer evidenced surprise then and did something strange—he stepped toward the window and sniffed. It was an animal gesture and it, more than anything that had occurred before, filled the woman with soul-deep dread.

"Yes," he said in a deep whisper, "yes, I see now. I remember that scent, and it pleases me more than you can know. It is just that my destiny will be fulfilled now. It is destiny that you have come to me to bring the answer I need just at this time; it will be all I need to begin my conquest of your pathetic homeland again. And this time there will be no damnable Dutchman to stop me."

"What? I demand you release me and tell me to whom I speak!"

The pale prince stepped back and gave an elaborate and sarcastic court bow to his captive. "Of course, Lady Harker who-is-not-Harker. My title is Vladimir, Prince of Wallachia," he laughed, "but I prefer the name that honors my father's position in the Order of the Dragon. You may call me Dracula."

Chapter Twenty-Nine: Legacy of the Dragon

"The Castle of the Dracul was built on the bodies of his own countrymen," the old priest said, "and mortared with their blood."

The sun had gone down and Howard, Magda and Father Janos, after sharing a meal, were sitting and drinking tea. The other two had dissuaded the Texan from going to the castle till first light and were explaining the history of the fortress.

"The master of that castle was Vlad III called Ţepeş, the impaler. He was *voivode* of Wallachia, losing and regaining his throne three separate times before he was murdered in 1477. His cruelty was legend so that the Ottomans called him *Kazkh Voyoda,* the Impaler Lord."

The Texan nodded. "My pal Howie wrote me of him when we were talking about the wars in Eastern Europe. Howie said this fella signed his letters Dragulya, honoring his father Vlad Dracul."

"Yes," Magda said. "Dracula, son of the dragon who died but did not die. It was said he made a bargain with the Devil to rise from the grave; to exist by drinking the blood of the innocent."

The night sounds outside the *vardo* had a comforting familiarity to the Texan. Owls hooted and somewhere up in the mountains a distant wolf called to a loved one. The small fire in a cast-iron stove in the *vardo* kept it cozy. It might have been a pleasant evening with friends at any other time, except that the subject discussed was so dark and the reason for Howard's presence there was so dire.

"When I was young, almost fifty years ago, the scourge of the undead, the blood-drinking vampire was upon the land," Father Janos said. "They are the unclean things that cannot abide fresh running water nor sunlight or tread upon holy ground. They fear little of this world, however, save blessed objects and garlic flowers." The old man's blind eyes sparked with remembered vigor. "I fought them. I fought them from Budapest to the Burgho Pass itself. But always when one was destroyed—a stake driven through their black heart, their head cut off, or their undead flesh exposed to the cleansing rays of the sun—another would rise."

Howard studied Magda as she watched the old man and saw love in her expression. She was clearly seeing him as he had been, young and strong and there was some pride in her expression too, as he related his tale.

"Then I realized that the Castle of the Dragon was the center of the evil, the source of the contagion. But an Englishman called Harker came and Dracula left with him before I could stop him. Yet I was able to raise the populace then." Janos was animated now, seeing the events as they had happened so many years ago, his age falling away with the tale. "We drove his servants away, purged the building with fire and salt and holy water. The Roma took all they could and I thought we were rid of the monster, but months later he returned, driven out of England by one he always called 'the Dutchman.'"

"That would be a fella called Van Helsing," the Texas said, "according to Howie Lovecraft's letters; he found a manuscript that some guy named Stoker wrote based on newspaper accounts, in imitation of that Varney the Vampire book. His story used real names, so it was never published for fear of lawsuits."

"You are well-read, for an American," the priest replied.

"Thanks, I think," Howard said with a laugh. "Gotta read a lot to be a writer, sir."

"Just so," the old priest agreed. "When Van Helsing and the others drove the blood-thirsty one from England, Dracula came back here, and they pursued him."

"To the shame of my people," Magda interjected, "many of them served Dracula before he left for England and despite Janos rousing the populace they once more fell under his thrall when he returned."

"It was in the chase when the Son of the Dragon was brought low that I was crippled," the priest said. He gave a wan smile. "My eyes left me on their own only five years ago. The Good Lord saw fit to let me see many, many sunsets and see three generations of our people born." He put his hand out and Magda's hand found it in a practiced gesture. "And I have been blessed in other ways."

Howard felt almost embarrassed by their closeness, and Magda noticed and made to remove her hand from the priest's, but he held tight.

"It is I who have been blessed. Janos has done much to help my people, but some do not see it that way. The young, those who do not remember fully how bad it was when the monster reigned in this valley, they are seduced by the quick dollar and the illusion of power. They do not realize it was Dracula who had the power. They are only pawns."

"You think that vampire fella's followers are up there now?" Howard asked. He had to concentrate to keep the fear out of his voice—not for himself, but for what might have happened to Gwendolyn.

"I have not heard of activity up at the castle for some time," Magda said. "But then, few ever venture near it, even now."

"But Gwendolyn did?" He had given up the pretext of calm and realized he was leaning forward in his seat, his weight on the balls of his feet as if he was ready to leap to his feet and fight.

"Be calm, young man," Janos said. "You must have faith; I have seen her in my mind, and she is well, you are not too late."

"I pray that, Padre, I pray that hard."

"What do you want with me?" Gwendolyn demanded of her jailer. The pale figure in the hall twisted his features into a scowl, directing the force of his personality at the English captive.

"With you, nothing, woman," Dracula said, "but with your parents. They surprised me; your mother was stronger an individual then I thought her to be."

"If you speak of Wilhelmina Harker," Gwendolyn said with a sob, "she was not my mother."

The Wallachian noble laughed a cold laugh. "No, the Harker scent is on you, but there is another scent, an older scent I remember. I meant your birth mother."

"You knew my parents?"

"No, but the Harkers did." Dracula raised a spider hand and clenched it into a fist as if he were strangling some unseen foe. "Wilhelmina, my thrall, was a cunning vixen. When she killed your birth mother, she obtained information that I want. She planned to use what your real parents had found to enrich herself and her line. She may even have plotted to oppose me directly someday. That information will enable me to return to that vaunted isle that I was driven from—me—killer of the Turks, savior of my people!" His bloodless lips curled back in anger to reveal fang-like teeth. "And you have fallen into my hands now."

It was hard for the girl to process all the Wallachian was saying and she shook her head. "I don't know what you are talking about."

"Do not lie to me, woman. I want the key."

"What are you talking about? What key?"

"The key to the treasure!"

"I don't know anything about any treasure. You may have anything the Harkers had, I would be rid of them!"

"I want what the Harkers took from your real parents and kept from me as a lever to raise their real whelp."

"Who were my real parents?" she pleaded with a sudden spike of hope. "I know nothing about them. Please tell me."

Dracula was suddenly at the window of the cell between eyeblinks, so quickly that she jumped back. His red-rimmed eyes filled the slot. "I will find the truth; I could enthrall you but to do so would dull the hidden memories, for I see that you do not realize you know what I need to know."

With no more comment, the nobleman turned and left.

The stunned girl rushed to the slot and called, "No, please, tell me about my parents. Tell me!" Dracula paused and turned, his smile feral and frightening.

"Tell you? It is you who will tell me many, many things. It is you who will strip your soul for me to gaze at and who will beg me to take all you have and more." He laughed leaving the girl to sob in desperation.

Chapter Thirty: In the Devil's Domain

Bob Howard stood on the plain before the Castle of the Dracul filled with apprehension. He had forced himself, at Magda's insistence, to wait for actual sunrise before venturing across the valley to the steep and narrow path that led to the fortress.

He had also decided to leave his precious typewriter behind with his other gear at the Gypsy woman's *vardo* and, not surprisingly, that case's absence at his side made him feel like he'd left a limb behind. He grinned as he thought, *I suppose it's a phantom limb all us storytellers have.*

The realization then came to him that the absence of that case was not half as disturbing as the thought that Gwendolyn was not at his side as he ventured up the path toward the castle—or the fact that he might indeed find her in such a place.

He thought about the old Romany and her *taltos* companion, both knowing their days were short as they progressed into the winter of their lives yet moving on with courage. *Death to the old is inevitable*, he thought, imagining himself talking to Gwendolyn, *and yet somehow, I often feel that it is a greater tragedy than death to the young. When a man dies young, he misses much suffering, but the old have only life as a possession and somehow to me the tearing of a pitiful remnant from weak old fingers is more tragic than the looting of a life in its full rich*ness.

He had a flash, a whimsy of a dream, that saw himself and Gwendolyn in the far future, side by side on some porch, looking over some fertile valley. He felt both joy and a little fear at the image as he thought, philosophically and with typical Gaelic melancholy, *I don't want to live to be old. I want to die when my time comes, quickly and suddenly, in the full tide of my strength and health.* Then he looked up once more at the ominous castle. *I might just get my chance.*

Even with the warming sun's light, the area around the castle was shrouded in gloom; the rough trail, barely wide enough for a wagon, was in deep shadow all the way up to the plateau where the castle stood.

Howard had read all of Mina Harker's journal several times and knew his enemy better for it. He read of Jonathon Harker's imprisonment in the very castle he was approaching, of three vampire brides in thrall to Dracula and Mina's own mesmeric enslavement that followed. Was something of that fate awaiting Gwendolyn? He tried to put it out of his mind, but it was constantly there.

Howard had learned of the Wallachian nobleman's attempt to invade England to bring his plague of vampirism to that sceptered isle and, through the intercession of Abraham Van Helsing, being forced to flee back to his Carpathian Mountain stronghold.

Howard put a hand on the Bowie knife at his hip, the one that fellow Texan Quincy Morris had plunged through the lord vampire's black heart. Now Dracula's followers might have Gwendolyn. The Texan knew he was walking into the lion's den, and he was glad to do it for the lady's sake.

Howard assessed the fortifications with a historian's eye. *No attacking force could catch them by surprise,* Howard thought as he dismounted and tied off his skittish mount to a bare shrub. *And a handful of men could slow an army to a crawl with them bottled up in that pathway up here.*

He stood trapped between the solemn purpose in being there to look for Gwendolyn and his awe at the history of the place.

Howard looked behind him at the plain below, visible from the wide ledge before the castle proper. He knew that on that plain, the monster called Vlad the Impaler had once executed ten thousand human beings, hoisting them on sharpened stakes to die horrid, lingering deaths while he ate lunch among the carnage.

No wonder the Roma and the villagers consider this place evil. He was a hero to his people for driving the Ottoman Turks out, but even his own people feared his ferocity and sadism. The Germans considered him so bloodthirsty they thought him in league with the devil.

The Texan left his mount tethered behind the fold in the land to keep it concealed from the castle proper and moved toward the ominous structure. He was glad he had his grandfather's six-gun holstered under his arm and the Bowie knife on his belt.

Every step closer to the dark stone of the fortress seemed to increase the writer's anxiety, sending chills up his spine.

This is wrong. I'm letting my imagination run away with me. He laughed and out loud said, "Easy, Bob, lead and steel always take down spooks; if it can hurt me, I can hurt it."

Nevertheless, he moved slowly, alert for any danger, his own pep talk having not dispelled the sense of foreboding and doom that seemed to settle around the building like a miasma.

The most eerie part of the experience was the dead silence all around—no birds sang, no breeze stirred the stunted foliage. The very air hung heavy with menace.

The remains of the moat, now little more than a wide ditch partly filled with brush and rubble, foretold the state of the interior of the building. The drawbridge was down, indeed, the mechanism to raise it was rusted and clearly had not been used in many years.

The Texan eyed the boards of the walkway with skepticism, testing each with a tentative step, worried the decaying wood might not hold his burly form.

"Gwendolyn girl, you are impulsive and brave, but coming up here was not a good idea," he whispered aloud as he passed under the stone archway into the fortress.

The sun had no power in the courtyard of the castle. The shadows ruled there—they were deep and black as night.

Howard halted at the arch of the entrance and surveyed the open space ahead. A gallery ran around the courtyard, which like the rest of the castle, was hoary with age and in disrepair. Gaping windows like soulless eye sockets looked down on the Texan and made his skin crawl.

He tested that his six-gun was loose in the holster before stepping from the arch to expose himself by entering the open space. He felt as if a hundred eyes were watching him from the dark pits of the windows, though in the rational part of his mind he knew that was not the case.

Or is it? Comanches could be having a party up there in all that space. Why not Gypsies?

He did his best to not race across the space, to keep his steps appearing casual, but with each step, he felt as if he were about to trigger a land mine. He had never felt more exposed or vulnerable and sighed in relief when he achieved the castle with no incident.

The massive door of the main entrance to the castle great hall would have been unmovable had it not been ajar. The Texan squeezed into the entrance and waited for his eyes to adjust to the gloom within.

The entrance hall to the castle was huge and weakly illuminated by shafts of light that struggled through the ruined windows high up on the inner wall of the building. There was a broad staircase that rose into the indistinctness of a second floor and archways that yawned into the darkness of the interior ground floor of the keep.

"Not too bright of me not to bring a flashlight," Howard whispered. When he felt his eyes were as adjusted as they would be he moved off slowly, heading up the stairs. "Might as well go where the light will do me some good."

The stairs were stone and though they showed age they were solid. Howard's boot falls echoed loudly despite his attempt to creep.

I guess I'll make a bad Comanche after all.

At the top of the stairs he moved into a wide corridor that truly showed the decay of the building, as each room he came to was festooned with cobwebs and what little furniture was left—the heavy pieces that could not be carted away by looters— was showing wood rot. In all, there was not even the scurry of rats or hint of any other form of life. As the search progressed the Texan was torn between a desperate hope to find some sign of Gwendolyn and hope that he would not find her in such a vile place.

Though the place was empty there was a sense of wrongness, a miasma aura of lingering evil to it that made the hair on the back of Howard's neck stand on end. As if every stone of the building had absorbed and retained the essence of all the evil that had happened there, so long ago.

It was the same in room after room. *Ain't no one been here for a long time, and I can see why—this place is pure Weird Tales territory, like something Howie Lovecraft would write about for sure.* He stood at the top of the staircase as the shafts of light increased angle, their weak light now tinged with gold, and debated his next move.

"Never forgive myself if I left and didn't see what's down below," he said with a sigh, "and I don't want to come back tomorrow. Gotta risk it." He started down the steps, then thought better of it and went back into the third room he'd investigated where the remnants of a couch were left. He pulled a leg off it and then wrapped some of the couch's stuffing's around the end, using matches from his pocket to light it and create an ad hoc torch.

"That will have to do," he said when it was lit. He brandished it to be sure it was solid, watching the flickering shadows dance around the disused room then turned and descended the steps to walk through the ground floor of the castle.

Almost immediately he found signs of recent occupation on the first floor's rear rooms—places on the floors where the dust had been disturbed or cobwebs moved aside.

Howard stopped and listened. At first, he heard only the wind's faint moan through the empty windows of the building but then, faintly he heard the muffled sounds of voices.

He crept forward, the six-gun in his hand now, holding the torch low and to the side so it had less chance to 'announce' his arrival. The voices came from a door that was slightly ajar.

Howard put the torch behind him and realized there was a faint, flickering light coming from the doorway.

"There you go," he whispered. He came to the edge of the door and peered beyond to see stairs that went down to a subterranean chamber. Somewhere down below another torch was burning and vague shapes danced and writhed on the stone walls.

Howard paused, able to identify the voices now—a man's voice, low and guttural and a woman's, shriller. He could still not make out the exact words, but it sounded like an argument. It was hard for the Texan to keep from charging down the stairs yelling for Gwendolyn, yet he knew he had to keep to stealth 'til he knew the reality of what was below.

Howard set the torch down and slipped into the space beyond the door to descend a wide set of curving stone steps. The echoes of the stone space distorted the words of the speakers so he could not even tell what language they were speaking in. Nothing was discernible but that it was a woman and a man in angry conversation.

Dungeon! Howard smiled. *No castle is complete without one.*

Near the bottom of the stairs, a single torch blazed in a wall sconce and set the shadows dancing madly. They lapped across the dark opening of a narrow corridor, sending a sliver of flickering torchlight slithering across the stone floor like a tentacle of some eldritch beast.

Howard flattened himself against the wall, holding his breath as he inched toward a doorway down the narrow hallway from which the voices originated. The Texan took a deep breath, pushed the door in and vaulted through the doorway, yelling, "Stick 'em up!" and feeling a bit silly as he did as if he were in one of his pulp stories.

Chapter Thirty-One: Return of Evil

"But I don't know anything," Gwendolyn called after Dracula. "I would tell you to be free."

"You do not know what freedom is." The Wallachian prince turned back and said, "I fought for the freedom of my country. I cut the bonds of mortal life to free myself from the oppression of time. I know freedom."

"Please," Gwendolyn sobbed. "Please."

"My freedom was taken from me centuries ago," Dracula said. "I spent years in an Ottoman dungeon. Then I regained my freedom when I was given the powers of the dark arts; when I learned that life was in the blood." His eyes reflected red like a wolf's eyes in the torchlight.

"But over the years I was opposed, my own people turned against me, hounded me, forgot what I had done for them, and the Turks invaded and occupied Budapest. I was forced to sleep, to rest and wait."

The nobleman lowered his voice so it was barely a whisper. "It was long before I could regain my strength but then I set my sights upon your little island. Jonathon Harker was the wedge to drive through the armor of your kingdom, and then his wife who I made mine."

His features twisted to a savage expression. "But that damned Dutchman foiled me, and I was driven to flee; me, who faced the might of the Mohammedans!" He clutched at his heart. "They drove a blade into my chest."

Gwendolyn gasped and this made her jailer laugh. He grabbed his own throat in a caressing gesture. "But though they burned my body and buried me, my faithful Romany gathered my remains and drained the blood of virgin sacrifices to feed me back to this mirror of life. I was reborn to my current undead state. When I returned to my castle it was looted, my treasures gone." His eyes narrowed in anger and his features became those of a predator.

"That Harker woman, she had the key to the wealth I need to renew my assault on that damned island of yours, and now..." He hissed, raising his voice in anger. "You have, somewhere in your memories, that same key, whether you know it or not. And I will have it!"

The scene in the room Howard entered was nothing like what he expected. A Romany woman was seated on a dilap-idated divan, gesticulating wildly at the Gypsy Dimitri that Howard had encountered in the village.

"Hold it there, varmint," Howard ordered. "You and I have some talking to do. I'm looking for someone."

The arguing couple were frozen by the sudden appear-ance of the Texan but a third Gypsy, standing off to the side of the stone-walled room—behind the arc of the opening door—was not.

The third Romany moved as Howard spoke and smashed a chair down on the writer's extended gun hand, knocking the weapon from his grasp. As the gun skittered to the floor Dimitri reacted by drawing a long thin blade from his waist sash.

"Now we gut you, gadji dog," Dimitri said with a satis-fied growl. "He is mine, Gorge," he called to the other Romany then advanced with delicious anticipation on his features.

Bob Howard cursed once when the chair smashed into his hand but wasted no time on recriminations or his own pain. Instead, he sprang at Gorge as Dimitri took his first step forward.

The burly Texan slammed into the shorter Romany and bowled him over. The two men rolled across the rough stone floor. The surprised Gypsy had no chance to draw his own knife and spent all his energy resisting the superior strength of the writer.

Dimitri was on the pair of wrestlers before they had rolled a full rotation but could not lash out with his knife for fear of stabbing his friend.

"Hold him, Gorge!"

"I am trying," the Romany yelled but could barely force the words out as he used most of his strength just keeping the Texan from throttling him.

Howard kept the struggling man close to him and worked to keep Gorge between him and Dimitri's flashing blade.

The Romany woman, meanwhile, had risen from her divan and produced her own slim blade. She charged across the room but discovered she could find no better position to attack Howard than could Dimitri.

The Texan realized that his situation was growing more dire with each labored breath as the Romany slipped his hands in to choke him, so he let Gorge roll on top of him. Then the Texan tensed his massive arms and bucked his whole body to launch the Gypsy into the air. Gorge smashed into Dimitri and the two tumbled back into a food-laden table.

Howard attempted to rise but the woman was upon him with her poniard darting at him like a striking viper. He barely avoided a slash at his head and shot a muscular hand out to grasp her wrist.

"Easy, ma'am, I just had a haircut last month."

He made his way to his feet but found he had grabbed a tiger's tail with the woman's arm. She clawed at him with her free hand and snarled like a trapped beast.

Howard had no time to be subtle; he could see the two men regaining their feet, so he pulled the girl to him, grabbed her around the waist and bodily hurled her across the room, aiming her at the divan. She landed hard enough to knock the wind out of her and leave her stunned.

Howard whirled to face the two Romany but now he was aware of what he faced, and he pulled the Bowie knife he'd gotten at the Harker estate.

"Tell me where the English lady is, fellas, and we can avoid all this."

The two Romany split, moving to flank the Texan but he did not let them get to the periphery of his vision before he slashed toward Dimitri on his right.

"Okay boys," Howard gave a warrior grin. "If that's the way you want it, let's see how you do when you're face to face with a fella instead of bushwhacking him."

As Howard expected Gorge immediately lunged at the writer's back. Snake-quick the Texan whirled from his feint and cut Gorge on the back of his knife hand, disarming him.

Dimitri went for Howard's exposed back but again, the tactical mind of the Texan had anticipated the sneak attack. Instead of holding position or pivoting back at the second attacker, Howard charged into the wounded man, slamming his shoulder into the man's sternum to send him flying against the stone wall.

This gave Howard room to maneuver. He waited to spin and face Dimitri till there was a good six feet between the two men.

"The Master will reward me for your head," Dimitri hissed with a triumphant smile on his face.

"The master?" Howard asked, "What master?"

"The only Master," Dimitri snarled. "He who was dead but returned. He who will make us all richer than any *gadji,* that will raise us Romany once more to kings of the earth. The Son of the Dragon, Dracula."

Howard's features were stoic as he steeled himself to do what must be done to save Gwendolyn. He took a breath and quoted one of his poems in a quiet voice, "*Raven-father, If I fall, Let me do it face to foe, Let the skalds sing, Of this wondrous thing— Of A warrior who loved And lived In the shade of his fear Yet stepped forward to embrace The battle crow…"*

The calm of the Texan seemed to unnerve the Romany, who glanced at Gorge, but the wounded man was moaning and holding his bleeding right hand.

Howard noted the glance. "Just you and me, Hoss, *mano-e-mano*. You got the stones to look me in the eye and throw down?"

Now the Texan let a smile slide across his lips, but it was the cold expression that had terrorized the Romans when they faced the Celts of Gaul or the English when they landed in Ireland.

The Romany's confidence drained from his expression, but not his determination to see the attack through. He growled and sprang forward with a slash of his blade.

Howard knew Dimitri's long, slender, double-edged knife was a fighting knife; its only purpose was to kill. He also knew that the design of the weapon emphasized thrusting over slashing.

The Texan had a traditional nine-inch Bowie knife, a wide, heavy blade with a thick spine and a clip point that gave him the capability to stab though it was more specially suited to chopping slashes. The legend had it that Jim Bowie had the knife designed to allow him to fend off swords in duels which is why it had a thick spine to handle the impact of sword blows.

It was clear to the writer that however fearful the Gypsy might be of the Texan he had experience with knife fights. He held his blade close to his body, his left hand extended to shield the knife and prevent any chance of it being knocked from his hand, not at all the 'fencing' like stance one sees in films. Any real knife fighter would take a forearm cut rather than lose his weapon.

It's all theoretical with me, Howard allowed himself to muse. Howard's grin got wider but with no humor left in it, only the fatalistic Celtic joy at living in the moment and to the limit. He had played with swords with friends, had many bare-knuckle icehouse fistfights and witnessed several real knife fights on the muddy streets twice back in Cross Plains. He knew any real-world knife fight would be a quick and bloody affair, with all those involved often cut up like so much meat.

"This ain't gonna be a long dance. Better get to it!"

Chapter Thirty-Two: The Long Road

Howard realized if the two men closed there would be blood for certain and Howard could be out of it, done with his quest and he might not be able to continue. Yet, the Texan knew he had to push on forward, had to survive, not for himself but for Gwendolyn. So he decided to go against his own nature and follow through on his challenge—to face off directly and as two warriors.

"Last chance, Hoss," Howard said in a flat tone. "We stop this now and you take me to the English lady, and I'll let you walk away from here."

"So," Dimitri spat, "you have come for the English slut?"

Howard snarled a curse, broke all the rules and threw his Bowie underhanded with all his might. The heavy knife was not aerodynamic and never meant to be thrown, but his fury at the insult was such that he threw with velocity so that the blade flew straight at the Gypsy as if fired from a rifle.

Dimitri had no choice but to try and dodge the blade and at the same time try to ward it off with his own knife. He only half succeeded with both.

The Bowie struck the Romany with the flat of the blade on his right shoulder. He was not cut, but by then it did not matter, because the Texan was on him with stone-hard fists.

Dimitri had no chance at all to raise a defense and went down, unconscious under the barrage of irate Texas knuckles. Only then did Howard's fury at the insult spend itself and he backed away from the prostrate man, turning to face Gorge and the girl.

"Now you two folks are gonna take me to where Miss Harker is before I get really angry," Howard said. "And watch your language."

Gorge's cries of pain had dropped to a steady sob and the girl was on her feet now, her own knife in hand and a savage expression on her face. She looked at the Texan as he picked up his knife and his six-shooter and decided to stay her fury.

"Why should we help you?" the girl said in heavily-accented English. Her cat-like eyes darted from Howard to the door, but he saw her intent and stepped to the portal, pushing it closed with his back.

"Because if you don't I will tear this place down around your ears looking for her and that will just be the start. You don't want to make me get upset. I ain't pleasant when I'm upset."

The Romany woman folded her arms and stared at the Texan with venom in her expression.

She's calling my bluff. There was no way he would strike the woman, at least not in cold blood and she sensed it. He stared back at her trying to think how to apply leverage on either of the two Romany then he noticed something.

"No!" He raced across the room so quickly she recoiled and gasped when he snatched at the choker she was wearing, yanking it from her neck violently.

"Where did you get this?" he snapped, holding the choker up for her to look at. It was the cameo that Gwendolyn treasured as the only real link to her real mother, the one she had said she'd had since she was a little child.

"It is mine!" the Romany girl yelled back.

"It was Gwen's," Howard said through gritted teeth. "She always wore it—she would never take it off of her own accord. Where is she?"

The aspect of the burly writer was suddenly so frightening in his fear for the kidnapped girl that the Romany blurted out, "Budapest!"

"Budapest?" he said. "She's not here?"

"No," she continued. "When we sent word to The Master we had captured her here and he found out who she was he had us bring her to him."

"Your master—Dracula?"

"Dracula!" she said like it was a prayer. "He is unbeatable."

"He wasn't here?"

"No, he has been there on some mission for months. We only stayed to keep others from defiling his home. He says he will rebuild it to the glory it once was in our grandparents' time. I believe him. He will and then you gadji will bow down to us." Her eyes shone with religious fervor and the Texan knew she was telling him the truth as she knew it.

"Where in Budapest?" Howard asked.

"I do not know," the woman pleaded. "I swear on my mother."

The Texan nodded then stepped away from the Romany, back to the door to open it.

"You all stay nice and calm now and keep yourself in here. You stick your head out this door anytime soon and I'll blow it off, either one of you." He pointed at the still unconscious Dimitri. "And you tell your pal there this is the last time I see him with any conversation; next time I see his ugly face I just shoot first; no talking at all."

Howard backed out of the room and sprinted up the stairs, his mind already racing ahead to how he would get to the Hungarian capital and how, in the vast city, he had any chance of finding the kidnapped girl before it was too late to save her from the undead monster called Dracula!

"Dracula," Father Janos said in a breathless tone. "I was afraid it was so; the evil has returned."

"But in Budapest," Magda said.

Father Janos said, "I have not been there in two decades, but it is a city with much history and the home of one of the greatest of the *taltos* of tradition, Kampo." The old priest leaned forward, gripping the arms of the chair, his blind eyes staring off into memory. "They say he ate lunch in Buda at the same table as King Matthias and was always poorly dressed. Many asked the King why such a pauper was eating at the same table as he, but King Matthias insisted on this tradition for he knew that a *taltos* was the spiritual defender of our homeland."

Howard had told Magda and the priest what he had learned, and they had once more persuaded the Texan from immediately leaping on his horse to race off for the nation's capital.

"You must plan," Magda said. "You are facing an evil larger than any one man can combat; an ageless foe who will have prepared well."

"I can't just do nothing," Howard protested. "Sitting around here I'll lose my mind." He held up the cameo that was Gwendolyn's that he had taken from the Romany girl. "Gwen needs me."

"Yes, my impetuous American," the priest said, "but you will do her no good if you fall before the first encounter with the dark one. You must plan to confront him in whatever lair he has occupied."

The Texan collapsed into a chair and listened while the priest continued, "When the Turkish army attacked the Kingdom of Hungary, Kampó, so the story goes, spewed fire from his mouth and he fought with his iced body against Turkish metal. I was never so strong a *taltos,* my writer friend, but in my heart, I know you can be. For the fire of your prose may serve you as much as the steel of your thews."

"I trust my good right arm as well, Padre," Howard said, "and sure as shootin' my Celtic gift of gab is strong, sir, but Magda is right; I'm going against something bigger than I ever imagined existed outside of Howie Lovecraft's tales, or the secret letters he wrote to me and said to burn. He knew things, things I only saw as legend and myth. He somehow knew they were real; that a monster like Dracula could be real. But I've seen in Mina Harker that this kind of evil is real and vile as life can be."

"That is the strength of so much of the evil of the world," the priest said. "The sane, the modern 'sane' world thinks of all the dark remnants of mankind's past as fantasy, myth— a child's dark imaginings; but that is not so. As there is a higher power that I believe in with all my heart there is a lower—the darkness—the evil forces of the devil that I fight with all my being. Both are as real as the bullets and bombs of modern man."

The priest reached out and his feeble hand grabbed Howard's and the grip was suddenly strong. "But you are an agent of the light and that higher power, my friend. With our prayers and with planning you will bring the forces of good to bear on this ancient evil and perhaps, with God's good help, we can finally bring an end to it for good."

"A man's only weapon is courage," Howard said, quoting one of his own stories, "that flinches not for Hell itself, and against such not even the legions of Hell can stand."

The old priest smiled. "The Lord has sent the very one to confront Dracula and win, I think."

"Amen to that, Padre," Howard said. "I sure hope so."

Chapter Thirty-Three: Amongst the Enemy

A low dense mist spread from the cold surface of the midnight Danube and crawled up over the banks like a sentient being. On the west bank, its tendrils barely made it up the steep slope and crawled only a few blocks into the hilly Buda Castle district before fading to a ghostly dew. On the east bank, the thick mist moved unhindered along the flat terrain of Pest, winding through the narrow, twisting streets like tendrils of some eldritch creature seeking prey.

Those streets were deserted at that hour, the shutters of the homes closed tight against the rising wind, the damp cold and a deep-seated fear of the legends of the country. These legends had spawned a new terror that had come to the city recently.

Ellena Czeny was well aware of that new terror, yet she had to leave the house and move up Jozef Varos Street to the Center Market to prepare her family's stall for the next day's sales. Her brother would normally do it, but he was sick with a cold and could not. She was next oldest so it fell to her to open the linen stall. He had tried to argue with her not to go, but he had not the strength to stop her, his fever having weakened him. She had left extra early as she did not have experience setting up by herself.

The girl walked rapidly through the narrow, twisting streets, constantly looking over her shoulder. Had anyone been watching, even a casual viewer would have seen clearly that she was terrified.

There was no one on the street, however. The windows were shuttered and the only sounds other than her footsteps on the damp cobbles were the distant sounds of boats on the busy Danube River. Through the fog, from across the river, the muffled sound of the bustling nightlife of the unafraid Buda District was dream-like in the darkness.

Ellena carried the newest batch of tatting to add to the stall's wares in the basket suspended by a strap on her shoulder and now she held it to her tightly as if to find comfort from it. She tried not to think of the reason the streets were deserted. "Blessed Mother," she prayed aloud, fingering the rosary her grandmother had given her, "keep me in your arms this night."

"You are always in her arms, my dear." A voice from the shadows startled the girl so that she dropped her basket and jumped.

"Do not be afraid, my dear," the stranger that emerged from the darkness said in a soothing voice. He spoke in Hungarian and had a cultured voice though his accent was a country one and his phrasing almost ancient in construction. "There was no intent on my part to startle or upset you."

The stranger was a thin, older man who was dressed lightly for the cold with only an old black frock coat. He had a hooked nose, and a mustache and pointed beard that had a single streak of white in it.

He smiled and his eyes, though intense, were warm and inviting.

"Oh, sir," Ellena said with relief at the obviously cultured man whose calm manner put her at ease. "I did not see you, sir."

"It is quite alright, my dear," the stranger said with a gentle tone. "The night is dark and the streets strangely quiet."

"Have you not heard about the killings?" she asked in a hushed whisper. As she spoke she looked around in fear.

"Killings? No," he said, his voice had the effect of calming her fears. "I am new to the city of late." He smiled, brushing his long white mustache with the back of his hand. "Well, not new to it, exactly, but I have not been back here for many years, so it all seems new to me."

She picked up her basket and shouldered the strap and began moving again toward the Market Center. The silver-haired man walked beside her with an easy, relaxed stride that was oddly quiet, his feet making no sound on the cobbled street.

"It is because of the killings that no one is out this night," she said. She felt at ease with the well-dressed man, as if he were an old friend whom she could confide in. "Three girls have been found dead in the last month on these very streets." She crossed herself.

"May I help you with your burden?" the stranger offered. Before she could answer he took the basket from her. "We may walk more quickly this way," he said with a smile that went all the way to his intense eyes.

"Thank you," she said, blushing a little at his attention.

"Tell me more about these terrible things."

"I know the cousin of one of the dead girls, Jenna Bodi," she said. "He told me that the girls were all found with their throats horribly torn, as if—as if by the talons of some wild animal."

"Ah," the stranger said with a satisfied nod of his head. "A wild animal. Yes, that is exactly what the authorities would let themselves believe, and of course it is why the throats *were* torn."

"What do you mean?" Ellena stopped at the corner of a street, the yellow light of an ancient gas streetlamp suddenly reflected in the eyes of the stranger so that they captured her stare like flaming beacons.

"Well, my dear," he said. "I did not want the authorities to suspect my presence here; not yet."

"Your—" She began but the words stuck in her throat as the meaning of his statement dawned on her. It was then she tried to scream but the eyes of her killer held her frozen as surely as if her throat was gripped by his long-fingered hands. Then he dropped the linens to the ground and sprang on her.

The weight of Dracula bore the girl to the ground as he sank his fangs into the throbbing food source of her jugular vein to feed.

\#

"You are the man from America?" A muffled voice came from behind the thick door. It was a sunny day on the small street off Szilagyi Erzsebet, in the City of Budapest. The streets in the castle district were all narrow and cobbled and it had taken Bob Howard more than an hour to find the address that Father Janos had given him in the maze. It was four days after his fight in Dracula's castle.

"If you count Texas as from America," the writer said with a chuckle. "Father Janos sent word I was coming?"

"Yes," the voice said. It was accented, but not with a Hungarian accent as the writer had expected but distinctly French. The door opened and the voice said, "Come in, *monsieur*."

The Texan entered and the door was quickly shut behind him. After the bright sunlight, the space within was dark and he had to blink for a few moments till his eyes adjusted and he could see his host.

"You made good time in coming, *Monsieur* Howard."

"Holy smokes!" he exclaimed when he saw who greeted him. "Sorry, Sister!" he quickly added as he removed his Stetson.

Before him stood a petite nun in a white habit and wimple. Her cloth-framed face was lit in a warm smile and might have belonged to a woman of thirty or sixty.

"I am Sister Maria," she said. "Janos was not clear in his telegram; he only said that you were here to continue his work as a *taltos*."

"You, uh, know about his work? About that?"

The religio waved the Texan inside what Howard now saw was a small curio shop. He was led through the shop to a curtained doorway beyond which was a small sitting room.

There were several chairs, a bookshelf filled with leather-bound volumes and a table set for a meal.

"You will join me for midday tea?"

"Uh, sure, ma'am," he said. "Thank you." He set his typewriter and suitcase down, removed his jacket and sat in an offered chair. When he did he noticed the sister's gaze went to the shoulder holster he wore.

"Oh, I'm sorry ma'am, but—"

"Do not apologize, Mister Howard," she said. "I know of many of Janos's adventures—of the many battles he fought in the name of the Lord in years past." She sat down opposite Howard and proceeded to pour tea for the two of them. "I cannot help but think that he has sent you here because of the recent deaths."

"Deaths?"

"Four young women have been found dead in Pest—across the river—in the last month," the nun said. "The most recent girl was found murdered last night." She poured him tea and the Texan lifted the cup that looked tiny in his meaty hand.

"I don't mean to be cold, Sister. But deaths in a large city like this—"

"Sadly true, there is evil everywhere, but these girls were killed horribly, as if by some wild beast with their throats savagely torn."

She leaned forward and dropped her voice to a whisper. "These deaths were unusual in other ways in that it appeared a wild beast killed them in the middle of the city, a wolf or wild dog. I have been told that there was no blood at the scene of the murders. None; though there should have been much." She crossed herself and shuddered at the image she had conjured with her words.

"Dracula," Howard murmured. The nun went white and crossed herself again.

"The cursed one!" she gasped. "That is why you are here?"

"Yes. He is why I am here; I did not know it for sure until a few nights ago but somehow he is back from the dead and killin' again." He then proceeded to tell the nun of his whole mission, of what had happened in England and all that had happened in Stregga.

She listened with frozen features, her tea untouched.

When he was done with his recitation she stood. "I will have to make some calls. There are others who must know of this and who will be able to help us; we cannot fight this horror alone."

She started to move to the front of the shop but stopped to look back with a smile.

"Father Janos was not alone in his fight in the old days, nor are you now. We will find your lady, Mister Howard and bring the monster of Wallachia into the cleansing light of the Lord."

"Amen to that, ma'am. Amen."

Chapter Thirty-Four: War in the Streets

There was no day or night in Gwendolyn Harker's cell. She was fed porridge, bread and cheese through a slot in the door by a taciturn Gypsy who never answered any of her entreaties. He only returned her pleas for freedom with a noncommittal grunt and a stony look.

Of the Wallachian Prince she saw nothing for three meal periods, which she judged to be at least two days. She once more searched the room minutely, inch by inch in hopes of finding her mother's brooch but concluded that it had been lost when she was captured by Dracula's underlings and that, even more than her incarceration, made her feel hopeless. She knew now, with a certainty, how Bob Howard felt as he waited for his moment in the arena in her parents' underground slaughter ground.

The fear of what to come gripped her heart like a clutching hand.

Time lay heavy on her hands with no way to mark its passage and she thought she might go mad from the silence and seeming hopelessness of her state. She wondered at prisoners who spent years incarcerated and it began to play on her mind. She fought the panic of the thought that she might be locked up for a long time and pushed it from her mind.

Robert will find me. Somehow he will find me.

She distracted herself by exploring her cell in detail but found no obvious means to affect an escape, nor any objects she could fashion into a weapon. The bed was a stone platform piled with straw, the toilet 'facility' a small hole in the stone floor and her water supply was in a stone basin built into the wall and filled from the outside of the cell with a slow drip.

"Oh Robert," she said as she sat on the primitive bed and sobbed in despair. "I was a fool; I should have waited for you to come with me."

Her thoughts of the Texan brought a wry smile to the disheveled woman's face. She tried to do what he had told her in one of their conversations. "*You gotta focus when things are darkest on something light; it was all that I could do some days to put words to paper when Mama was dyin', but she used to tell me, 'Son, the hope is in the poetry, in the words,' so that is what I've set my stock by and it got me this far.*"

Gwendolyn set her mind to remembering a poem Bob had sent her in a letter. She visualized the words in his bold handwriting, as he always wrote the letters to her by hand to make them more personal, and then recited one of them out loud.

"*Battle Crow, my lover, calls, Across the field of jarls, Where brandished swords and great shield walls, Are beckoning me fall., My cry to her is loud and clear, My heartfelt hail of lust, My charge is swift, my axe is sure—Its keen edge holds no rust; The bouquet that I send to her, Is red and bright and warm, A gift of precious life she craves, 'Fore she will take me home, So, lover, hold me in your arms, Enfold me in your wings—Transport me to the drinking halls, To sup w' warrior kings!*"

"Bravo!" The voice of Dracula startled the prisoner from her reverie. The Wallachian's piercing eyes were like burning orbs staring at her from the small window in the door. "Proud words; warrior words. Whose words are they?"

She shot to her feet and set her shoulders back, announcing with pride, "They are the words of Robert Ervin Howard of America, Prince. He is—he is my friend."

"Ah," Dracula said, his voice like a well-aged wine. "*A gift of precious life.*" He laughed softly. "It is good your friend understands life and death so clearly, for to understand them is to value both. He was the one you sent the papers to in Paris?"

She gasped. "How—"

The Wallachian laughed softly. "I know all that goes on in my domain, my dear. I do not know what you sent, but once I knew who you were I had you watched—my fool agent did not think to stop the packages you sent, but he did find out to whom they were destined. Fortunately, I have agents in many places; I can tell you that your poet received the packages."

"You did not have him harmed?"

Again the laugh that was like an animal growl. "My Paris-based Romany agents failed to obtain the package you sent, and your 'poet' escaped with them. They regained his trail while he was on a train but once more he was lucky, this poet, and he escaped. So far they have lost track of him."

Now it was Gwendolyn who laughed a laugh with hope in it. "He will not stop until he finds me," she proclaimed.

"You have much faith in this poet; trust me, Madam, I do not fear poets."

"You should,' she said. "He is from Texas and not at all what most think him to be."

"He, like you, are cattle to me," the Wallachian said. "But you can be allowed to hope; hope is good. I have hope myself to regain what is rightfully mine. The treasures of the past will restore the glories of yesterday, I will have again what was mine. And you will help me with that."

"I told you," she pleaded, "I do not know what you want from me."

The face in the window disappeared for a moment then the sound of a bolt sliding back made Gwendolyn gasp.

The door opened and Dracula entered slowly as if floating across the floor at her in a nightmare.

"You will help me, dear lady whether you wish to or not," the Walachian said. "For I know you have—inside your mind and memories—just what I need to rise once more to my true position."

With that, the pale nobleman advanced on the woman with a predatory smile.

Within two hours of his arrival at the curio shop, Bob Howard sat in the back room with the nun and four others she had contacted to help him hunt Gwendolyn and the monster that had kidnapped her.

The Texan was surprised that most of them were his age or younger, with only one gray-hair that seemed old enough to have worked with Father Janos in times past.

"I remember Janos as young and vital," said the older man, whose name was Karl. "He was fire and steel in those days. I, who was ten years his junior looked up to him for his devotion to The Lord and because he was a good man." He looked guilty when he added, "I was not with him that day when he fought the Dark One and lost his legs; now is my chance to be with him-."

"I have only heard of it," one of the others said. He was Andros, a young Hungarian with blond hair and a perpetual smile. "But I know in my heart it is a battle that must be fought. It is my time to help."

The other two were a brother and sister pair of Romany who sat quietly but watched all with intensity.

"Why are you here?" the Texan asked. "Not to be looking a gift horse in the mouth, but it is good to know things like that if it comes to a showdown."

The siblings, Ivan and Illyana, were barely in their twenties and it was the girl who spoke.

"Ivan and I, we are ashamed that our people have helped this monster, my—our father was one who was seduced by the promises of Dracula and became one of his disciples. My grandfather died while serving that monster in the fight against the men from England. Our father made us promise to reclaim our family honor. Now we can do it and avenge him by destroying that monster."

"There it is then," the Texan said. "We all got our reasons, and we have resolve, but what we don't have is a plan."

"How do we find this beast?" Illyana asked. "He is a cunning killer with as many years of hunting we of the light as all our ages combined."

"That's the key, sister," Howard said. He stood before a map of Budapest that he had asked the nun to furnish. Now he turned to it and his writer's mind began to whir and he could see the map as a thing alive.

"If we think of Dracula as a beast, a hunting animal, a predator," Howard said, "we hunt him like one. We track his hunting habits, mark his 'kills' and figure out the pattern—because there has to be one. Animals are creatures of habit. When we do that, we can find his lair."

"And then?" Andros asked.

"We put the animal out of his misery and ours, permanently!"

Chapter Thirty-Five: Death Hunt

The conclave of Dracula hunters went on for some time as they made plans for their campaign against the monster, deciding on what supplies they would need and debating the best method for tracking the midnight killer.

Howard decided that, first off, he wanted to see the actual places that the victims had been found.

"I figure the only way to really find Dracula is to see why he chose those spots, those women. Was it because of the location, was it because of who they were or some other factor."

"It is not safe to go to those places at night," Ivan spoke so softly it was almost a whisper. "Better to wait for daylight. I know where two of the girls were found."

"I will find out all the locations," Andros added. "I know a constable who likes his beer and I will meet him tonight to lubricate the information out of him."

"Ha," Howard said, "yup, people are the same all over. Okay, then tomorrow I will visit the sites of the murders and see for myself."

"And we will gather the supplies you suggested," Illyana said.

"I had better find me a place to bed down in the meantime," Howard said, "I confess, I am a bit tuckered after the last two days."

"That is not a problem, Mister Howard," Karl said. "This is my curio shop, and these rooms are mine—I will make up a bed for you in the storeroom."

"Good," Sister Maria said. "Then it is time for me to head back to the convent. Mother Superior is lenient with me, but I still have duties to perform." The nun stood and smiled. "And I think some extra prayers tonight are in order."

"I think we can all agree with you on that, ma'am, with no doubt at all," Howard said.

The darkness had settled on Pest with an abruptness and with it came an eerie silence as the city dwellers, now all aware of the series of murders despite lack of official confirmation, shuttered themselves in their homes.

No one walked the streets save the police force, now all at full alert and walking in pairs. The pall that fell over the town was thicker than the fog that crawled along its streets and even the police walked with fear in their steps.

The Bodi family lived in a small cottage on Koher Street off of Ohegy Park. Yarnia Bodi was a simple cobbler who had a comfortable business near the market district and rode his bicycle daily from his shop to home. Usually, he would come home for dinner and then bike back for a few more hours at his workbench.

Not this night.

His wife, Kitterina insisted that he stay home. He objected saying, "I am a man, I will be fine; and I have my tool bag and hammer with me, my kitten."

She shot back, "But I and Ivanka would be here alone."

And he could not argue with that.

The three, father, mother and their five-year-old daughter were sitting by the fireplace later that evening after a full meal and enjoying unexpected family time reading, when the knock came at their door.

"Who would be out at this hour?" Kitterina asked.

"We shall see, Kitten," Yarnia said. He put his newspaper aside and went to his tool belt from which he snatched up his hammer and walked to the door.

"Who is it?" Yarnia asked.

There was no answer save a second knock, more insistent this time.

The cobbler looked back at his wife who shook her head.

"Go to your room, Ivanka," Kitterina whispered.

"But Momma—"

"Go!"

The blonde girl rose, recognizing the 'do it now or else' tone in her mother's voice, so she closed her book and went into the back.

"Who is it?" Yarnia called louder at the door.

This time his admonition was met with silence.

When the cobbler moved to unlatch the door, his wife jumped up and stopped him.

"No. It could be some sort of trick."

"But what if someone needs help?" he asked.

"No!" she hissed. "They could yell to us or knock again."

"I have to see, Kitten." Yarnia slid back the bolt despite a gasp from his wife. He raised his hammer over his head and eased the door open a crack to glance out.

"Yarnia!" Kitterina whispered as she crossed herself.

After a long moment, the cobbler pulled the door open, and his wife saw that there was no one outside. He closed it quickly and rebolted it.

"I don't understand," he said.

"Leave it, husband, and come to bed. This is not right."

"Mama," Ivanka called from the doorway to her room. "The nice man at the window was cold."

The two parents turned to see the little girl holding the hand of a tall mustached figure dressed in black.

"She is very well mannered," Dracula said. "She invited me in to get warm. You should be very proud."

Then the Wallachian prince, Dracula, smiled to reveal his fangs and the killing began.

Despite being tired from his trip, Bob Howard could not sleep. The cot in the storage room in the back of the curio shop was not uncomfortable but the swirl of events of the last weeks was like a vortex of thought within him.

He thought back to Big Carney and his time in New York and tried to imagine how he would have reacted if he had magically appeared to tell his then-self what was to come. His world then was—while not what anyone would call mundane—not one peopled with blood-drinking monsters and the occult. Even though Howie Lovecraft's letters spoke of a dark and sinister world Bob had only half believed him. Now he knew that the shadows were deeper in the world than in some of the stories they both wrote.

In all the images hovering in the mist that kept play across the screen of Howard's mind, Gwendolyn's face was in the center. She was looking at him, pleading for his help. He recalled the look of fear on her face as she raced after her brother's horse and the joy in her eyes as she listened to him read his poetry to her for the first time.

He could not help but be afraid he was too late to help her, and that fear pierced him like a hot knife. When he had learned of the murders in Budapest, he had been terrified that he was already too late, but he took heart in the fact that the Gypsy had said he had been ordered to bring Gwendolyn to Budapest. There had to be a reason.

If Dracula wanted her harmed, why would he have her brought here? It has to do with her heritage, something that is connected to the Harkers or even her real parents, I'm sure, but what?

He fingered the cameo choker he'd found with the Gypsy girl and held it up to stare at it in the pale moonlight that streamed in through the window. He imagined the ivory cameo really was the image of Gwendolyn's real mother, for in studying it closely he could see a resemblance. The detail was lifelike and finely wrought so that it seemed captured between breaths.

Soon, however, he became fascinated with the intricate background behind the portrait. At first, it appeared to be just complex geometric shapes, but the more he stared at it the more there seemed to be a distinct and deliberate pattern to it.

But what is it a pattern of?

The parallel lines, the more he looked at them, seemed to be very specific, but he could not fathom what they meant. He fell asleep staring at the choker, dreaming that the ivory portrait came alive to be Gwendolyn and she was calling out his name, "Robert, Robert—I need you!"

He did not sleep well.

Chapter Thirty-Six: Revelations

Gwendolyn was startled when the door to her cell was yanked open and two Gypsies entered. The two of them had drawn knives and stared at the English girl with stoic intensity.

"What do you want?" she said. She stood, but she was tired and hungry and rising quickly made her dizzy, so she reached out to hold the wall and steady herself.

"Have a care, my dear lady," Dracula said as he glided into the corridor outside the room. "We do not want harm to come to you; at least not yet."

The Wallachian prince smiled and beckoned Gwendolyn out. "If you will please accompany my aides I would like to show you something."

Dracula looked less sallow than the girl had seen him before, and moved slowly, almost torpidly. His smile was languid and his eyes half-closed. It reminded Gwendolyn of a snake that had just fed.

"I will not tell you anything," she said.

Dracula laughed. "I don't want you to tell me anything you don't want to, dear lady." His eyes widened and bored into her with lambent intensity. "But do come out. Now!" He did not raise his voice, but she felt the strength of it reach into her soul and compel her to step through the door.

The nobleman walked ahead with Gwendolyn several steps behind and the two Romany guards flanking her. The narrow corridor was lit by naked electric lightbulbs. The nature of the walls changed as the corridor meandered, from set stone to roughly-carved naked rock. It was clear to Gwendolyn that they were also descending gradually into the earth. There was a low rumble that came from ahead, faint and low as if of distant thunder. Along the walls were large carved niches, empty, but it was clear they had held something—or someone.

Burial spaces, Like the catacombs beneath the Vatican. But why empty?

She had her answer after the entourage rounded a final curve and came out into a large chamber. It was at least two stories tall; what had clearly been a natural cave as big as a football field had been reshaped to a space much like a gallery. In the center was a large round fountain, clearly long disused and in ruins.

There were many dark openings leading to a dozen other corridors on two levels all around the large central space. Ladders led to the second tier. It was all lit by naked lightbulbs strung overhead that ran into the dark mouths of those openings.

In the center of the open space, piled in hideous stacks that reached to shoulder height around the destroyed fountain, were hundreds of human bodies. Mummified human corpses! Many had broken arms or legs and the remnants of richly colored clothing.

Across the space a half a dozen Romany with shovels and picks were moving around the space, climbing ladders or stringing more lights. Some had miner's helmets on. Standing apart from the bodies was a small pyramid of stacked boxes, each marked 'Danger Explosives.'

While Gwendolyn watched, several workmen dropped off new bodies and removed a stick of dynamite before heading back up one of the ladders with the stick. In a few moments, the men came running out of the corridor they had entered followed by a loud rumble and a fine spray of dirt propelled by a muffled explosion.

The whole scene, lit by the garish exposed bulbs, looked like a scene from Dante.

Dracula paused at the entrance to the large gallery, surveying all that was before him, hands on hips and his face lit with a satisfied smile.

The Wallachian prince turned to look at Gwendolyn. "They are all mine here, both living and dead." The implications of his statement made the woman gasp. "At least many of those," he pointed to the stacked mummies, "might be mine."

"But those explosives," Gwendolyn said. "Your men could be killed."

"What does it matter? They serve me—living or dead makes no difference. It is all for my purpose; this catacomb was used to hide the treasures of the city when the Ottomans laid siege to the city and conquered it in 1541. While the Turks occupied Budapest it sank to the level of a pitiful village, wretched hovels, unpaved streets, miserable mud-plastered fences, hogs wallowing in the streets."

Dracula's anger was palpable at his ancient enemies, almost a physical force that came off him. "For more than a hundred years the hated Turks occupied the city; in that time those who knew the secrets of where the monies were secreted died with their secrets. Many of the tunnels have collapsed and must be excavated, sometimes by explosives. Whatever it takes, I will have that treasure; it is only right I use it to restore myself. You will make that possible."

"I don't know—"

"Your real father was an architect hired to certify the stability of these tunnels and he made a survey of them—and in doing so he discovered the treasure. I know he had to have done so; that Harker woman who escaped me, she planned to use it someday to finance the ascendancy of her son through the White Glove Society on your island... thinking I was no longer a factor. Then when I returned to this semblance of life she kept that fact from me, or so she thought."

"But I do not know anything!"

Dracula ignored her plea and strode to a throne-like carved wooden chair set near the fountain in the center of the space. Behind it, resting on a raised platform was a long elaborately carved oak coffin, its lid open to reveal a brocade interior.

Beside the throne was a carved oak table covered with papers and charts. The nobleman sat in the chair with a self-satisfied sigh.

"You see, English lady, I know the human mind, intimately; in the recesses of yours is the key, it must be. Your real parents would have talked about such a find in your presence. So, I will find those words in your mind; I must. These fools I have searching have done nothing but blunder about in these tunnels for months."

Dracula waved a hand and two of the Romany seized Gwendolyn and pulled her to a stake that had been driven into the stone floor of the gallery. There was a long chain attached to it that ended in a steel collar. The two men forced the collar around her neck.

"Stop, stop," she screamed. "I know nothing, let me go!"

"You know and you *will* remember," the Wallachian said smugly. He sat back in his chair and basked in his coming triumph. "I became what I am when my desire to defeat the Turks caused me to call on dark forces, powerful forces that have given me many resources and powers. I am sure you saw some limited expression of them with your adoptive mother. I could make you my puppet, but that would not unlock the memories within your child-brain. Other means to ferret out the information might well leave you a vegetable. I am sure you do not wish that either. After all, I will be looking for new brides and you would not be an unfit replacement for the Harker woman!"

The intensity of his lambent eyes sent a chill down Gwendolyn's spine. "I will use all those methods to find the answer I wish if you do not give me what I want, but now I have fed well, I am among…old acquaintances," he waved at the piles of corpses, "and I am sure you will search your memories well for what I want before I have to resort to drastic steps."

Gwendolyn was stunned by the actions of the Romany and his words, and for a long moment after the collar was locked on her neck could not find her voice. Finally, she drew herself up and said, "If I knew anything about your treasure do you think I would ever tell a monster like you anything to further your plans?"

Dracula laughed softly. "It is good to have spirit; I like that in my brides, to a point." The Wallachian then turned his back on his prisoner to consult one of the maps on the table by his chair, dismissing her as if she were a chained pet.

"Robert," she whispered to herself as she sank to her knees. She tried not to cry at the sense of hopelessness she felt. "Please come soon; I am losing hope!"

Chapter Thirty-Seven: On the Track of Evil

Howard was up early, eager to investigate the sites of the murders in hopes of finding some clue to where Dracula might be holding Gwendolyn. He rode across the Danube to Pest on a bicycle with Ivan to show him the way. It was an adventure in itself with the Texan not having been on a bicycle since he was ten.

After several adventures with near falls and collisions, the two made it to the furthest of the locations. The intention was to work backward toward Buda from the sites, hoping at each site to find some hint of their prey.

"Gotta hunt him like the animal he is," Howard said. "And the best way to track a predator is to learn his habits, see his hunting pattern and that will lead us to the lair."

Outside the home where the Bodi family were slaughtered, Howard discovered crowds of gawkers and a number of police officers.

"A whole family," Howard said with disgust while he and Ivan hung at the back of the crowd that had gathered. The morning was chilly and everyone was huddled in heavy coats against the cold, their collective breaths forming a small cloud over the gathering.

"I will see what I can learn," Ivan said with a mischievous grin. He moved to the front of the crowd like a ghost with true Gypsy skill. Howard stayed with the bikes and surveyed the street up and down.

Pest had little of the baroque facades of Buda across the river but was a solidly built city stretching out on the flat plain. Howard knew it had been ravaged by the Turks who tore down the older medieval churches and used the stone from them to build mosques. These had, in turn been torn down and the materials used to rebuild the churches. The narrow streets and wide boulevards spoke of age, of adventures and wars, plagues and history.

"And now," Howard thought as he looked back toward the river, "somewhere out there is a monster and he has the gal that has found her way into my heart." His frustration at being forced to plod along looking for clues when he wanted to rush to wherever she was galled the Texan. He stood savaging the handles of the bikes until Ivan returned sometime later to tell him the details of the murders.

"And you say the other murder victims were found on the streets?"

"Yes," Ivan said. "This was the first time such a thing happened inside a building."

"He is getting desperate, then. Not waiting for easy prey but actively hunting it down." He shuddered at the image of the dead family that Ivan had related to him, especially the little girl. "Let's get going," the Texan said. "Nothing more to learn here."

They remounted their bikes and rode to the next site. And the next.

By the time they approached the third of the murder locations Howard had begun to form a hypothesis about the undead prince's hunting patterns.

"All these sites are just off the main avenues, but they are all out here in Pest," Howard said as the two rested after surveying the last of the known sites that they attributed to Dracula's handiwork. "I think that his hiding place must be somewhere in Buda."

"Why do you say that?" Ivan asked.

"Dracula may be morally an animal, but he is a cunning one with human-level intelligence, right? I think he would be smart enough not to hunt near where he is hiding for fear of bringing heat down on himself. I think if we map out all the locations where he hunted, those spots should be farthest from his lair."

The Texan pulled over to the side of the road at the Chain Bridge that connected the hilly Buda district with flat Pest. Howard looked at a map of the city and pointed out to the Romany where all the murders were. "See," Howard said. "Everyone on major routes back toward Buda!"

"I see," Ivan said. "But how does that help us? It is said the undead ones cannot cross running water."

"Have you looked down there?" The Texan pointed over the side of the bridge. Below the Danube was a jagged sheet of white.

"I had not realized," Ivan said. "It does not freeze often, but still Buda is a large city; how will we find Dracula?"

"I don't know, Ivan." The Texan leaned against the bridge and stared out at the hills of Buda ahead of them trying to plan what to do next, how to narrow down his search when he saw a familiar face. Howard leaned in to conceal himself behind Ivan.

"That's one of Dracula's men," Howard whispered.

"Are you sure?" Ivan asked. "After all we all look alike to you Gadji."

Howard ignored the dig. "That's Dimitri. Him and I tussled face to face at Dracula's castle near Stregga."

The thuggish Romany was walking across the bridge talking with two others of his tribe, paying no attention to his surroundings.

"He might see me. You'll have to follow him," Howard said to Ivan.

"He will not see me," the Romany said with a smile.

"Don't take it for granted. He's a Gypsy too and a squirrely one."

"When I see where he goes what shall I do?"

"I'll go back to the curio shop and wait there," Howard said. "Call when he lights somewhere, but don't do anything—and keep yourself safe."

"Do not worry, American," Ivan said and opened his coat to show off a sheathed knife. "I am not a child."

"Never a thought, Ivan, but that bunch scares me; just take care. I'll mind your bike."

Then the Romany was gone into the crowd like a ghost before Howard had finished his statement.

Howard made his way laboriously back to the curio shop with both bicycles and had Andros contact the others of their little group to be ready. Within the hour they were all at the shop and waiting for the phone call from Ivan.

The Gypsy's sister was distraught at her brother following Dimitri, but Andros and Howard both reassured her that Ivan was more than up to the challenge.

"Your brother will be fine, "Howard told her. "You know there is no one better to track a Romany than a Romany."

She tried to put on a brave face, but the girl's concern did not disappear—especially when the last member of the group, Sister Maria arrived.

"Is it true, you have found him?" the petite nun said as she entered the curio shop.

"Not yet, sister," Andros said. The shop owner was loading six shells into the Winchester 42 pump action .410 grade with a full choke he had elected to use. He had spent much of the day specially preparing 3-inch shells for his own gun and special ammunition for the other shotguns the group had selected to use in their battle with the undead lord.

"But I thought—" she began.

"I saw one of his known deputies here by the Chain Bridge, Sister," Howard said. "Ivan was going to follow him and call here when he—"

Just then the phone rang.

For a moment no one moved, then Andros reached to pick up the receiver.

"Hello," he said. Everyone in the room held their breath while they listened. "Yes, yes, Ivan. Where? How can that— I know. You are sure he has not left? Alright, we will come right away." He then hung up and turned to face the expectant group.

"Well, where is he?" Ivanka asked.

"He said the man went into Saint Matthias Church and did not come out!"

"Dimitri went into the church?" Howard said. "How can that be—Dracula can't step foot on holy ground!"

"By the Blessed Virgin," sister Maria exclaimed. "I think I know what has happened—and where that monster is; he does not have to step onto holy ground—I think he is under it!"

Chapter Thirty-Eight: Holy War

Gwendolyn Harker felt like an animal on display as she sat chained by her neck to the stake. The Gypsy workmen continued, like drone ants, to drag out the ruined corpses of the dead of Budapest—blasting and digging in the side tunnels all around the   gallery. The workmen, for the most part, ignored her even after Dracula took to his coffin and closed the lid to allow him to 'sleep.'

"When the sun has set and my powers are once more at their peak," the Wallachian prince said, "then, dear lady we will begin deep discussions of what you know; I would suggest you reflect on your memories while I rest or unpleasantness is inevitable."

When he closed the lid to his wooden tomb two muscular Romany took up posts at its head and foot and made it clear by their attitude that they would defend it to their death.

Gwendolyn had never felt more alone.

Through long hours she watched as the Romany workers went about their graverobbing and ignored the prisoner, making a point, it seemed, to never even look in her direction or at the casket of their overlord. The guards of the coffin never spoke a word, nor, as far as Gwendolyn could tell, changed expression or posture the entire day.

Time weighed heavily and the tension worked on the prisoner's nerves so that eventually Gwendolyn slept, huddled on the ground, tethered to the stake by the collar.

She was awakened abruptly by sharp laughter and sat up to see the Romany Dimitri standing over her.

"You are not so proud now, are you English lady?" Dimitri said. "You and all your kind will learn to bow before the Romany people."

"You mean kneel before that monster you follow," Gwendolyn said. "Grovel like a dog as you do before him?"

The Romany darted forward and slapped the woman, knocking her to her knees with the violence of the hit. "You will not be so quick to speak when The Master is awake; you are nothing but a prized pet."

"And he will not be so happy with you for hurting his prize, will he, you traitorous two-faced thief!"

Dimitri raised his hand to strike her again, but she knelt defiant, thrusting her chin out at him. Something in her expression stayed his hand and his eyes darted to the coffin and the guards, who were watching the exchange with sharp glances.

"Bah," woman," Dimitri said, stepping away from her. "You are not worth the trouble." Then he laughed and sneered, "Neither was your cowboy."

"My cowboy?" She took a step toward her tormentor. "Bob! What do you know about him?"

The Gypsy knew he had hurt the girl with his statement and smiled. "The fool came looking for you at the castle of The Master."

"What did you do to him?" She moved forward until the chain stopped her.

Dimitri just laughed. "You will find out when I tell The Master." He turned to walk away but a voice as cold as the grave stopped him.

"What do you have to tell me about this poet-cowboy of Miss Harker's?"

The lord of the undead had risen from his coffin and was already standing beside it. He brushed some earth from his long coat and moved smoothly across the cave floor to his throne.

"Master," Dimitri mumbled and dropped to a knee, bowing his head.

"Speak!" Dracula insisted.

"The American came to your castle, Master; he was searching for the girl."

"I told you he would come for me!" Gwendolyn exclaimed.

"You destroyed him?" The Wallachian prince held out a hand and one of the guards who had stood by his coffin put a goblet in it then held a mewing cat over it. The guard produced a knife and slit the animal's throat and drained the pumping blood from the dying cat into the goblet. "Well?"

"He came to the castle and uh-- took us by surprise," Dimitri mumbled, "I fought him, fiercely but..."

Dracula drained his goblet in a single gulp then tossed the cup aside and growled, "But what? Is this poet dead?"

"No, Master, he...he escaped."

"Then why are you here?"

"He...uh...He made Helena tell him where we had taken the girl."

"What!" Dracula shot upright and fixed his subordinate in his glare. "You mean he knows I am in Budapest."

"But he does not know where, Master," Dimitri was on his feet and backed away. "I punished her for revealing the information, Master. She will tell no one anything again. I came to warn you."

"Warn me?"

"They do not know where you are, Master."

"I told you Robert would come for me!" Gwendolyn stood upright with a new strength and stared her captor down. "And he will destroy you, regardless of what happens to me."

The Wallachian ignored her and flowed forward toward Dimitri who froze, unable to move. Dracula seized him around the throat and lifted the Gypsy off the ground to hold him at arm's length.

"You will not tell me you have failed ever again," Dracula hissed. He tossed the gypsy ten feet into a pile of mummified corpses, scattering the bones. "Leave my sight and do not let me see you again until you have killed this poet, or I will suck your soul dry!"

A moaning Dimitri crawled from the pile and limped off, up the main tunnel.

Dracula turned to face Gwendolyn and his expression was not pleasant. "Now, English woman," he hissed, "I have no more patience; you will give me the information I want; now!"

"What do you mean, Sister?" Howard asked the nun.

"The Matthias Church was built over the remains of the Church of Our Lady in the 13th century and that over a natural cistern," she said. "An underground river, really, an offshoot of the Danube. It has long been dried up, but during the Turkish occupation many—fearing the desecration of the Christian dead—began to bring their dead down to this cavern in secret. Tunnels were dug and, like the catacombs in Rome the dead were laid to rest there."

"But the unholy cannot walk upon consecrated ground," Andros said.

"It was never officially blessed," Sister Maria said. "There was no priest and, when at last the Ottomans were driven out it was deemed best that no one entered the caverns again. Everyone simply thought it was enough that the dead rested beneath the holy church itself."

"Then it seems the perfect place for a rat like Dracula to go to ground," Howard said. He took up his Remington 12-gauge, which was pump-action and gave him five rifle shots. He placed the weapon in a canvas bag to allow him to carry it through the streets of the city. It had been loaded it with the 'special load' they were all using in their shotguns, that all had a secret ingredient they hoped would give them a solid chance against Dracula. "We better head out to meet Ivan."

Sister Maria moved to pack a sawed-off double-barreled shotgun into a small carpet valise.

"Whoa, Sister," Howard said, "I don't think it is a good idea you come with us."

She fixed the Texan in her unwavering gaze and with a fixed smile on her face said, "I am Hungarian, Mister Howard. We have been fighting for our land for ages. It is only fitting that I, as a woman of God, am also ready to fight for the soul of my land beside you all."

"But there might be people there, sister," Howard said. "Dracula is bound to have some Romany beside Dimitri."

"If they serve the fiend then they are lost already," she said. "They cannot be helped; I will pray for them and hope that I do not have to take life, but if it occurs, I will face the Lord with a clear conscience and answer for my actions. Besides, you are using my ammunition; I wish to see its effect."

"So be it," Howard said to the group. "Let's saddle up and go hunting. The sun's going down soon!"

Chapter Thirty-Nine: Into the Belly of the Beast

The plaster and marble facade of the Matthias Church loomed over the scene, a pseudo-Gothic Cathedral that was at the center of Buda's castle district.

There was a huge equestrian statue of King Stephen—who later became a saint and was the founder of the Hungarian state—in the plaza before the impressive, ornate cathedral. It reminded all the monster hunters of their mission; to save not only the state but possibly the world.

The group approached from the northwest side of the church where two streets converged, their weapons in carrying cases.

Ivan stepped from a shadowed alcove from the Fisherman's Bastion across the plaza from the church.

"Here, here!" the Gypsy boy called. The group moved to join him.

"Is he still in there?" Andros asked.

"Yes," Ivan said as he exchanged a hug with his sister. "I found two of our tribe I know and trust to watch the back entrances; they have not seen him leave and I have not left here. I called from a store and kept the door in sight at all times."

"We need to have an idea where he is in there," Howard said.

Sister Maria handed the carpetbag to Karl. "I will go in."

"Sister—" Howard began.

"What could be more natural than one of my order lighting a candle in hope?" the nun said. She gave a sly smile to the Texan and walked calmly across the plaza through the afternoon crowd.

The little party stayed tucked in the shadow of the Bastion and waited.

Howard, as was his want and habit, even in the anxiety of waiting to attack, found that his mind went to the history of the buildings around him. The city of Budapest began as Aquincum, a Celtic settlement that became the Roman capital of Lower Pannonia.

We Celts started a lot of things.

The Hungarians came in the 9th century only to be pillaged by the Mongols and then, later after the Battle of Mohacs there were nearly 150 years of Ottoman Turkish rule.

Now another battle was about to be fought, not in its streets but beneath them and it might well be the most meaningful of the battles fought there.

The young Romany girl, Illyana, interrupted the writer's meditations.

"Do you think there will be much fighting?"

He looked over at her and gave a smile. "I reckon, there will be but we are on the side of the angels, so don't be afraid."

"Are you not afraid, my American friend?" The gray-haired Karl asked.

"Of dying? I reckon, but no more than the next guy," Howard said. "But honestly, I've seen death all my life and it holds no terror; for me the real horror would be a life without meaning or purpose; I had to climb into the pages of books to find mine back home. Now, I only really fear dying before I can help that little lady in there to be able to live her life. That would be meaning and purpose enough if it's my time."

"Do you think we can fight the undead one with these?" The girl held up her rifle. "They say he has died more than once."

"Anything that can hurt me, ma'am," he said, "I figure I can put a good hurt on as well, especially with the load Sister Maria got for us."

Just then Sister Maria came back came out of the main door of the church, looking very small against the grand facade and scale of the cathedral. She walked slowly, almost reverently across the expanse of the square, her solemn expression giving the watchers no clue as to what she had found inside the sacred space.

"The Roma we seek," the French nun said when she was safely in the midst of the group, "was not in the church, but I noticed several of his tribe lingering near the entrance to the Trinity Chapel, on the left before the entrance to the sacristy."

"Guards?" Andros ventured.

"It would seem so," Maria said. "I saw two leave the chapel that seemed to me to be disheveled, as if they had been working, and their clothing was soiled."

"Then that's it, folks," Howard said. The group began to move, as casually as possible, across the plaza according to their plan. The siblings split off to the right to enter the church from a small door near the choir area, across from the sacristy. Andros and Sister Maria took a wide arc to the left to enter the main entrance separately and from an angle. The Texan and gray-haired Karl walked straight for the main entrance.

"We must act quickly," Karl said as he looked up at the gray sky. "The sun will be going down soon. Dracula is most in his power in the time of darkness."

"If'n he's underground how much difference can that make?"

"Some think that the undead, the vampire is helpless during the day," Karl said. "And it is true they are weakened by healing rays of the sun, but Dracula and his sort are not really weak as a babe—on the contrary, his dealings with the Dark One have given him great power, but like many predators he is truly nocturnal. His vision is better in the dark, his energies more in the shadows. He will be strong no matter when we attack him, but with the sun still in the sky he cannot flee as easily."

"You're saying that we are in for a hell of dust-up down there, regardless?"

"Yes," Karl said as the two men approached the massive main door to the church.

"Well," Howard said, "let's get to it then!"

The two men slipped into the gothic splendor of the church ahead of Sister Maria, Andros and the siblings. By previous plan the two men would move up the left side of the church past the St. Stephen's Chapel and head up the side aisle straight ahead toward Ladislaus Chapel, which was just beyond the Trinity Chapel.

Howard and Karl paused by the large baptismal fountain at the main entrance and Karl stopped to dip his fingers into the water and then blessed himself by making the sign of the cross.

The cathedral was spectacular, not quite on the scale of Notre Dame or Westminster, but still would have mesmerized and taken Howard's breath away were he not on so solemn a mission. Everywhere was color—gold, crimson red and brilliant blue—within the tile floor, the gold leaf walls and on the arching, vaulted ceiling that soared above them several stories.

Stained glass windows tinted the afternoon light golden, and it was surreal for the Texan as he and the Hungarian walked slowly, and as casually as possible up the aisle. Howard had taken off his Stetson and was holding it down by his side in an attempt to blend a bit, but he still stood out among the few townsfolk in the church.

Two Romany were kneeling in a pew across from the Trinity Chapel and looked almost as out of place as the Texan did, their attitude anything but that of supplicants in search of solace. They both seemed to notice Howard and Karl just as the two men broke into a dead run.

The Romany pulled knives, but Howard and Karl swung their canvas gun bags at almost the same moment and both of the Gypsies were knocked to the ground.

Howard drew his six-shooter and pointed at the fallen men. "Stay down or you will not be able to get up." The two glared at him but froze where they fell.

Illyana and Ivan appeared then and proceeded to tie the men up while the men spewed many Romany curses at the two siblings they considered traitors.

Sister Maria and Andros joined the group then, pulling out their guns.

The few worshipers in the church noticed the commotion and reacted with confusion till Sister Maria stood up and spoke in a loud clear voice to them in Hungarian. They all listened then crossed themselves and left.

"What did you say to them?" Howard asked as the group moved into the side chapel.

"I told them we were doing the Lord's work, that there was an infestation of evil below and we were going to clear it out." When the others looked at her with incredulous expressions she shrugged. "They are good Catholic people and listen to nuns. I also asked them to pray for us."

Despite the circumstances, the Texan smiled. "Can't argue with any of that, ma'am." He donned his Stetson and removed his shotgun from the case. "Let's go."

The group removed their weapons from their carry bags and moved off cautiously into the side chapel. The space was small by comparison to the cathedral, but still larger than any church Howard had ever been to in Texas. It was used for daily masses, or special occasions, as were the other side chapels, but now there was a sawhorse barrier set across the opening to keep out the regular churchgoers.

"They had to have someone from the church in on this," Howard said indicating the barrier.

"All they would have to do is bribe a caretaker," Andros said. "Or even threaten his family as well; there is not much they would not do to protect their master. The priests would not question their own man."

The six adventurers spread out once in the chapel, scanning right and left for any sign of an entrance to the subterranean lair. It was Howard who saw the dirt scuffing on the mosaic tile floor. He followed the trail to a space behind the altar.

"There is a door here," Howard whispered. He looked back at the others and the unspoken question was "Who will go first?"

Howard used his thumb to tilt back his Stetson and shrugged. "I guess I—" Just then the door opened and the Gypsy, Dimitri, stepped through.

There was a frozen moment when the Romany went stock still at seeing the figures standing before him. The group was stunned for a split second as well but almost as one all raised their weapons.

Dimitri exclaimed, "*Atkozott!*" and darted back through the door before anyone could squeeze a trigger.

Chapter Forty: Hell Below Heaven

Howard, at the lead of the group, raced forward after the Gypsy, plunging through the narrow doorway only steps behind Dimitri. It was a stone-walled corridor that went along level for a bit then began to slope down and widen.

Dimitri pounded down the stone floor as if he were on fire, quickly rounding the angle of the hallway and out of sight. Howard could not match the panicked speed of the Romany and when the writer lost sight of him, Howard slowed to a fast walk.

He's gonna raise the alarm for sure. We're committed now. Howard held his shotgun in his left and drew his pistol and he moved forward with new caution. Behind him he could hear the others moving up on him, but he kept his focus forward, now alert for ambush. Dimitri had not cried out and that made Howard suspicious that there might be some sort of trap ahead.

The corridor had stone block walls and torches in sconces that created deceptive shadows that Howard feared could hide ambushers. He slowed down his walk as he came to a doorway along one wall. It opened to a bare stone room and had bars in a small window in the door.

Some sort of cell.

The others had caught up with him now and they all moved down the hallway scanning right and left. The worked stone block walls gave way to rough-hewn walls from the native rock and the incline was clearly moving downward. Then they rounded a bend and walked into hell!

"I have been patient, woman," Dracula said to Gwendolyn. He stood, looming above her, his lambent eyes fixing her as if she were a butterfly pinned to a board. "But I must have the information you have in your head. And so now I will call on all the power of the dark lords I serve to rip that memory from your mind; I warn you there will be little left of you when I am done."

"I will never give you any help," she spat at him. "You will never succeed. And my death will only mean that Bob Howard will destroy you utterly."

The Wallachian allowed himself a *sotto voce* laugh. "Your faith is amusing to me. Now look into my eyes and see your destruction."

She could not look away, her attention arrested as if cold, dead hands had taken hold of her and drew her into the dark lord's mind. She felt her very soul slipping away from her as she journeyed into her own past.

She saw her childhood with the Harkers, the isolation and separateness she felt, even when Jonathon visited his guilty affection on her. She saw the cold glances, again, from Momma Mina, now recognizing them for what they were. But she saw another face with eyes like her own that she saw in the mirror every day. It was a kinder face, a loving face and the smile and loving words were just at the edge of her memory.

"Mamma," Gwendolyn whispered.

Then behind that smile, she saw a sterner, yet still-loving face. Her father! She saw him laughing with her as she took her first steps and felt his arms holding her on his lap while he worked on a big table. She could almost see what he was doing, bent over a tiny ivory oval—

Suddenly Dimitri ran into the cavern and screamed, "We are under attack!"

Abruptly Dracula turned away from his prisoner and hissed a growl at the interruption. "What are you babbling?"

Dimitri ran directly to throw himself to his knees before his lord. "Master, Master!" He cried, "Save me, the cowboy is coming, he is going to kill me!"

Gwendolyn felt her head-clearing, a chill racing up her spine. "Bob?"

Dracula sprang at the kneeling Romany. A taloned hand slammed onto Dimitri's skull and jerked him straight up to the full extent of the Wallachian's arm, suspending him with his legs kicking in the air. Dracula hissed, "You disappoint me!"

Dimitri tried to make a sound of protest, but Dracula jerked his wrist so there was an audible snap, and the Romany went limp.

Just then Bob Howard and the group of hunters burst into the cavern.

"Gwen!" The Texan called when he saw her.

The Romany workers at first did not realize that their sanctum had been invaded but their master yelled, "*A fegyverekhez!*—To arms!"

All at once, the Gypsy workers within earshot dropped their shovels and drew knives to turn toward the invaders.

"Robert!" Gwen cried when she saw the Texan who froze when he saw her situation.

Dracula dropped Dimitri's lifeless body to the cave floor and turned to glare at Gwendolyn with contempt. "Your poet?"

"Yes!" she yelled in triumph. "I told you he would come for me!"

The Wallachian prince flowed to grab Gwendolyn by the hair. "You will watch me destroy him before I snap your traitorous neck." He dropped her to her knees and turned to face the Texan.

"Get your hands off her, you filthy sidewinder!" Howard yelled. He charged at the Wallachian but the two bodyguards of the undead lord had already made their way past their master and went straight for Howard.

The Gypsy workers charged the intruders, but Andros and Sister Maria fired their shotguns into the massed attack, dropping the first wave by shooting low at their legs with birdshot. The Romany hit the ground screaming in pain.

The bodyguards came at Howard with ten-inch knives swinging at him like scythes, but he did not dare fire his pistol or shotgun at them because Gwendolyn was directly in the line of fire. Instead, he dodged to his right using his shotgun to parry the slash of the first attacker.

The blow was so hard that it knocked the shotgun from the Texan's hand. The Romany slashed back, and the blade cut into Howard's left arm, biting deeply.

Howard cried out in pain but was able to jump back to avoid a third sweeping cut.

The Texan dropped to one knee and fired the six-gun up into the chest of the first bodyguard so that Gwendolyn was not in line.

The second attacker yelled a war-cry and swerved around his companion to stab at the kneeling Texan.

Howard had no choice but to throw himself backward to avoid the knife tip. He hit the ground on his wounded left arm which brought another involuntary cry of pain from him, and the attacker leaned in to press his attack on the fallen writer.

The move placed the bodyguard out of line again and Howard fired from the ground sending two forty-five caliber bullets through the man's chest. The now-dead Gypsy fell forward onto Howard as Gwendolyn screamed.

The other Romany were charging out of the side tunnels now and Illyana and Ivan rushed to meet them knife to knife while Andros and Karl moved to cover the brother and sister and keep them from being overwhelmed by numbers. The siblings fought with manic fury, all the while screaming curses in Romany, calling those they fought, *marime*—unclean—and traitors.

Sister Maria ran for Gwendolyn, but Dracula interposed himself, looming over the tiny nun like death itself. She never flinched.

"Begone, spawn of Satan!" she crossed herself and raised her sawed-off shotgun to aim it at the monster, but he was on her with the speed of thought, slapping the gun from her hand and grabbing her by the throat.

"Take your God and your vows and precede me to hell!" He squeezed his hand into a fist and crushed the nun's throat in a spray of blood.

Gwendolyn screamed.

Howard threw the dead Gypsy off himself and rose like a cat at the scream.

"You son of a bitch!" The Texan yelled. He fired his last two bullets from his six-gun into Dracula in a spasm of fury till the hammer clicked on empty.

Dracula laughed, ignoring the bullet holes in his chest. He shook the gore from Sister Maria's murder from his hand then licked his fingers clean.

"Is that the best you have, poet?" He slowly advanced and looked at the sobbing Gwendolyn. "I will tear him apart before your eyes, woman and make him curse his own poetry and his God."

Howard was on his feet now. He holstered his grandfather's six-gun and pumped the shotgun to load a shell.

"That little lady is in a better place than you'll ever be, you skunk," Howard said. "And I'm the one to send you to your master in hell."

Epilogue: Poetry and Death

Howard did not rush, but rather deliberately strode toward the Wallachian prince, his shotgun pointed at the dark lord's stomach. His arm was streaming blood, but he ignored it, his whole being focused on the undead monster.

The sounds of the battle behind them seemed to fade as the last of the braver Romany workers fell before the guns and knives of Howard's companions. The rest of Dracula's horde that had no heart to fight had fled into the tunnels.

All living eyes in the room focused on the two tall figures as they stepped closer.

Dracula amused himself by pushing a finger into the holes made by the Texan's pistol and smiled, his canine fangs clearly visible. He looked at the fresh blood on the Texan's arm and licked his lips.

"Will you not regale me, poet, with words to usher in your destruction?"

Howard's jaw was firmly set, his steely gaze locked with Dracula's. His breathing was regular, his steps as slow as if he were in lockstep with five pallbearers.

"Bob," Gwendolyn whispered.

"It's alright, Gwen, I've faced bullies before and this dead smelling dog ain't no different. He ain't nothin'."

"Do you not fear for your mortal soul?" Dracula laughed. "All the rest of these sheep, even my Romany, tremble in terror of losing even a single day of their miserable lives and have a horror of what comes beyond. I have embraced that beyond."

Now Howard gave a derisive snorting laugh. "I don't fear dyin', Hoss; I fear not livin'."

The Texan was now an arm's length from the Wallachian, his shotgun barrel between them. He glanced over at the table that was set by the throne, the maps on its surface and suddenly he knew why Dracula was in the caverns and he knew what had clawed at the edge of his thoughts when he looked at Gwendolyn's necklace.

Her father carved a map of these tunnels into that cameo. Some secret he wanted his little girl to have, and this carrion is hunting it.

"Not having any luck with your treasure hunting, are you, Hoss?" The Texan could see the Wallachian's eyes widen at the taunting surmise and knew he had guessed right.

"Well, I got the secret of it, varmint, right in my pocket. If you want it, you gotta take from me."

The two foes stood, eyes focused two forces of nature. It was clear to all in the cavern that they were polar opposites of power, the dark and the light.

Dracula reached out and pulled the shotgun's barrel to his stomach so that it was snug against him.

"No more words, poet?"

Howard spoke in a whisper at first, then his voice gained strength, "*Within my soul, A warrior cries, A prisoner of my life, With mundane, Walls and soft Footfall, Of petty, sordid strife.*"

Dracula's expression, a frozen mask of contempt, began to subtly change, a curious light shining in his eyes. Howard's steely gaze never wavered as he continued. *" Oh where are the Fields of Agincourt, The plains of Roark's Drift too, The fields of Acquilonia, Or the gates of Timbuktu? To wish for far horizons, To long for Maidens fair, To pray for an adventure To pine for some new dare? But the wanderer within me fights wherever evil rears and with my fist and with my heart I've overcome all fears!"*

Dracula hissed a challenge and pushed forward to grab for Howard and the Texan pulled the trigger of the shotgun.

The discharge was like a cannon blast in the silence of the cavern, echoing off the walls to magnify the sound tenfold.

Almost as loud was the scream of agony from the Wallachian prince who was blown back from the barrel with a hole the size of a fist through his stomach. He stumbled to his knees, growling like the wounded animal he was, and looked at Howard with shocked eyes.

"Hurts, don't it?" The Texan pumped the shotgun to load another shell and stepped closer.

"How?" Dracula hissed.

"That fine woman you killed had the idea; we loaded the shotguns with silver and ivory rosary beads that had been blessed by a priest and dipped in holy water. Now to put you down like the mad dog you are—"

The Texan had overplayed his hand however as he stepped too close to aim the gun down at the gasping vampire. Dracula sprang up at him, knocking him backward to the ground.

Howard's weapon went flying and the wounded Wallachian was on him with his taloned hands driving for the writer's throat.

Howard managed to get his hand on the dark lord's wrists and just barely was able to hold them from crushing his windpipe by main strength. The breath of the growling monster smelled of death and Howard could see Gehenna in his eyes.

Dracula opened his mouth and lowered his head toward the Texan's throat, saliva dripping from his lips.

Howard smashed his forehead up hard into Dracula's nose with a satisfying crack, the Texan growling himself in Celtic fury.

The Wallachian reared his head back and roared a curse of annoyance.

Howard yelled in anger and heaved the body of his attacker off him and drew his Bowie knife, driving it into Dracula's heart to the hilt.

Dracula screamed in anger and reached for the handle of the blade when suddenly his head exploded!

The Texan scrambled backward and got to his feet, grabbing for his shotgun. He whirled to point it at Dracula, but the monster was writhing on the ground with half his face gone. There was no blood, for the undead nobleman had none of his own, but it was still a horrid sight, made more so by the unhuman, guttural noises issuing from the mutilated figure.

Howard did not hesitate but pumped four more shots into the fallen form, all but obliterating the nobleman.

Then the Texan looked up to see who his savior was. Gwendolyn stood at the full extension of her neck chain holding Sister Maria's sawed-off shotgun, the barrels still smoking.

Howard ran to embrace her and they all but collapsed into each other's arms.

"I was so afraid…" she began.

"Shhh," he said. "Me too, Gwen. Me too."

"But I never gave up hope."

"I know," he managed as he crushed her to him, "and it gave me the strength to keep on comin'."

The other hunters came to stand over the corpse of Dracula, emptying their own shotguns to obliterate the remains with blast after blast.

When the echoes had died, Karl, tears in his eyes, knelt by Sister Maria's body. "We will wash this place with holy water, then seal it up with explosives so that no one can ever bring that monster back."

"The shame of our people has been erased," Ivan said. "And we will sing of Sister Maria's courage for generations to come."

"And of the cowboy who came to save our people from the scourge," Andros added.

Howard, his arm around Gwendolyn's waist, looked at the scene before him and said, *"My sword thirsts for blood, Edged to sup'on thee, which of us will be set free? Fire, fury, axes red, living always envy the dead- Warriors calling we who wield steal, Ne'er to surrender, Ne'er to yield."*

Gwendolyn smiled, "I told Dracula to be afraid of Irish poets from Texas. I'm glad he didn't listen."

The End

Post Script:

I have used the names of some famous real people in the telling of this tall tale, none with malice or disrespect and, I hope, all with proper reverence. In any case, all were used with a sense of fantastic whimsy and no offense was intended.

The Dramatis Persona of this novel:

Robert Ervin Howard: (January 22, 1906 – June 11, 1936) was the consummate pulp author who wrote in a diverse range of genres. He wrote westerns, detective tales, horror stories, historical adventures, boxing stories, humorous tall tales and virtually invented the sword and sorcery subgenre of fantasy with his Solomon Kane, Bran Mac Morn, King Kull and Conan of Cimmeria tales, blending he-man action with dark fantasy that reflected a deep, Celtic melancholy and fatalistic view of the world.

He wrote with equal aplomb for pulps as diverse as *Weird Tales*, *Argosy All-Story*, *Oriental Stories*, *Fight Stories*, *Magic Carpet*, *Sport Story*, *Star Western*, *Cowboy Stories*, *Masked Rider Western*, *Smashing Novels*, *Top-Notch*, *Thrilling Adventures*, *Golden Fleece* and other magazines.

Howard was born and raised in the state of Texas. He spent most of his life in the town of Cross Plains. He taught himself to box and sword fight and often engaged in 'icehouse' fights—bare-knuckle competitions with the roughnecks in his area.

From the age of nine he dreamed of becoming a writer of adventure fiction but did not have real success until he was twenty-three. His main outlet and lasting fame was the pulp magazine *Weird Tales*.

He was introduced (via correspondence) to H.P. Lovecraft by an editor at *Weird Tales* and the two 'veteran' writers were soon engaged in a vigorous correspondence that would last for the rest of Howard's life.

Howard was successful in several genres and was on the verge of publishing his first novel when he committed suicide at the age of thirty. His mother was terminally ill with tuberculosis before she had even met his father and so was slowly dying throughout Howard's entire life.

A theme in most of his writings was that the atavist in us all, the barbarian, would always triumph over civilization. If he could see shows on television these days, he might find himself proven right.

His divergence from our reality in this book is the moment, seated in his car on a Texas road that he does not shoot himself in grief but returns to the hospital to have his last moments with his dying mother.

I have used some of Howard's own poems and even quotes from some of his letters to provide his 'dialogue' but have used many more of my own poems and 'words' to bring this version of R.E.H. in the interest of spinning a good yarn. I think Bob, the pulpster, would understand and maybe even approve. If you want to read further on his amazing, but too short life, I suggest the excellent book *Blood & Thunder: The Life and Art of Robert E. Howard* by Mark Finn.

William Henry Pratt (November 23, 1887 – February 2, 1969), was an English-born actor better known to the world under his professional name as Boris Karloff.

He studied to go into the consular service. He dropped out in 1909 and worked as a farm laborer and did various odd jobs until he happened into acting. His brother, sir John Thomas Pratt, became a distinguished British diplomat. Karloff was bow-legged, had a lisp, and stuttered as a young boy. He conquered his stutter, but not his lisp, which was noticeable all throughout his career.

Though he had a long and ultimately successful career his early years were very hard—performing Shakespeare in Canadian lumber camps and doing manual labor once he came to California. It was here that he injured his back, an injury that plagued him for the rest of his life.

He actually played the African villain in the silent version of "Tarzan and the Golden Lion," his only black-face role.

His moment of 'alternate reality' in this story comes when the Hungarian actor Bela Lugosi (who had risen to fame portraying a fictional vampire—in this world named Varney) changed his mind and decided to play Frankenstein's monster, thus denying Karloff his star turn in 1931's James Whale's *Frankenstein*.

Mina and Jonathon Harker are fictional creations of Bram Stoker for his novel <u>Dracula </u>(1896) as is Quincy Morris, the Texan friend of the pair who died in the book and whose Bowie knife was used in the battle against the vampire king at the end of the novel— though the bloodsucker was stabbed with Quincy Morris' Bowie and beheaded by Jonathan Harker's Kukhri.

Dracula:
Vlad III of Wallachia was known as Vlad Țepeș (or Vlad the Impaler) in Romania. He was *voivode* (or prince) three times between 1448 and his death. His sobriquet as 'the impaler' is connected to the impalement that was his favorite method of execution. The Ottomans called him Kazkh Voyoda (Impaler Lord).

Vlad himself signed his two letters as "Dragulya" or "Drakulya" in the late 1470s. His name had its origin in his father's title, Vlad Dracul ("Vlad the Dragon"), who was a member of the Order of the Dragon. Dracula is the Slavonic form of Dracul, meaning "the son of Dracul (or son of the Dragon)".

Vlad was murdered in January 1477. Books describing Vlad's cruel acts were among the first bestsellers in the German-speaking territories. And these Bram Stoker used as inspiration for his novel <u>Dracula</u> in 1898.

Varney the Vampire; or, the Feast of Blood was a Victorian-era gothic serialized story which was the epitome of the penny dreadful type magazine. It was one of the influences on Stoker's <u>Dracula,</u> but in this world the book was the one that was made into a film starring Bela Lugosi and not Stokers unpublished pseudo-history about Vlad Tepes.

Author's Biography

Teel James Glenn was born in Brooklyn and has traveled the world for more than forty years as a stuntman, fight choreographer, swordmaster, jouster, book illustrator, playwright, storyteller, bodyguard, ballyhoo for a haunted house, and actor.

His stories have appeared in scores of magazines like *Weird Tales, Mystery Weekly, Sherlock Holmes Mystery, Mad, Black Belt, Blazing! Adventures, Black Cat Weekly, Crimson Streets, Cirsova* and *Fantasy Tales*. He has over three dozen books in print in multiple genres.

He was awarded Best Pulp Writer by the 2012 Pulp Ark, The original version of A Cowboy In Carpathia won The Pulp Factory Award for best novel in 2021 and his novel Not Born of Woman was a finalist in the Pulp Factory, Silver Falchion and Shamus Awards.

You can keep up with his adventures at theurbanswashbuckler.com.